By John Inman

Laugh Cry Repeat

"*Laugh Cry Repeat* is a powerful story, a novel hard to forget for the themes it speaks of…"
—Scattered Thoughts and Rogue Words

"This story captivated me… A perfect finish and happy ever after."
—Open Skye Book Reviews

The Hike

"Once again, John Inman assures his spot as a topnotch horror writer who uses a deft hand to weave in just enough romance to ease the tension and keep the reader on the edge of their seat."
—The Novel Approach

"*The Hike* is one of my favorite stories of the year so far."
—Joyfully Jay

Love Wanted

"This book simply blew me away. The writing and storytelling were outstanding, and I couldn't take my eyes off it once I started."
—OptimuMM

"I really liked this one… I highly recommend it to all."
—Love Bytes

By JOHN INMAN

Acting Up
Chasing the Swallows
A Hard Winter Rain
Head-on
The Hike
Hobbled
Jasper's Mountain
Laugh Cry Repeat
Love Wanted
Loving Hector
My Busboy
My Dragon, My Knight
Paulie
Payback
The Poodle Apocalypse
Scrudge & Barley, Inc.
Shy
Spirit
Sunset Lake
Two Pet Dicks
Words

THE BELLADONNA ARMS
Serenading Stanley
Work in Progress
Coming Back
Ben and Shiloh
Ginger Snaps

Published by DREAMSPINNER PRESS
www.dreamspinnerpress.com

WORDS

JOHN INMAN

Published by
DREAMSPINNER PRESS

5032 Capital Circle SW, Suite 2, PMB# 279, Tallahassee, FL 32305-7886 USA
www.dreamspinnerpress.com

This is a work of fiction. Names, characters, places, and incidents either are the product of author imagination or are used fictitiously, and any resemblance to actual persons, living or dead, business establishments, events, or locales is entirely coincidental.

Words
© 2018 John Inman.

Cover Art
© 2018 Aaron Anderson.
aaronbydesign55@gmail.com
Cover content is for illustrative purposes only and any person depicted on the cover is a model.

All rights reserved. This book is licensed to the original purchaser only. Duplication or distribution via any means is illegal and a violation of international copyright law, subject to criminal prosecution and upon conviction, fines, and/or imprisonment. Any eBook format cannot be legally loaned or given to others. No part of this book may be reproduced or transmitted in any form or by any means, electronic or mechanical, including photocopying, recording, or by any information storage and retrieval system, without the written permission of the Publisher, except where permitted by law. To request permission and all other inquiries, contact Dreamspinner Press, 5032 Capital Circle SW, Suite 2, PMB# 279, Tallahassee, FL 32305-7886, USA, or www.dreamspinnerpress.com.

Trade Paperback ISBN: 978-1-64080-155-4
Digital ISBN: 978-1-64080-156-1
Library of Congress Control Number: 2017919741
Trade Paperback published June 2018
v. 1.0

Printed in the United States of America
∞
This paper meets the requirements of
ANSI/NISO Z39.48-1992 (Permanence of Paper).

Prologue

ET OSTENDE incipit... and the show begins

Washington Square Park lay knee-deep in snow on this dawning Sunday morning. Located in Lower Manhattan, the park was a favorite gathering place for Greenwich Villagers. A tall marble arch stood at one end, celebrating George Washington's inauguration as president of the United States in 1789, and the park's ten acres of grassland and trees were a rare and well-loved commodity for New Yorkers in any season.

Modeled after the Arc de Triomphe in Paris, the 74-foot tall Washington Square Arch stood grand and imposing at the foot of Fifth Avenue. Behind the arch sprawled the park's fountain, the pool of which, at the moment, was frozen as stiff as marble itself.

The air was cold enough to kill a homeless person in six hours flat and discourage even the staunchest of joggers from venturing out. For opposing ends of the social spectrum, home treadmills and homeless shelters were the rule of the day. The truly elite sat safely insulated high in surrounding high-rises, sipping Kenyan coffee from bone china and peering down at the frozen city through frosted windows fifty floors up, as untouchable as gods.

New Yorkers are a brave, sturdy lot, but this weather had most of them stymied, which explains perhaps why the lone figure standing at the northwest corner of Washington Square Park on this freezing January dawn was there at all. That person was not a New Yorker.

It might also be true that people with murder on their minds do not feel the cold as the rest of us do. But we shall leave that for the experts to decide.

The figure in the shadows was tall and lean. If one could have seen beneath the scarf wrapped tightly about the face, the figure might also have been handsome. Or maybe not. Warm woolen gloves protected the hands, and the body was shielded from the cold by a long, heavy coat that reached all the way to the ankles, a pretentious piece of clothing in any weather except the one in which the figure now stood. The hair might have been blond or dark, ginger or gray, short or long, since at the moment it was hidden beneath a woolen watch cap pulled low over the head. And the ears were tucked snug and warm beneath the watch cap as well. In truth, the cold only touched the figure's eyes, and those were as blue as ice themselves, so perhaps immune to the winter's chill.

The wind whipped past as the shadowy figure stood beneath one of the park's grandest trees, studying the hotel across the street.

The towering tree was an English elm and it was more than 300 years old, its far-reaching limbs bare of foliage at the moment due to the season. In summer, the tree spread its leafy boughs wide, welcoming passersby to partake of its cooling shade. In historical circles the tree was known as the Hangman's Elm. It acquired that name not by any flight of whimsical New York fancy, but because of a legend that stated traitors were hung by the neck from its branches during the American Revolution.

Being an executioner of sorts, perhaps it was not inappropriate that our lean figure should be standing beneath the naked boughs of the Hangman's Elm on this January morning, fingering a two-foot length of clothesline tucked in a coat pocket. A garrote, it is called, and the person we are watching knew its uses better than most. At the moment, in fact, it was a most beloved possession.

Sliding the velvety length of narrow cord through slim fingers, the figure wound it caressingly about a gloved hand. The cord's hidden strength comforted, even while it both fed and soothed the figure's anger. A shudder that was almost sexual passed through the body as the eyes above the scarf narrowed in either desire or fury. Or perhaps both.

Those steely, cold eyes focused outward again when a cab pulled up to the front of the Washington Square Hotel, situated on the adjacent corner. A man and woman exited the taxi's back doors. The cabbie popped the latch on the trunk. Looking miserable and put-upon, he thrust open the driver's door and jumped out to extract the couple's luggage. He didn't wait around for a thank-you but merely dropped the cases at the couple's feet and leaped back into the warmth of the cab. As he pulled away, turtling off at a median speed of five miles an hour, his snow chains crunched on the asphalt, leaving two jagged scars in the pristine snow.

The couple grabbed their luggage, their breaths clouding about their heads, and hurried through the hotel's front doors to escape the cold.

The figure beneath the tree smiled, for patience is always rewarded.

Noting the security camera above the hotel entrance, the lone figure pulled the watch cap lower and drew the scarf more securely about nose and mouth, again leaving only the eyes exposed.

Moving for the first time in thirty minutes, the figure dusted snow off long sleeves and stepped out from under the Hangman's Elm to cross the street, clomping awkwardly through the snow. Somewhere off in the distance, the sound of snowplows rose on the frigid air. They were beginning the monumental task of clearing the city streets. Soon they would reach this end of Greenwich Village, and when they did, all footprints would be obliterated. Beneath the scarf, the figure smiled again, knowing it was one less thing to worry about.

To dislodge the powder from soles and trouser cuffs, the lean figure stomped on the hotel's front steps, then dusted the latest coating of snow off the long coat and stepped boldly through the front door.

The clerk behind the counter barely looked up at the figure wrapped so thoroughly against the cold, clearly assuming it was one of the registered guests who simply didn't want to die of frostbite on this horrid winter's morning. The bellhop, waiting idly by the check-ins' luggage so he could manhandle the bags upstairs and hopefully wangle a tip for his efforts, didn't look toward the arriving figure either. He merely shivered at the sudden infusion of cold air whipping through the lobby when the front doors opened. He tapped a foot impatiently as the desk clerk checked the couple's reservations and handed over the obligatory touristy brochures, as if anyone in their right mind would be sightseeing in the middle of a blizzard.

The visitor strode boldly across the lobby. Ducking into the teeny elevator with its brass and mirror interior—the only elevator in the building available to guests—the figure pressed a gloved finger to the button reading 3 on the panel. After an interminable period of time, the antique elevator finally jerked itself awake and began to climb. As the elevator rose, the rider stood casually, humming a gentle tune from beneath the scarf in a remarkably sweet voice. One hand still fingered the length of clothesline hidden in the pocket of the snowy coat.

On the third floor, after waiting another interminable amount of time for the elevator doors to open, the figure stepped out into the hall, all the while listening carefully to the sounds of the sleeping hotel. The elevator doors remained open, and in this way the visitor knew the new arrivals had not yet been shunted off to their rooms, which might very well be on 3 as well. So there was little need to hurry.

The hallway was narrow and veered off in odd directions. Gleaning the lay of the land quickly enough, the snowy figure set off in search of room 311. It was at the very end of the hall, just past the stairs leading down—not only to the lobby, but also to a back exit from the hotel that opened onto MacDougal Street. One could not enter the hotel from this door, but one could easily leave it, slipping away onto the city streets like a whisper of air leaking through a subway grate.

The visitor checked the door leading into the stairwell to assure it was unlocked. That done, a shadowed pair of eyes scanned the hallway ceiling, seeking security cameras, of which there were—believe it or not—none. The figure smiled broadly and without further hesitation, strode directly to room 311.

From behind the door, no sounds could be heard, just as there were no sounds coming from any of the rooms surrounding it. Nor was there any noise from the elevator down the hall. The elevator merely hung there, doors open like a gaping maw, waiting to be fed.

Aside from that gentle tune still issuing from behind the figure's scarf, there was nothing to be heard at all. The Washington Square Hotel was as still as death.

Pulling the garrote from the coat pocket and gripping it securely, the visitor gently tapped at the door to room 311. No answer. And only silence came from inside when the figure stepped closer and pressed an ear to the cool wood. The visitor tapped again.

This time a mumbling could be heard, then a muted thud, as if the person inside had fumbled for a lamp switch on a night table.

"Yes?" a groggy female voice called out. "Who is it?"

For the first time, the lean figure slid the scarf down out of the way so a lowered voice would carry. "Hotel staff, ma'am. There's been a bit of an emergency, I'm afraid. I'm sorry to disturb your sleep."

That should do it, the visitor thought. Just distressing enough to pull the sleeper awake without scaring her to death or encouraging her to call the desk to find out what the hell was going on.

"Just a minute," the woman called out, her voice followed by a swish of bedclothes, then the rustle of footsteps dragging over carpet. The doorknob jiggled from the inside, and a moment later the door eased open a crack. Through the opening, a sleepy eye appeared. Again, the voice said, "Yes?"

One solid thump with a driving shoulder snapped the chain lock on the hotel room door, and the door flew inward, striking the woman in the face. She cried out in pain, then sudden terror. Before she could find a scream inside her fear, the intruder barged through the doorway and quickly pushed it closed again, sealing them inside. The lean figure roughly caught the woman as she turned to flee, a gloved hand covering her mouth to silence her from behind. She cast her eyes, no longer sleepy but filled with panic now, over her shoulder, gaping in fear. The woman was clearly unable to speak, unable to understand quite yet what was happening. But she would know soon enough.

Clad only in a nightgown, her pasty body smelled sleep-warm and yeasty, which disgusted the attacker. The woman's breath was sour with terror. She mumbled something and tried to bite the hand that held her, for which she earned a vicious yank of her hair from her captor's free hand.

Her knees almost buckled, and the intruder fought to hold her upright. Seeing an easier way to get things done, the attacker forced her forward and pushed her bulk down onto the bed, landing on top of her as she fell.

Even with a hand across her mouth, the woman wrenched her head to the side and tried to scream. A quick punch in the face silenced her.

Using body weight to hold her in place, the attacker looped the clothesline around the woman's throat and drew it tight, cutting off her air.

Her eyes grew round with horror, and her tears spilled onto the bed.

The garrote tightened. The smell of the woman's fear grew rancid. A sudden reek of urine filled the room, which disgusted the intruder even more.

As the victim's reddening face ballooned and her tongue slipped from between her lips, blackening already from lack of oxygen, the shadowy figure pressed lips to her ear and offered her the last human voice she would ever hear.

"Your pen is poison," her attacker whispered. "Your words are filth."

The woman tried to twist around, tried to see the person who was killing her, struggled to understand what the words meant, why the person was doing this, what she had ever done to warrant such hatred, such fury.

"No," she almost managed to garble. "Please." But the figure hovering over her simply tightened the garrote and smiled down with icy eyes as cold as the winter dawn outside.

Yet again, the intruder leaned in to whisper in her ear. Lips brushed over tender skin like a lover's kiss even as the garrote clawed across her gullet, tore into her larynx, and snapped the hyoid bone, squeezing her life away.

"Your pen is poison," the muffled figure said again, and before the words were fully uttered, life had vacated the woman's eyes. Those eyes stared emptily now at the snowflakes brushing across the hotel window, at the sky lightening to the east with the promise of a dawn they would never see.

Her attacker kept the garrote wrapped tightly about her throat for a further thirty seconds before rising from the bed to stare down at the woman. Her nightgown was stained where she had wet herself in her last moments. Her stillness, her killer thought, was a vast improvement over the sounds she made when living.

The figure paused in the doorway before slipping away. The room was now soundless, the terror inside waning, cooling like a forgotten cup of coffee. But still the killer could sense the fear that had lived there only moments before. And in that sensing, felt content.

"Disgusting bitch," the intruder muttered. Five seconds later, soundless footfalls trod the back stairs, heading quickly down two flights through the old building like a wisp of smoke before wafting at long last through the exit onto MacDougal Street.

Ducking beneath the awnings where the snow was shallower, the lean figure headed uptown on foot, the only pedestrian on the street. Two blocks from the hotel, the garrote went down a sewer grate. Knowing how enthralled the police could be with trace evidence—fiber, lint, hair—the gloves, coat, and watch cap found their way into a trash can on the corner of Fifth Avenue and Twelfth Street, where they would likely never be found. As for the scarf still wrapped snugly about the killer's face, that would remain. After all, it was a favorite.

Shivering now, the figure hurried along the frozen street, lungs and eyes burning with the cold.

Blocks later, when the dawn finally broke and the day began to lighten, it did so with the clarity of clean, cold glass. Our escaping killer hustled along the empty street, slipping through the icy wind. Teeth chattering, the lone figure hurried on as crisp snowflakes speckled the scarf wrapped tightly below watering, jubilant eyes.

The world was purer now. Less stained. One notch closer to being kind.

Hunkered against the cold, the figure stole through the shadows, smiling into the bitter wind.

Only a few more notches to go.

Chapter One

MILO COOK sat behind a long wooden table inside the doors of the Andiron Bookstore in Coronado, California, hoping to snag each and every book shopper as they strolled in off the street. The problem was, there was no one strolling in.

Granted, Coronado, California, was a Navy town, but it was also a touristy resort mecca, known for its pristine beaches. Situated across the bay from San Diego with its back to the ocean, Coronado sat upon a tied island, connected to the mainland by a tombolo known as the Silver Strand. Despite its beauty, however, Milo was beginning to believe the city was populated by illiterates. Didn't anybody read in this town? Didn't anybody like a good story to wrest them away from their humdrum lives? They were gobbling up tons of gelato from the shop down the block. Didn't any of them crave something a little more cerebral and a little less fattening? Like fiction, for Christ's sake?

That was Milo's stock in trade. Stories. Fiction. And if nobody wanted to read such things, Milo might end up living in a cardboard box behind a dumpster somewhere in pretty short order. Not a pleasing prospect by anyone's definition. Milo enjoyed his comforts. Like, say, a roof over his head and food on the table, not to mention an occasional bag of Dog Chow for his mongrel, Spanky, who was undoubtedly sitting back in Milo's San Diego home right this minute, twiddling his thumbs (well, assuming he had any), waiting for his lonely, miserable day to end just as much as Milo was.

The scarred oak table Milo sat behind (on a chair so hard it felt like it was made of granite and squeaked rather alarmingly every time he moved) held unsold copies of Milo's latest novel. Alongside the books stood a placard with Milo's picture and name and a few scattered excerpts from complimentary reviews his newest book had gleaned. For writers, there was no such thing as modesty when it came to foisting one's books onto an unsuspecting public, thereby ratchetting up their sales. It had occurred to Milo in a moment of morbid whimsy that authors work on the same principal as serial killers. The higher the body count, the more famous they become. After all, there are only so many readers scattered around the planet, while there are writers everywhere, dangling copies of their latest masterpieces in front of each and every reader they run across.

A woman stepped in off the street, and Milo immediately molded his lips into his patented author's smile—welcoming, humble, wise. The woman's gaze skipped over him like he was merely another parking meter, or fire hydrant, or any of a thousand other inanimate objects, and peered off into the store's interior. *A discerning reader? Looking for the latest Grisham, Brown, or, please God, Cook?* But his silent question was instantly answered when the woman barked, "Aha!" and bustled off toward the bathroom in the back of the store.

Milo kept his smile intact until she returned some minutes later. Once again her eyes skimmed over him like he didn't exist as she headed straight out the door. She did look considerably relieved to have found a public toilet, however, and for that Milo was happy for her. He was also pleased as punch to see she was dragging a three-foot streamer of toilet paper that had stuck to her shoe.

He dug into his sport-coat pocket and plucked out a piece of Juicy Fruit gum, quietly peeled it from its wrapper, and popped it into his mouth. He settled in again to wait, avoiding the eyes of the sales clerk, who kept glancing his way, either in pity that the poor writer was getting so few nibbles, or in annoyance that the writer was taking up so much space for nothing. Milo couldn't quite be sure which.

There are few things more exciting for a writer, Milo mused, than to be parked in a bookstore, offering himself to the masses for slavering admiration and the chance to buy one of his books and cop a free autograph. And there are few things more humiliating than when the masses have better things to do with their time and clearly wouldn't recognize a decent book—or a world-renowned writer—if one leaped up and bit them on the ass.

Milo Cook had been writing for years, although he was only twenty-eight. His first book had done all right. His second book had done a little better. The sales of his third book had topped the other two by a considerable amount. It was too early to judge the numbers on his latest endeavor, although so far the reviewers had been kind. Not effusive perhaps, but kind. And for that Milo was grateful. Nothing can kill a writer deader than a bad review. And in some cases literally. Milo knew one poor soul who drank a bottle of Drano after a particularly cruel review, which even in Milo's eyes was taking artistic sensitivity a bit too far.

Milo glanced at his watch. He had been sitting at this table for three hours now, and during that time he had signed two books. *Those* books had been purchased elsewhere and, by the looks of them, none too recently. In fact, both books had probably been tossed in the trunk of a car, forgotten, and quite possibly never even read, until the owners saw the sign touting Milo Cook's presence for the sake of signing books and thought, well, why the hell not? I've got nothing better to do. Might as well get the scribbler's autograph while I'm here. Maybe it will up the book's resale value on eBay.

Milo poked another piece of gum into his mouth to augment the first. The reek of Juicy Fruit wafted around his head like swamp gas. He pattered his toes underneath the table, doing a little impromptu tap-dance routine to kill the time—keeping it quiet, of course, so he wouldn't look like a fool. He stared out through the bookstore's plate-glass window at the multitudes passing by on this gorgeous Southern California afternoon. None of the passersby glanced his way or had the slightest inkling he existed at all. At one point in the day, he heaved a sigh and rose from his chair to snag a book off the shelf across the aisle. He had been staring at that book for the last two hours. Lugging it to the front desk, he tossed it and his credit card onto the counter. The clerk tried not to smile as she rang up the sale but was not entirely successful.

Finally, her own wit got the better of her, and as she slipped his purchase into a bookstore bag and returned his credit card, said congenially and with infinite pity, "I think you're missing the point. People are supposed to be buying *your* books, not you buying *theirs*."

"Funny," Milo answered with a tooth-grinding smile and returned to his lonely table by the front door to continue his exercise in abject humiliation.

He settled back down at the oak table he was quickly beginning to hate and let his gaze wander once again through the bookstore's front window. There was a print shop across the street. He might have just enough time to jog over and have a ten-foot banner printed up. A banner to be splayed across the front of the bookstore reading, quite possibly, "Fine, then! *Don't* come and meet the author!" Or would that be petty? He snickered and stuffed a third stick of Juicy Fruit into his mouth.

Oddly enough, it was at this point in the day when things started looking up.

A shadow fell over the bookstore's front door. The little bell over the door jingled merrily, signaling a live one entering the premises. Milo looked up and saw a handsome man of perhaps as many summers as himself blinking away the sun's glare and focusing instantly on the hapless writer sitting all alone at the tacky wooden table.

Since the hapless writer was himself, Milo sat up a little straighter, resurrected his patented author's smile, and instantly regretted he had a wad of Juicy Fruit in his mouth big enough to choke a hippo.

Being an aficionado of tall men—holy cow, was he ever—Milo sat speechless with admiration when the guy had to duck his head to step through the shop door. He had clearly been banged in the forehead a few times in the past when navigating doorways and had no intention of doing it again. How sexy was that? Once inside, the man reached up and pushed his thick, dark hair out of his eyes. The hair was chestnutty in the sun's light and curled around his ears. It was long enough down the back of his neck to be perpetually mussed by the movement of his collar. His face was lean but inviting, with a very sexy five-o'clock shadow darkening the cheeks. He appeared a likable sort. He wore an uncontrived smile on his face. It looked at home, that smile, as if it were a permanent fixture. His eyes were hazel, his lips full and expressive, his body trim. He wore tennis clothes—white polo shirt, white shorts, white tennies and socks—and all that white played up his tanned arms and legs, and a smidgeon of bronze chest at the base of his throat to perfection. He also wore a Pride bracelet on his left wrist, a simple braid of varicolored wire.

Put simply, the guy was a hunk, and judging by the bracelet, gay. Being a gay man himself, and single, and sort of horny, and being always attracted to long, hairy, suntanned legs and the men they come attached to, Milo was instantly fascinated.

The stranger's gaze swiveled around the store before returning to land yet again on Milo's face. When they did, his expressive lips spread wide in a smile that exposed an array of snow-white choppers. The man slid his hands down his shirtfront, smoothing the fabric as if trying to present himself in the best possible light—as if he could do otherwise looking the way he did—and it was that simple display of insecurity that truly captured Milo's interest. Like the guy's movie-star looks hadn't done that already.

Those beautiful, long legs carried the man directly to Milo's table, and Milo's neck creaked when he looked all the way up the guy's towering frame to return a smile.

Trying not to choke on his gum, Milo asked, "Six four?" And instantly regretted it. *Damn. Why do I always start blabbing before I engage my cerebral cortex?* It was a question he had asked himself on numerous occasions. Especially when coming face-to-face with particularly sexy males, and this guy certainly qualified as that.

The sexy male in question blushed but didn't seem to mind the question. "Six five actually. Maybe even a little over."

"Well, you carry it well. A fan of tennis too, I see."

"Yes. Are you?"

"Well, I watch men's tennis on TV." *But only for the legs.* That last thought remained mute. Milo wasn't a complete fool.

The man's blush deepened. He trailed his fingers over one of the copies of Milo's latest book adorning the table in front of him. Tearing his eyes from Milo, he lifted the book to stare down at the cover. He flipped it over, gazed at the picture of Milo on the back, then shifted his gaze back to Milo's *living* face, which he was sure to notice was not nearly as photoshopped into gossamer perfection.

"I'll take it," the man said.

"You mean the book?"

"Yes. The book."

Milo was astonishingly pleased. He wasn't sure why. Believe it or not, he had actually sold books before, although by the swell of gratitude that instantly infused his heart one would never have known it. "Wonderful," he said around the wad of Juicy Fruit. "Would you like me to sign it for you?"

"Please," the man said, dutifully handing the book over.

While Milo jotted "Tennis anyone?" on the book's title page, prior to extravagantly swirling his signature below like a pompous ass, the man reached across the table and tapped the sign Milo had placed on the table showing excerpts of his new release's best reviews.

"That's me," the man said. "BookHunter. That's quoted from my review in the Huffington Post."

Milo stopped scribbling and stared at where the man was pointing. Then he lifted his eyes again to the man's face. He tried to shift the wad of gum around in his mouth to a spot that wouldn't interfere with what he was about to say, because this was important.

"You're BookHunter.com?" Milo asked. "The reviewer?"

The hunk gave a shrug. "In the flesh."

Milo stared down at the book he had just signed. "But you must already own a copy of this. Why would you buy another? And by the way, I'm honored to meet you. Honest."

He scooted his squeaky chair back and stood up, sticking his hand out across the table. As they shook, Milo couldn't help noticing that his hand fit quite neatly inside the other's.

"I'm at a bit of a loss," Milo said, reluctantly pulling his hand away. "You know my name, but I don't know yours."

The man blinked. "I'm Logan Hunter," he said, his ears glowing red now as well as his cheeks. Again he tapped the placard. "BookHunter.com, like I said. I founded the review site a couple of years ago."

"And you reviewed my book."

Again his blush deepened. "I did. I love your writing."

Milo blinked. Compliments to his writing always caught him smack in the heart. "Thank you, uh—"

"Call me Logan."

"Logan." He gasped when the wad of Juicy Fruit tried to slide down his throat.

Logan Hunter's smile went from embarrassed to teasing in the thump of a heartbeat. "You should spit that out before you choke to death."

Milo nodded as his eyes watered up. He gazed around for a place to deposit the gum. There wasn't a wastebasket in sight.

Logan pulled a slip of paper from his back pocket. "Here. Use this."

"Oh, no, I couldn't. That's probably important."

Logan flapped it in his face. "It's a note I wrote to myself to stop by and see you. Now that I'm here, I don't need it anymore. Take it."

So Milo did. With the gigantic lump of gum out of his mouth, he found it immensely easier to talk. While he was setting the paper-wrapped wad of gum aside, still not sure exactly what the hell to do with it, Logan had slipped the book from his hand and began reading what Milo had scribbled. His grin told Milo the inscription was acceptable.

"Why are you buying this book if you already own it?" Milo asked again.

"I only own the e-book, and that was an ARC from your publisher," Logan said. "Advanced Reader's Copies rendered digitally are well and good for reviewing, but for the books I love, I want hard copies to keep on my shelf."

Milo blinked in surprise yet again. "Gotcha. So do I, actually." His gaze skittered to the book in Logan's hand. He hated asking, but he couldn't stop himself. "So you really loved it?"

Logan's gentle gaze settled over Milo like a warm blanket. "Did you read my full review?"

"Y-yes."

"Then you know I loved it. I've loved all your books. I reviewed them too, you know."

"Yes. I know. And thank you again."

This time when Logan shrugged, it was quaintly self-deprecating. "Reviewing books is what I do. You don't have to thank me. It's my job."

A reasonably comfortable silence settled around them. Milo sat back down in his chair. He felt a little guilty about it since there wasn't a chair available for Logan. Still, it once again put his head on a level with the guy's crotch, so he couldn't complain too much.

God, I'm a slut.

"How about a bite to eat?" Logan asked, smiling down at Milo. "Somewhere casual. I'm not exactly dressed for the Ritz."

"Really? You want me to go out to dinner with you?"

"If you want to call it dinner, sure. You eat, right?"

"Well, yeah."

"Then what's the problem?"

Milo's eyes dipped to take in the Pride bracelet on Logan's wrist.

Logan caught the glance and grinned. "Don't let your writer's imagination get the better of you. It's not a date. Just a bite to eat."

"No, I—I know…."

"If you're up for a little social interaction, we can talk about your writing. I've never met a writer yet who would turn down *that* invitation."

"And you still haven't," Milo said, making them both laugh. "But should you really be asking me out to dinner? How do you know I'm not in a relationship?"

Logan's dimples deepened. "In the first place, I'm asking you out to eat, not make love. And in the second place, according to your bio, you live with a dog named Spanky. If you had a significant other at home, one that's human, I mean, you probably would have mentioned it."

"Oh." Milo gave an almost audible gulp. He was a bit mesmerized by how incredibly sexy it was to hear this man utter the words "make love." It *really* kicked his writer's imagination into high gear. With bells and whistles and the whole nine yards. *Yowza.*

Totally unaware of the weird thoughts rampaging through Milo's head, thank God, Logan glanced around the store, looking for the clerk. "I'm going to go pay for this book, then maybe we can leave. It's almost five o'clock, and I would imagine you're bored enough by now. It doesn't look like there have been many readers lining up to bask in your glory."

Milo barked out a little laugh. As laughs go, it wasn't a happy one. "No, you're my first sale."

"In that case, I'll buy two." He snatched up another book, opened it to the title page, and slid it over to Milo to autograph. "Say something generically literary. It'll be a Christmas gift for my mom."

Milo did as commanded, jotting "Happy reading!" above his signature.

Logan glanced at it and tucked the book under his arm with the first. "Good, then. I'll pay for these while you pack up. Is that acceptable to you?"

Without an ounce of shyness, Milo said, "It's the best offer I've had all day. Give me two minutes."

He watched as Logan Hunter, aka BookHunter.com, aka hunk extraordinaire, aka loving son to his dear old mother (and how sweet was that?), strode off down the aisle toward the cash register at the back of the store. As soon as Milo could wrest his eyes away from the long, hairy legs Logan strode away *on*, he started packing up his stuff.

He didn't even *try* to hide the smile on his face as he tossed his unsold books haphazardly back into the boxes they came in. True to his word, in two minutes flat he was packed up and ready to go.

"I HAVEN'T met that many reviewers," Milo said.

Logan grinned. "I'm sure you haven't missed much. We're a surly lot, some of us."

Milo rolled his eyes, but not in a mocking way. "I don't believe that."

Logan frowned, then just as quickly smiled. "Neither do I. Most of the reviewers I know are great people. They love what they do."

Milo smiled back. "I agree 100 percent."

While he appreciated the words, Logan thought he saw a bit of reluctance in the way they were expressed. Logan knew perfectly well that some book reviewers could be hurtful. Judging by that wary look on Milo's face, he had been targeted a time or two himself. Logan was grateful when he saw Milo whisk the gloom away with a smile. He suspected, although he had only known Milo Cook for a few minutes, that this particular writer's default mood was one of open optimism and good cheer. That was a nice change. Some of the authors Logan dealt with were not only socially inept, but about as cheerful as a toothache.

With Logan's help, Milo had dumped his book-signing paraphernalia and two boxes of unsold books in his car down the street. He and Logan were now waiting for their orders at a hamburger joint two blocks from the bookstore where Milo had just endured the most miserably pointless afternoon of his life, or so he informed Logan prior to ordering the biggest hamburger on the menu.

Logan aimed a smile across the table. He had to admit, he was intrigued by this writer sitting across from him. And it wasn't just Milo's books that intrigued him.

That surprised Logan more than anything that had happened to him in a very long while.

Milo Cook stood perhaps five ten, a good head shorter than Logan. His hands were expressive, his smile quick, his eyes as green as new leaves freshly sprouted on the branch. And those lovely green eyes stared out from beneath the longest eyelashes Logan had ever seen. Milo's unruly hair was reddish and streaked with blond. The streaks came from the sun, not some hairdresser's magic potion. That much was obvious. Milo's tan was even deeper than Logan's, and while he didn't appear as muscled as Logan, he did have the lean, graceful look of a runner, perhaps, or a swimmer.

While they waited for their food, Logan studied the man in front of him while trying not to *look* like he was studying him. "You must be out in the sun a lot. Are you a runner?"

"Surfer, swimmer, all-around beach nut," Milo said. "That's when I'm not glued to my computer, sitting on my ass in my writing cave trying to string words together so I can make enough money to buy dog food, that is."

"Ah, yes. For the aforementioned Spanky."

"Exactly."

Logan settled back in his seat. His legs were so long they bumped against Milo's legs under the table. "Oops, sorry."

"No problem," Milo said, readjusting his legs to get them out of the way.

Silence settled over them, and suddenly Logan felt uncomfortable. Well, not uncomfortable really, just *anxious*. Maybe even a little guilty. It had been a long time since he found himself interested in another man. And it had certainly been a long time since he had asked one out for a meal.

After fiddling with the salt shaker for a minute and taking another glance at the menu on the little sandwich board sitting on the table because he didn't really know where else to aim his eyes, Logan cleared his throat and asked, "What made you want to be a writer?"

"Are we doing an interview?" Milo asked.

"No. Just chatting. So are you working on something new?"

Milo groaned. "Sounds like an interview. And if you really want to know, I'm always working on something new."

"Good. You're far too talented a writer not to be writing." Logan could tell his words had hit home. An appreciative light hit Milo's eyes, and before he could say "Thank you" or any other of a hundred mundane things people say when they've received an unexpected compliment, Logan crowbarred his way back into the conversation. "So answer my question. What made you want to be a writer?"

Milo smiled. It was a truer smile this time, Logan thought. With less shyness in it, he was happy to see. It never ceased to amaze him how a heartfelt compliment affected people.

"I suppose you want the real answer," Milo sighed, a tendril of ginger hair falling over one eye before being impatiently tucked back into the mass of curls atop his head.

Logan returned the smile. Gently prodding. "Of course."

Milo readjusted his silverware, then twirled the ring on his finger, which Logan noticed was a gold and onyx number. Quite nice. Simple and masculine. For some reason, Logan tucked his hands under the table to hide the silver band on his own finger. He didn't bother to analyze the psychology behind why he did it. Instead, Logan watched as Milo gazed out the restaurant window for a second. When his eyes returned to Logan, he appeared resigned.

Milo fiddled with his fork while he talked. "Well, since you want the truth, I won't give you the long-suffering artist baloney about leaving my mark on a heartless world and struggling to write tales that will last and how my books are my only progeny, what with me being a fruitcup and all. I'll just tell you the truth. And the truth is—I don't know why I write. It's simply something I've always done. Something I've always loved. It's been my outlet since grade school. It's a tough business, but I can't imagine living my life outside of it." He paused, looking a little embarrassed, as if thinking maybe he had said too much. Then he leaned in, settling his eyes on Logan. "My turn. What made you want to be a reviewer?"

Logan laughed. "Oh, believe me, I'd rather be a writer than a reviewer, but I don't have the talent or patience for creative writing. Still, I love books, so being a reviewer is my way of staying close to them, I guess." He studied Milo with an admiring gleam in his eye. "Of all the writers I've spoken to over the last couple of years, you're the first to ask me why I wanted to be a reviewer."

"I'm nosy."

"No. I think it's more than that."

"Well, whatever it is, I'm glad our two livelihoods brought us together. If it wasn't for you, I wouldn't have made any sales today at all, and I'd probably be sitting at home eating a bologna sandwich."

Logan pouted like a three-year-old, or pretended to. "And here I thought you liked me for my critiquing skills. Now I learn it's only my Visa card you're enthralled with."

Milo laughed. "The tennis shorts didn't hurt either."

To Logan's amusement, Milo instantly looked appalled by what he'd said. His ears went fiery red, and his mouth formed a horrified little O. In fact, he looked so shocked, Logan almost burst out laughing.

"I'm sorry," Milo said. "I don't know why I said that."

Logan reached across the table and patted Milo's hand, still trying not to laugh. "Don't look so embarrassed. I forgive you. Trust me, it's nice to know I can still turn a head now and then."

Logan stared down at his hand. The way Milo's skin felt beneath his fingertips was something he could not have anticipated. It was— *electric* somehow. He yanked his hand away.

"Yes, well...," he stammered, flailing around for something to say before spotting the waitress wending her way in their direction between the tables, laden with plates.

Milo didn't seem to notice anything amiss, and for that Logan was grateful. He swallowed his surprise at the rush of desire that had surged through him, brought about by nothing more than touching Milo's hand.

Resurrecting his beaming smile for the waitress's benefit, Logan exclaimed, "Ah, here we go. Food!"

MILO WAS down to dragging his last french fry through a raggedy puddle of ketchup when Logan collapsed back into his seat and patted his belly.

"God, I'm stuffed."

"Me too." Milo grinned as his final bite of lunch disappeared between his lips. "I'll have to come here again," he mumbled, chewing and then tucking his mouth behind his fist to disguise a delicate burp. "Good service. Good food."

"Good company," Logan added. He patted his mouth with a napkin and puckered his lips over the end of his straw, slurping the last of his soda, making as much racket as a four-year-old. Over the fountain glass, Logan's gaze fell squarely on Milo's face. "So do you live in Coronado?" He plunked his glass down and pushed it aside.

Milo shook his head, admiring for the umpteenth time the warmth that radiated from Logan's hazel eyes. He admired, too, the little golden flecks he could see in them when the light fell on Logan's face just right. "No," he said, blinking himself back to the moment. "I live across the bay. A little gentrified section of San Diego known as South Park. You?"

"Manhattan."

Milo blinked in surprise. "Then what are you doing here? And how in the world did you manage to cross an entire continent and end up stumbling onto me sitting all alone in that stupid bookstore?"

Logan shrugged. "Just luck, I guess." Then he laughed. "Actually, I've been apartment hunting. I've decided to move here. The New York winters are frankly killing me. Do you realize that at this exact moment in time while it is seventy-three degrees here in the merry month of January, it is five degrees below zero in Manhattan, with a foot of snow clogging up traffic and making life miserable for millions of grumpy, frostbitten New Yorkers?"

"No kidding?"

"No kidding. And you may not know this, but at that temperature your boogers freeze inside your nose in ten seconds flat. It's most disconcerting."

Milo snorted in merry disgust. "I guess it would be. So you're packing up and moving all the way to the West Coast just to keep your boogers from freezing?"

A playful grin twisted Logan's mouth, causing a dimple to kick in. "Do I need a better reason?"

Milo shook his head and chuckled. "Nope, I guess not. I complain when the temperature in San Diego drops below sixty."

"Pansy. And actually I've already moved. Everything I own is sitting in a van not more than two miles from here at this very moment. I'm just trying to find a place to put it. A place that feels like home. And by the way, I don't recommend driving across the country while towing your car behind a moving van. It's a pain in the neck."

Milo eased back in his seat, studying Logan more closely. He offered up a cluck of sympathy. "I'll bet it is. But that still doesn't explain how you ran across me sitting like a lump inside that bookstore."

Logan shrugged. "I keep track of my favorite writers. I knew you were signing today. It had been on my agenda all along to stop by and meet you. Having a bite to eat together was a spur-of-the-moment decision. And a pleasant one."

Milo's ankle touched Logan's foot under the table. He pulled it away, although he certainly didn't want to. "Pleasant indeed," he said. "And thank you for asking."

Again Logan shrugged, but Milo thought he seemed pleased. "Don't mention it."

A friendly silence settled between them before Milo asked, "And you're moving to San Diego alone? No lover? No better half? What about your mother? Is she boxed up in the moving van, or did you leave her to freeze like a Popsicle in a New York City snowdrift?"

To Milo's surprise, Logan paused for a couple of ticks, as if something Milo had said disconcerted him. He recovered quickly enough, but Milo thought he detected a little bit of forced good cheer in Logan's answer when it finally came. Or maybe it was just Milo's overblown writer's imagination tinged with the inferiority complex he had been battling since grade school. Both had been known to show up at odd times before.

"No lover," Logan said, his gaze steady again. "No better half. As for my mother, she lives in Florida. I'd rather set myself on fire than live in Florida. In fact, for the better part of the year, you might as well. It's hotter than hell in Florida. Strangely, elderly Jewish ladies don't seem to mind the heat. And just between you and me, I'd also rather set myself on fire than live in reasonable proximity to my mother."

"So you're Jewish and your mother's annoying. No clichés there. Any pets?"

"Nary a one. Is that a character fault?"

"Well, it is, but a few of your other attributes nullify it."

"I hope you're not talking about my tennis shorts again."

Milo grinned. "Well, now that you mention it. And by the way, if you just came from the frigid East, how can your legs be so tanned?" *And sexy*, he didn't add.

Logan grinned as well. "Bloodlines. My mother's parents were Egyptian. They migrated to the States during the Suez crisis."

"After the founding of Israel."

"Exactly. Anyway, nice coloring, Egyptians. Saves me a fortune on sunlamps and Coppertone."

"I imagine it would," Milo said. "Prying question number two. If you haven't unpacked yet and all your stuff is still sitting in a moving van across town, how can you be dressed for Wimbledon?"

"I spotted public tennis courts on El Cajon Boulevard." He vaguely waved a hand eastward. "Somewhere in *that* direction. After manhandling that bigass truck for days on end, I needed to unwind and stretch my legs, so I dug through my luggage to find tennis clothes, then stopped and played a few games with a nice old lady whose legs looked like matchsticks and who beat me two sets out of three."

Milo laughed. "What a bitch!"

"That's what I thought."

Milo sat quietly for a moment, both men smiling at their easy banter. Then he asked, "And how exactly did you know I'd be book-signing today?"

Logan gave a lazy shrug. "Being a reviewer, I keep up with things like that."

"I hope you won't let the reading world know what a horrible flop it was."

"Your secret is safe with me."

"Phew!" Milo leaned in closer, his eyes delving. "Is that all you do? Review books? I mean, is that enough to pay the bills?"

"You're right. You *are* nosy. But no. I also edit for a select group of writers, I submit book reviews for a variety of publications, and I write business copy for an ad firm in New York. All of which are jobs I can perform online. Away from the snow. Anywhere, in fact. Or more precisely, here. In close proximity to one of my favorite novelists."

Milo's cheeks heated. "Flatterer."

Oddly, Logan blushed again too. It was a sight Milo was beginning to enjoy. He also enjoyed the way Logan's eyes squinted at the corners when he laughed. And the way the bridge of his nose wrinkled up when he smiled. Milo rested his elbows on the table and studied Logan's face more closely. It really was a hell of a face. And that five-o'clock shadow was sexy as hell.

"I can't believe you're not taken," Milo heard himself say. "And yes, I'm still being nosy."

To his surprise, Milo caught a glimmer of unease in Logan's eyes. He had spotted a couple of them during the course of their conversation, but this one beat the others hands down. He was about to apologize for going too far when Logan's eyes drifted to the window, as if something there had captured his attention. As Milo's gaze followed, Logan began to speak. Milo turned back to listen, but Logan's eyes never left the window. His voice was a little breathless, as if he were looking back, at his past, at his life, at something only he could see.

"I had a lover. We were together for three years. Last March—I can't believe it's been almost a year already—Jerry died in a car crash. In the snow, in fact. During a blizzard. He was twenty-seven at the time. I think maybe that's another reason I'm leaving New York."

"Too many memories?" Milo quietly said.

"Yes. Too many memories."

Logan shifted his gaze back to Milo as a drowsy smile returned to soften his face. He heaved a quiet sigh. "Now you know everything there is to know about me. What about you? No exes I should hear about? No romances in the works?"

Milo ran his fingertip through a ring of moisture on the table left there by his soda glass. "I really didn't mean to snoop that much, Logan. I'm sorry. And I'm sorry for your loss too. I can't—I can't imagine what that must have been like for you."

Logan gave him an accepting nod, his eyes fixed on the table now, on his hands resting there in front of him. For the first time, Milo noticed the silver band on Logan's ring finger. Somehow he knew there was a story behind that ring, a story he would love to hear but knew instinctively not to ask about.

"Thank you, Milo," Logan said, jarring Milo's attention from the ring. "And don't be ashamed of snooping. That's what writers have to do, I think. But still, it doesn't let you off the hook. I want to hear about your love life. How many lovers have you driven mad tap-tap-tapping at your keyboard day and night while they're trying to sleep? How many partners have you pissed off by tacking their most annoying faults onto a character in one of your books? And how, pray tell, does someone who looks like you find himself living with a dog named Spanky and not a handsome, worshiping Adonis?"

Since the tip of his finger was wet already, Milo flipped the moisture at Logan's face, making him jump. After they'd both chuckled at that, although Milo knew he was being infantile and no doubt Logan knew it too, he decided to share a few secrets. It was the least he could do after Logan had revealed so much to him.

"Thanks for the compliment, if that's what it was," Milo said, grinning. Then his face grew more serious. "My Adonis and I broke up a long time ago. His name was Bryce. Another writer." Here, Milo rolled his eyes. "Well, he was trying to be. He never got the breaks, though. Couldn't make his first sale. I'm not being catty when I say his stuff wasn't good enough, but truthfully, it wasn't. I never quite had the nerve to tell him, though. I loved him, after all. At least I thought I did. I didn't want to hurt him. Still, I think now it would have been better if I'd been honest."

"So what happened?" Logan asked. He was leaning forward with his elbows on the table, his chin in his hands, taking in every word.

It almost embarrassed Milo that Logan was so absorbed in what he was saying. But he couldn't stop now. He might as well finish the story. Logan had been open with him. Tit for tat, and all that.

"Bryce just up and left. No, that's not right. I suppose we sort of left each other. Truthfully, our relationship seemed to meander into self-destruct mode without any help from either one of us. He eventually moved away. Left San Diego, I heard. I'm not sure where he ended up. It could have been anywhere. Bryce had money he'd inherited, so that was one thing he never had to worry about. Anyway, I hope he's happy. We had a good time together for a while, and I know a lot of gay guys who haven't had that much. So I'm not complaining."

He pulled himself out of his own thoughts and looked at Logan as if they were good friends already and this was the first time he had seen him in a while.

A kind light warmed Logan's eyes, like he knew the exact moment when Milo pulled himself away from his memories and back to the present. He reached out and patted Milo's hand.

"Thank you for sharing that with me," Logan said.

Milo nodded. "You too."

Suddenly Logan sat up straighter. He glanced at his watch. When his gaze traveled back to Milo, he appeared saddened by what he was about to say. Saddened but still determined. "I'm going to have to leave. I have an appointment to see an apartment in thirty minutes. I don't want to be late."

Milo jumped. "No. Of course not. Here, let me get this." He reached for the tab, but Logan beat him to it.

"No. I invited you," Logan said. "Dinner's on me."

Milo sat back. "Well, if you insist." A moment later he added, "It was nice meeting you. And thank you again for the reviews."

Logan gave a cavalier shrug. "Hey, it's what I do." He glanced at his watch again. "I'm going to have to run. I don't want to lose a chance on snagging that apartment. It's perfect."

"Yes, of course. Go. Run."

Milo watched as Logan laid some bills over the tab and scooted it to the edge of the table for the waitress. He rose and hovered over Milo for a second. He stood silent, shuffling from one foot to the other, as if unsure what to say.

Finally, he asked softly, "Can I call you sometime?"

Surprised by the shyness in Logan's voice, Milo looked up and said without thinking, "Of course. I'd like you to."

"Oh good, then," Logan said, the relief evident on his face, although he still looked incredibly embarrassed. His eyes skidded away from Milo to take in the restaurant and the diners scattered here and there.

Before Milo could reply, before he could think of a single thing to say, Logan laid a gentle hand on his shoulder, the lightest of touches, before hurrying away, weaving between the tables and slipping out the front door without a backward glance.

Only after he had disappeared down the street did Milo remember he hadn't given Logan his phone number.

Chapter Two

THE DAY after he met Logan Hunter, Milo rose early and donned pajamas—since he wore them to work in, not to sleep—and parked himself in his downstairs office to write. Milo's house stood on a lushly wooded canyon that rolled off to the south. On a clear day it afforded him a terrific view from his bedroom window of the distant Mexican mountains. From a bank of living room windows on the other side of the house, he could see the San Diego city skyline, three miles west. The view from his office, however, was less engaging, which Milo considered a good thing since it afforded less distraction. Too bad some other distractions weren't as avoidable. Properly stocked with a pot of coffee at his side, his workday began, as always, with Milo finding fault with everything he had written the day before. While beating himself up over that, he wasted a considerable amount of time wishing he could crank out pages like Stephen King, who, it was rumored, could jiggle a bowl of alphabet soup and come up with a novella and two short stories.

At the moment, Milo was knee-deep in writing a thriller. His last book had been a comedy. Milo liked to mix things up when it came to plotlines. He guessed he was doing something right since his readers hadn't deserted him yet.

His office was a bit chilly this morning, so Milo tucked his bare toes under Spanky, his big fuzzy dog of indeterminate breed, boundless loyalty, and infinite laziness, who lay snoring at his feet, as obsequiously fawning as ever.

While he wrote, Milo took occasional side trips to Facebook. He swore it would be the death of his career one day. Writers were always looking for an excuse not to write. Having Facebook a mouse-click away made dawdling a breeze. Unfortunately, most of his connections to the writing world—friends, reviewers, fellow authors, publishers, editors, readers, even a few morons who posted nothing but political crap and who had sneaked onto Milo's friends list when he wasn't looking—were maintained through social media. In Milo's eyes, it was a necessary evil.

Today his meandering path through Facebook, usually a total waste of time, but fun nevertheless, began with a surprise. A surprise that made Milo's sleepy eyes crinkle with happiness as he sat there gaping at the screen and slurping his third cup of coffee.

The surprise was a friend request from a certain BookHunter, reviewer of all things literary, or so he touted himself on his Facebook page.

Milo accepted immediately, and not ten seconds later a private message came through.

>BookHunter: *Good morning.*
>Milo Cook: *Good morning to you too. Did you get your apartment?*
>BookHunter: *I did indeed. Will be moving in shortly.*
>Milo Cook: *Congratulations! What part of town?*
>BookHunter: *Hillcrest.*
>Milo Cook: *Oh good. We're practically neighbors.*
>BookHunter: *Great! Oops, gotta run. I'm sitting in my rental Ryder truck with all my possessions piled in the back, and the movers I hired have just shown up. I'm sad to report there's not a cute one in the lot.*
>Milo Cook: *Some days nothing goes right. LOL.*
>BookHunter: *Ain't that the truth. Later.*

Smiling, Milo closed out the message box. He spent an enjoyable few minutes in the newfound knowledge that he and Logan now had a way to communicate with each other. He spent a few *more* enjoyable minutes remembering how Logan had looked in tennis shorts.

God, I really am a slut.

Shaking himself back to reality, Milo clicked his way out of Facebook and once again tried to concentrate on his Work in Progress. He'd succeeded for perhaps an hour, baby-stepping his way a little deeper into his preconceived plot, when a beep proclaimed the arrival of an incoming email. He tapped his way there and found a note from a fellow writer from his publishing house, Winter Press. Her name was Lillian Damons, a romance writer. Mutual fans, she and Milo had met at a writers' conference in Denver several years before. She was married to a book reviewer, Grace Connor. Milo had attended their wedding in Kansas City, where the two women now lived.

> *Dear Milo,*
>
> *My heart is broken. Grace was murdered in New York City two weeks ago. She was strangled in her hotel room. They tell me it was most likely either a rape or a robbery gone wrong. I've been in shock ever since. I can't stop crying. It took almost ten days for the NYPD to release her body. The funeral was held yesterday in Grace's hometown of Roanoke. Her family was gracious to me as always, but we are all so crushed with grief we can't accept it yet that Grace is gone. Maybe none of us ever will.*
>
> *I know you loved Grace, so I wanted to let you know. I pray they'll catch the monster who did this, but so far the homicide detective in charge of the case tells me they don't have many leads.*
>
> *What a cruel planet this world has become. My beloved Grace had heart disease too, you know. She must have been so frightened at the end. My own heart is broken now too.*
>
> *Stay safe, darling friend.*
> *Lillian*

Milo stared at the screen for the longest time as he read and reread Lillian's heartbreaking email. Finally he answered with an email of his own, extending the proper shock, empathy, sorrow, commiseration. Saying all the right words, denoting all the proper emotions.

And all the while he typed, a worm of guilt chewed through him. Guilt because in truth, Milo had not loved Grace Connor at all. He associated with her only because she was Lillian's wife, and Lillian was a friend. They shared a history, Milo and Lillian. Working for the same publisher. Attending conferences. Traveling once to Germany together for the Frankfurt Book Fair, the largest annual gathering of writers and publishers in the world. They had even cowritten a short story for one of their publisher's anthologies.

There was no such history with Grace, nor had Milo ever wanted there to be.

Almost without thinking, Milo signed his email with its empty platitudes and insincere expressions of comfort and sent it off. While it whizzed silently away through the ether, his true thoughts were not on Lillian's grief at all, but on Grace. On some of the reviews she had written. On the enemies she had made by being less than gracious with her criticisms of certain writers. Grace was not a popular reviewer with authors. She often took a hard stance on those writers whose skills she found wanting. Her words could be mocking, belittling, even bordering on cruel. Under a threadbare guise of humor and clever wordplay, she could rip a writer's fragile ego to the quick, and often did, seemingly for the sheer enjoyment of it. In fact, there had been a mean streak in her reviews that had discouraged more than one new writer from ever publishing again.

Milo had never wished her ill because of it, but there were certainly times when he felt she had gone too far. Yet even Milo knew his thoughts on her passing were tempered by the fact that she had never pointed her wicked pen at him or his own books. Not so for many in the writing community, Milo suspected. There were a few writers out there, he didn't doubt for a minute, who were hoisting a drink or two to Grace's untimely, and in their eyes, well-deserved demise.

Yet it had not been Grace's reviews that got her killed. Fate had done that. Wrong place, wrong time. Or maybe it was karma. And if there *was* a touch of justice involved, it was not up to Milo to decide. Still, there was no denying that in his eyes, a kinder victim would have warranted greater grief.

The coldness of that realization caused Milo to slump in his desk chair and close his eyes. Lillian was right. It was a cruel planet indeed. Even Milo wasn't immune to its lure.

THERE HAD always been a streak of social anxiety nibbling away at Milo's psyche. Simple duties that most writers take for granted were a bit of a chore for him. Book signings, readings, writers' conventions—all took a toll, jarring his composure and frazzling his nerves, but he had learned over the years to cope with his frailties. Most of his friends, in fact, would probably be surprised to learn he suffered from social anxiety at all.

Actually, large groups for Milo were less intimidating than smaller ones. Take tonight, for instance.

The South Park Reading Club had extended an invitation to Milo and two other local authors to attend their monthly meeting and perhaps do a short reading and answer a few questions for the members, all of whom were fans, the invitation stated.

Milo had accepted, of course. After all, these readers lived in his own neighborhood. He couldn't very well blow them off. Still, he had to concentrate on not breaking into a cold sweat or finding a thousand other ways to make a fool of himself. And so far he had succeeded.

In fact, with the reading of an excerpt from his latest Work in Progress behind him—he had been slated as the last to read, which didn't help his nerves any—the worst was now over. The small crowd, perhaps twenty people in all, were kindly attentive, clearly grateful Milo had deigned to grace them with his presence, and the cheese dip was especially good, which didn't hurt either. The group appeared to take in all extremes of the social spectrum, from the moneyed to the not so moneyed, from young to old to in-between. As always, it was their devotion to reading that brought them together. Social status had nothing to do with it. This was one aspect of book lovers that always gave Milo hope for the human species. For the sake of a simple tale on paper or in pixels, people could overlook their differences and come together as one to share a common passion.

Yes, so far the night was going swimmingly.

Then the Q and A began.

The first question out of the crowd came from a small woman with thick glasses and tightly permed graying hair. She looked like someone's grandmother. An ace at baking cookies, no doubt, and doling out endless reams of advice, all the while aiming a gimlet eye at friends and strangers alike.

That gimlet eye came into play now, as she cast a probing glance at each of the three authors sitting huddled on the sofa side by side with plates of goodies in their laps. The way food and utensils instantly froze in midair suggested the question clearly came as a shock to all of them.

"I wonder if each of you would give us an opinion concerning the recent murder of Grace Connor, taking into account that a goodly part of the writing community is not exactly heartbroken by her death."

Milo was holding a plate of cheese and crackers. One of the crackers was in his mouth at the time. He hastily chewed it up and swallowed it down as he noted the surprising lack of empathy in the old woman's eyes when she spoke of Grace's murder.

Happily, it was Juliet Karnes, the author on his right, who chose to answer first. She was a pinched, tweedy woman in her high seventies, if she was a day, who wrote sex scenes in her het romances that curled even Milo's hair. The very idea that she knew what a sex act *was* seemed fantastical at best. The fact that she sat sipping periodically from a silver flask and cussed like a sailor seemed a little out of character as well.

"Are they fucking not?" she asked coolly. "I mean, heartbroken by what happened?"

The old lady who posed the question gave a disapproving tut, whether at the question or the cursing Milo couldn't be sure. "Goodness me, it's all over social media. Excerpts of her many—shall we say—ungracious reviews. Unkind words she wrote about this book and that, lambasting one writer after another. Don't you have an opinion on her passing? A host of your fellow authors certainly do."

For the tenth time that evening, Miss Karnes tucked her flask back in her jacket pocket and smiled, not unlike a shark who's just spotted a lone swimmer with yummy-looking thighs. "Most writers know that reviews don't matter. And I for one refuse to garner news by trolling Facebook, or personal blogs, or any of a hundred other social media sites. It's all bullshit. I'll admit Grace Connor was a bitch, but I'm still not sure she deserved what happened to her. And I think it's a little premature to expound on the idea it was her reviews that got her killed. Did the killer drop an unfinished manuscript behind at the murder scene? I'm sorry, dear lady, but you seem to be talking out of your ass."

A few snickers could be heard, but the woman who posed the question merely muttered, "Well, I never!" Making a noble effort to unruffle her feathers, she turned to the second writer for his opinion, leaving Milo once again, it seemed, last on the program.

The second guest was Adrian Strange, a sci-fi writer with a fair backlist of science fiction novels on his Amazon profile, but who had never really seen much financial success from his work. Milo knew him as a prolific writer who had at one time turned out two or three books a year. After once reading a couple of his books, Milo felt Adrian Strange would do better at the money end of the game if he concentrated more on quality in his writing and a little less on quantity. Strange was a skinny, gangly man in his late thirties, not bad-looking but not really handsome either, whose long legs were at the moment tucked under the coffee table in front of him because there was simply no other place for him to put them. He was balancing a mound of food on his lap that practically overran the plate. Obviously, Mr. Strange wasn't one to pass up a free meal. Maybe his less-than-stellar royalty checks had something to do with that.

At the moment, he was chewing a sausage, but he didn't let that stop him. "I'm a firm believer in karma. People reap what they sow in this business. A slight, an unkind word, a cruel review, will come back and bite you one way or another. Grace Connor was a snake, and every once in a while a snake will slither across the wrong foot and get its head chopped off by a farmer with a hoe. As far as I'm concerned, the writing world is better off without her."

He had been speaking to the room at large, but now Adrian focused his attention on the spinster lady who asked the question. "You ask if I think her death was a direct result of her cruel touch in reviewing people's work. My answer is yes. And even if it wasn't, the result is the same. She got what she deserved."

With that, he smiled acidly and poked another sausage into his mouth.

Milo honestly couldn't believe what he was hearing. When expectant eyes at long last turned to him, he set his plate aside. He had suddenly lost his appetite. He stared down at his hands for a moment while the entire South Park Reading Club sat around, gazing at him expectantly, clearly waiting for his opinion. All except for Adrian Strange, who was forking up potato salad like the end of days was coming, and he intended to go out with a full stomach.

Milo cleared his throat. Hoping he wouldn't piss off the entire room, he chose to center his response on the lady who started the conversation. Perhaps that way the collateral damage would be minimal.

"What happened to Grace Connor was terrible. I don't think it's fair to hint that hordes of people were delighted to see her go. She was tough with her reviews, I'll admit. But she was also expansive with her praise. She didn't hate everything she read, after all. She never panned any of my books, at least."

Adrian Strange mumbled something incoherent under his breath, and Juliet Karnes bit back a sarcastic giggle while nipping at her flask again. For the first time, Milo noticed she had only three untouched radishes on her plate. No wonder she looked emaciated.

The old lady who posed the question was not to be swayed. "But her homosexual lover is a colleague and friend of yours. Perhaps if that were not the case, she might have gone after your second book, which in my opinion had a few plot holes big enough to drive a truck through that should have been remedied in the editing phase."

"Touché," Miss Karnes mumbled, clearly having fun now.

Milo laughed too. He noticed the hostess of the evening's activities looked immensely grateful when he did. Clearly she already thought the conversation was getting out of hand, and the last thing she wanted to do was offend the guests of honor, although in Milo's opinion most of the offending had been done by the guests, not the hostess. She cast a homicidal glance at the old spinster, and Milo wondered if his interrogator would find herself suddenly deleted from the mailing list for future club events.

Again, Milo focused his attention on the woman with the Coke-bottle glasses. "As it happens, you're right. I am a friend and colleague of Lillian Damons. But she and Grace were not simply homosexual lovers, as you put it. They were legally married wives to each other. I attended their wedding. And for my part, I considered Grace as much a friend as Lillian." This was a fib, but Milo didn't figure anyone in this room needed to know that. "It's almost as if you are accusing Grace of being murdered *because* of her reviews."

"And why not?" the bespectacled woman countered. "She ruined more than one writing career, I've heard. Who's to say one of those people didn't go after her for a little revenge?"

This time it was Adrian Strange who tried to stifle a chuckle, although Milo noticed he didn't try very hard.

Milo gazed at the woman with a far less charitable eye than he had before, and frankly, he was getting a little fed up with his fellow guests of honor as well. It took a goodly amount of willpower not to speak rudely to the lot of them. But in the end, he was saved by a rather hastily contrived question from the other side of the room concerning points of view in writing. Grateful to get off the subject of poor Grace, he turned away to address the speaker, while the woman who blamed Grace for her own murder muttered *"Harrumph"* loudly enough for Milo to hear, which was clearly her intention.

Milo orated for three minutes on omniscient and limited omniscient viewpoints, which the questioner had specifically targeted. All the while he spoke, he grew more disconcerted by the heartless way the woman with the bad perm and thick glasses had referred to Lillian's wife. He was none too pleased with the response of his two fellow writers either, but since it was the spinster who started it all, he decided to cast his final opinion on the matter at her. So the moment he finished the viewpoint lecture—and he could tell he should probably wrap it up by the glassy-eyed looks on his listeners' faces—he turned back to the woman. She was still looking shortchanged by Milo's answer and was soothing her frustrations by stuffing her face with chips and salsa. Milo surprised her so by redirecting his attention back to her, a glob of salsa slid off her chip and landed in her lap.

Milo kept his words cool, his contempt for the woman hidden. But there were things he wanted to say, and he was determined to say them. If the two writers at either side of him got an earful as well, so be it.

"Ma'am, I don't believe Grace's reviews had anything to do with her death. Nor does Grace's wife believe that. Sometimes the world has a way of sneaking up and bringing even the best of us to our knees. For the most part, it has nothing to do with the way we live our lives. It just happens. To the good and the bad. It could happen to you tomorrow. Or me. Or the lovely person who made this delicious cheese dip." A startled chuckle rolled around the room. It seemed to come from every attendee but the one he was addressing. That woman didn't look amused at all. "Writers may write of murder, ma'am, but most of us barely have the wherewithal to set it down properly on paper, let alone pull it off in real life. I think you, and all of us, should let poor Grace Connor's memory rest in peace. There is little need to speak ill of her now that she's gone."

"Very well," the woman said with tight lips.

Milo wasn't sure, but he suspected the stern stare the woman was getting from the hostess might have had something to do with her capitulation.

Anyway, she appeared to accept the rebuke by falling silent, and for that Milo was grateful.

As for the writers at either side of him, Milo had no idea what they thought of his words, because at that point in the evening, he centered his undivided attention on the crab salad, which really was delicious.

Later, after driving home and walking Spanky around the block, Milo fixed himself a drink to unwind. Logging on to social media to kill some time before bed, Milo quickly realized speculation about the motive for Grace's murder was far from limited to one old lady from the South Park Reading Club and a couple of mediocre authors who seemed a little too thin-skinned for Milo's taste. It was rampant, just as the woman had said.

There were few who did not believe Grace had brought it on herself, and many of the commentators didn't mince words, stating flatly they thought she deserved it. Some of the remarks were so cruel, and offered Grace Connor such little hope of a respectful passing, that Milo could only pray Lillian would steer clear of social media for a while. She had been through enough.

Disgusted, Milo shut down the computer and went to bed. Spanky leaped up right behind him and tromped around in a circle, making a mess of the covers until he had them just the way he wanted. Only then did Spanky heave a monumental sigh and collapse like a dead thing smack in the middle of the bed. Yawning and stretching, he used his paws to prod Milo a little more out of his way, managing in the process to hog 90 percent of the bed, which was a nightly ritual.

Milo, relegated to the very edge of the mattress as usual, grumbled kindly and patted Spanky on the head. He was rewarded with a lick for his patience.

Just before sleep found him, Milo's mind slipped to Logan Hunter and how tall and handsome he had looked in his snow-white tennis outfit the day they met. And how sweetly shy Logan had sounded when he asked if he could call sometime. The memory brought a smile that carried Milo into sleep. His dreams were sexier than usual, and when he woke in the morning, he was so horny he was ready to explode.

Taking himself in hand, he brought himself to climax before the sunrise lit his window. And as he did, it was thoughts of Logan that spurred him on.

Afterward, breathless, with his heart thumping like a piston engine badly in need of a tune-up, he licked away a smear of semen that had splashed across his lips, wishing it had been deposited there by Logan instead of himself.

With the night shadows slowly fleeing his room as sunrise lit the canyon outside, Milo threw his trembling legs over the side of the bed.

Trying not to disturb Spanky, which wasn't hard since the mutt could sleep through anything, even an early-morning masturbation party, Milo padded off to the bathroom to wash the come off his chest and chin and start the day.

As efficient as ever, he set up the coffee maker, and while it perked and filled the house with the delicious scent of fresh-roasted coffee, Milo jumped in the shower to soap himself down.

The next time I have sex with Logan Hunter, he told himself, squinting into the spray, *maybe it won't be a figment of my imagination. Maybe it'll be for real. Stranger things have happened, right?*

Smiling, with a wicked leer in his eye, he wondered what his chances were of actually making that happen. It might be a dangerous proposition. Milo really liked the guy, after all, and Logan Hunter couldn't have been more Milo's type if Milo had constructed the man himself to his own specifications.

Considering the fact they had spent a grand total of one hour together over burgers and fries, Milo suspected he liked him a little *too* much. But did Logan like *him*? That was really the big question here. And even if he *did* like Milo, did he like him *that* way? Plus, how was Milo supposed to know if Logan was even ready to start bedding casual acquaintances? Over hamburgers, he had made it pretty clear he still missed his lover. Poor guy. *And here I am wondering if I can coax him into the sack. What, like getting a decent review from the guy isn't enough, now I want to fuck him too? Jesus, it's never enough with me.*

Later, as he dried himself off, Milo remembered poor Lillian mourning the death of her wife and chided himself *again* for being a thoughtless twit. Maybe he should send her flowers. Hell, maybe he should send them *both* flowers. Logan and Lillian. One to woo, one to console. Or maybe he should do nothing, like he always did. Especially since he didn't have an address for Logan to send the flowers to anyway.

Milo stared at his dripping reflection in the bathroom mirror and sighed.

Why does life have to be so complicated?

Chapter Three

WITH A sigh of relief, Logan Hunter stomped the last packing box flat and kicked it toward the front door with all the others. On this crisp California morning, after a nonstop two days of work, his new apartment was fit to live in. His belongings were stashed away in their permanent niches, his furniture arranged the way he liked it, and his clothes closets neat and tidy for the first time in a decade. Of course, they wouldn't stay that way long because Logan was basically a slob. That inglorious fact had been proven and corroborated time and time again over the years. Jerry, his ex, had said this trait of Logan's to throw stuff all over the place and never actually pick up a single bloody thing was a toss-up between charmingly eccentric and infuriatingly annoying. Charming because he loved Logan, and through the eyes of love you can overlook a lot of faults. Annoying because when Logan's closets ended up looking like they had been cluster bombed, then rearranged with a bulldozer, as they inevitably did, Jerry's stuff was lost in the rubble as well.

Logan stood in front of his bedroom closet now, staring in at the neatly aligned clothing, most of it still rumpled from sitting in moving boxes all week. At least it was on hangers and off the floor for what was probably the first—and last—time in its life. And wouldn't Jerry have been surprised to see that.

As always, thoughts of Jerry turned Logan's mind inward. A sadness dimmed his eyes that was so familiar he didn't need a mirror to see it. He knew when it was there. He *always* knew when it was there.

He glanced down at his hand, staring for the millionth time at the simple silver band wrapped snugly around the third finger of his left hand. A matching ring still rested on Jerry's hand, Jerry's *cold and lifeless* hand, in a slot six shelves up on the east wall of the Peabody Mortuary in Calumet City, just south of Chicago. Calumet City had been Jerry's hometown, and Logan had flown his body back there for interment at the request of Jerry's parents. At the time, Logan had hated the idea of laying

Jerry to rest so far from Manhattan, but now he was glad. It had made it that much easier to leave New York.

Logan mindlessly twisted the ring on his finger, feeling the smooth, familiar perfection of it. For the first time he wondered if the ring felt lonely too. After all, its mate was gone just as Logan's was. They were both on their own now, he and the ring, and had been for over a year.

Maybe, just maybe, it was time to put the past behind them both.

He gripped the ring between his thumb and index finger and began to slide it off, but at the last second he stopped. No. He couldn't bear to part with this last remnant of Jerry. Not yet. Maybe one day, if love ever found him again, he would slip it off. Tuck it in a drawer somewhere like a hundred other mementos he had stashed away over the years, eventually to be forgotten or lost. But for the moment, Logan dropped his hands to his sides and left the ring where it was. Just as he left Jerry, still stowed securely in his heart.

Logan's greatest fear was that with Jerry still there, a new love, if one ever came along, would be unable to worm its way in and make room for itself. Still, while the ring was on his finger, and while Jerry slept in his heart, alive and well, at least in memory, Logan knew he would never completely move on. And that saddened him.

Especially now. For Logan knew beyond a shadow of a doubt that somehow, suddenly and inexplicably, things had changed. The tectonic plates on which he rested his life had unexpectedly shifted. Just enough to make him teeter, no longer balanced like he thought he was, no longer steady on his feet. And the reason for it was so surprisingly simple, even he understood it.

For the first time since Jerry's death, Logan had met a person who intrigued him. And he wasn't quite sure how to feel about that.

He heaved a sigh and closed the closet doors. Stepping into the second bedroom, which was now his office, Logan dropped into his desk chair and booted up his Mac. A moment later he was cruising Facebook. Well, to be a little more precise, he was cruising Milo Cook's Facebook page. Skimming through the photos, smiling at Milo laughing among a group of Winter Press authors at some convention or other, wearing a silly birthday hat behind a humongous cake with a forest fire of candles burning on it and a host of friends waiting expectantly for him to blow them out. Pictures at the beach standing shirtless in the sand in a baggy pair of swim trunks that barely clung to his slim hips.

Logan leaned in closer to the screen and studied Milo's body. It was beautiful. Not overly muscled, but slim and elegant, his legs aglow with blond hair, capturing the sunlight. Another trail of blondish hair wandered down from a trim little belly button to disappear beneath the drooping waistband of his shorts. Other details captured Logan's attention. The branching veins on his forearms and across the back of his hands. His ginger, sun-streaked hair tumbling around his face, stirred by the wind blowing off the water. The battered surfboard, obviously well-loved and well-ridden, lying in the sand at his feet. His nose whitened with zinc oxide, and his eyes squinting into the sun as he laughed, making a silly, impatient face as if coaxing the cameraman to shoot his stupid picture already.

Logan found himself smiling at Milo's happy, carefree expression. To look at him, one would never imagine he had a brain behind that silly grin, or that he was a successful writer with a seemingly endless string of stories in his head just waiting to be jotted down and offered up to a devoted world of readers.

Sitting back, Logan scrolled through more pictures, then even more. Clearly, Milo tried to keep his Facebook followers updated on his life and career. The photographs seemed endless. Then Logan's hand jerked away from the mouse as he found himself staring at one particular photograph.

It was a snapshot of Milo and a young man with dark hair. They were both in khaki shorts and hiking boots, fat backpacks strapped to their backs. Their hands were clasped as they stood, shoulder to shoulder, at the edge of a cliff. Behind them, the ocean, clearly the Pacific, sprawled out to the farthest horizon, its surface as smooth as hammered silver.

Logan focused on the man at Milo's side. He was a head taller than Milo, handsome, with brooding eyes and thin lips that were barely smiling. Still, he seemed happy enough as he stood there holding on to Milo with one hand and clutching a leash with a dog on the end of it with the other. Logan smiled. That must be Spanky. Brown and white, tail high, playfully nipping at Milo's sock.

Again Logan's gaze slid back to the man holding Milo's hand. Was this his lover before they broke up? It must be. Something about the way Milo clutched the man to him, and the merry light in his laughing eyes as he stared into the camera lens, told Logan that this was one of Milo's happy moments. And why shouldn't it be? He had love, he had youth, and he had his entire life and career ahead of him.

Logan wondered what it was that finally tore the two apart. Was it jealousy, perhaps, as Milo had hinted? Jealousy because Milo was successfully published while—what was his name? Oh yes, Bryce—while Bryce couldn't catch a break? Or was it something else. Infidelity perhaps. Or maybe it really had been as Milo said. That they simply grew apart, as couples sometimes do.

Logan studied Bryce's face for a moment longer, the crisp, serious angles of it, the dark, piercing eyes, the tight lips only slightly bent in a smile. Tearing his gaze from the screen, Logan logged off, shutting down the computer. Glancing to the left, he stared for a long moment at a picture of Jerry, waving and smiling at the camera, blithely unaware that he was leaning on the car he would die in less than two months later.

Turning away, Logan swallowed a familiar surge of sorrow. That sorrow, that emptiness, was almost an old friend now, he knew it so well. It was all that remained of the anger he had initially felt at Jerry's death. He thought back to those first few weeks after the accident, how the unfairness of it consumed him, how the fury of what had happened ate at him day after day after day. But in the end, the anger was too self-destructive for Logan to hold on to, and he had gradually allowed it to slip into grief. It wasn't easy letting his anger go, but in the end he had succeeded because he knew he would never survive if he didn't.

Now, grabbing his keys and his wallet, he cast one last look around the perfectly arranged apartment. Feeling totally out of place in all the order and neatness, he stepped through the front door and walked away. Out on the street, in cargo shorts and a T-shirt, he took a moment to relish the novelty of warm air flowing across his bare legs in the middle of January, and more than that, the novelty of standing a continent away from where he had spent all the other years of his life. This was a big deal for him. Moving to California meant a fresh start, a new beginning. It did not escape him for a second that he had left Jerry far behind when he did.

Maybe, just maybe, that was the only reason for moving at all. Logan chose a direction at random and set off on foot to explore his new neighborhood. But exploring wasn't the only thing on his mind on this bright, sunny January morning. He needed to think too, and the thoughts he contemplated were both troubling and exhilarating. Rising from the jumble of those cogitations stood the young man Logan had eaten with a few days before. Milo Cook appeared in his mind, handsome and smiling, as bright and shiny as a glint of crystal sunlight on a skyscraper window.

And while the beauty of that one young man filled Logan's head, he absently fingered the ring on his left hand, ever mindful of how painful—and how comforting—it would be to at long last slip it off.

ON THE morning of the last day Logan saw Jerry alive, they had made love, as they almost always did—gentle, sleepy sex after lazily pulling themselves awake to greet the new day dawning through their bedroom window. As always, one would be drawn to the welcoming, familiar heat of the other, and scooting across the bed, gather that heat into caring, needful arms. A self-conscious kiss would follow since neither had brushed their teeth yet. Snuggling close, each would breathe in the sleep-warm scent of the other's body. Moments later, whispered words of love would drift through the darkness, and after that, the temptation of iron cocks tenting the bedclothes would draw hungry mouths downward. Soon, what began as a simple cuddle became a craving neither man felt the slightest inclination to deny.

On that last morning, as they lay in their cocoon of postorgasmic contentment, still relishing each other's heat and taste, Logan had peered across Jerry's silken hip and eyed the heavy snow as it peppered the bedroom window with a pattering hush. Jerry taught fourth grade and had classes that morning.

"Maybe you shouldn't go," Logan remembered saying. "Traffic will be horrendous."

"Unless they call a snow day, I have to go. You know that. But don't worry. I'll drive carefully."

"The snow chains are in the trunk. Use them if you need to."

"Worrywart!" Jerry giggled. Then he drew Logan into a final bone-crushing embrace before slipping from beneath the covers and padding naked to the bathroom, laughing all the way because the floor was so cold.

Later, after the highway patrol had called, and days after that, after the funeral, after a cold, seething fury at the unfairness of it all had settled into Logan's heart, Logan thought back to that last spout of laughter echoing through the frigid morning darkness. How could Logan have known they would be the last moments the two of them would ever spend together? It seemed incomprehensible that a life-altering event such as Jerry's death could pass without so much as a glimmer of foreboding. And every time Logan thought back to that merry peal of laughter as Jerry raced across the room naked to get ready for work, Logan's heart would break all over again. How could it happen? How could a morning begin with such happiness and yet end in such an avalanche of pain and sorrow and loss?

And the loss for Jerry would be even greater. For he was left with an eternity of nothing, his laughter silenced, the beating of his loving, generous heart stilled forever.

That was what angered Logan most, what he fought so long to overcome. It wasn't what he had lost. It wasn't his grief at losing Jerry. It was what Jerry had lost. And how fate had erased such a good man from the face of the earth without so much as a blink of compassion.

That long-ago morning was the last time Logan had touched another man in lust. He had lived his life like a monk ever since. Yet somehow, he didn't regret his year of abstinence. Jerry deserved that much, at least. But now things were beginning to change. Logan could feel the change inside himself, rising up, floating to the surface. The hungers. The needs. The breathless longings.

It was time for Logan to rejoin the human race, and he damn well knew it.

THE BUZZ of a honey bee flying close to Logan's ear jarred him back to the present. He glanced at his watch, bemused. Good grief. He'd been walking for twenty minutes and didn't remember a thing. Chuckling at his own absentmindedness, he glanced around as if expecting all the other pedestrians to be looking at him like he was crazy. But of course no one had taken notice of him at all.

He wondered what Milo was doing. It was still early; he was probably writing. Logan should be working too, he suddenly realized. He might have relocated to the other side of the country, but his commitments were still the same. In fact, with the move and getting settled and all, he was a week behind on everything. He had ad work to finish, a blog to update, two book reviews to write, people to notify with his new address so they could get in touch with him if they needed to. He had Jerry's family in Chicago and his own family back in New York to reassure, because both clans had clearly thought he was nuts when he told them he was moving almost three thousand miles away.

Basically, Logan had a whole new life to set into motion.

He gazed around, still getting his bearings in this unfamiliar sun-drenched city of San Diego he now called home. Casting a last amazed glance at the smoldering California sky arching high above his head, he executed a jaunty about-face and headed back the way he came. Back to his new apartment. Back to his brand-new life.

And maybe, just maybe, back to all the other things a new life might one day conceivably entail.

Chapter Four

MILO HAD been up since 4:00 a.m., tippy-tappy-typing away at his new book. When writing, Milo was at his happiest. And most miserable. He had a love/hate relationship with the creative process. Some days his exact words would survive from the moment of creation all the way through endless rounds of his own personal edits, then after the story was contracted out (if he was lucky), they might even survive an endless string of his publisher's edits. Hell, they might remain unchanged from the moment a spark of imagination brought them to life, all the way to release day, when his book, polished to within an inch of its life, was delivered to a hopefully adoring public.

At other times, of course, his words didn't last five minutes. In fact, sometimes his words barely survived the process of being dribbled across the computer screen like so many bird droppings (an apt simile if there ever was one) before Milo turned right around and deleted the fuckers from the face of the earth.

Such was the case today. Every word that spilled onto the screen from Milo's head by way of his fingertips on the keyboard left a crappy taste in his mouth. Some days his words soared. Other days, they were stillborn. Today was a stillborn sort of day.

So it was with infinite relief that he was distracted from his incessant pounding of the Delete key by a beep on the computer heralding an incoming message on Facebook.

"Thank you, God," Milo mumbled, docking the page he was working on and logging on to Facebook, as grateful for the interruption as if the governor's reprieve had come through just before the warden pulled the switch and fried his sorry ass.

When he saw who the message came from he was even happier.

Yo! Good morning. I forgot to get your phone number. Assuming it's still available.

Milo grinned. It was Logan. He obediently typed his phone number into the message box and sent it on its way. A moment later the phone on his desk rang.

Milo answered in a horribly snooty English lord impersonation a la Terry-Thomas, right down to the impossibly soft *a*'s, an aristocratic lisp, and a condescending sniff, now and then, as if letting the caller know his tea and crumpets were being ruined, thank you very much for interrupting brekkie. "You have reached the home of Sir Milo Cook, internationally renowned master of the written word. If you are a doting reader, your call will be answered in the order it was received, probably sometime next week. Yes, he really is that popular. If you're a publisher and wish to offer a record-breaking advance for his next literary masterpiece, which isn't written yet and doesn't look like it ever will be, please enunciate clearly, stating the number of zeros you're willing to stick on the check."

Milo was rewarded with a wry chuckle on the other end of the line. "Jesus, you really are an ass. Funny, I didn't pick up on that the other day at lunch."

"It was closer to dinner than lunch. You said so yourself. And besides, you were paying," Milo haughtily explained. "I'm never an ass when somebody else is paying." He laughed at himself and dropped the ridiculous accent. Excitedly, and with the first hint of true sincerity in his voice, he asked, "So you said you got the apartment?"

"Got it. Signed a lease. Already moved in."

"Wow. That was fast."

"Depending on my motivations and how badly I want something, I can move like a wabbit when the need arises."

Milo sat speechless for a moment, wondering if Logan's persistence in getting back in touch was an example of his wanting something badly enough to "move like a wabbit." God, he sure hoped so.

After filling the lull in the conversation with lots of interesting thoughts, some of them pretty darn sexy and far more creative than anything he had typed into his manuscript that morning, Milo finally recovered his manners. "I'd love to see it."

"Then you shall," Logan said, sounding pleased.

"Really?"

"Sure. Why not?"

Milo thought he heard a smile in the voice, but he wasn't sure. When he glanced at his reflection on the computer screen in front of him, he wasn't surprised at all to see his own smile. He had known it was there since the moment his phone rang.

"I'll bring you a housewarming gift," Milo said.

"Just bring yourself," Logan answered. "That's gift enough."

This time the silence lasted even longer.

"All right," Milo finally said, speaking softly into the phone and holding it closer to his ear so he could hear Logan breathing on the other end. For some reason he liked that sound. He liked it a lot.

Logan eventually cleared his throat, as if even he thought the conversation was getting a little out of hand and a change of subject was needed. "There must be a lot of writers living in San Diego. Maybe you can help me connect with a few of them."

"Sure. I'd love to. We're like a big family. Everybody knows everybody. Plus there are reading clubs you might like to visit, book signings around town almost daily where you can meet a few writers and bookstore owners, coffee klatches where writers and readers get together and bitch about reviews. Well, no, you might want to skip those. We haven't hung any reviewers in effigy yet, but there could always be a first time. I'd hate to see you strung up from a palm tree, crisping in the California sun."

Logan laughed. "Creatively phrased, but yes, that would be a bummer."

Their conversation flagged, and before Milo could stop himself, he said, "It's good to hear your voice. I've been hoping you'd call."

Milo caught the teeniest intake of breath before Logan said, "Have you?"

"Yes. I really enjoyed the time we spent together the other day."

"Thanks, Milo. So did I. It'll be nice to have one friend in town at least."

"Do you mean to say you don't know *anyone* here?"

"Not a soul."

"You must miss New York, then."

"You mean do I miss the snow, the ice, the frozen boogers? No. But the city? Maybe a little. I'd kill for a Gray's Papaya kraut dog. Or a slice of pizza from that little walk-in joint on Fifth Avenue next to Bergdorf's. Or a quiet drink at the Stonewall, where even the barstools are steeped in history."

"Ah, a junk-food and gay-movement devotee with alcoholic tendencies to boot. I knew I'd find something we have in common. What other passions do you have?"

A lingering silence on the line indicated Logan was considering his answer very carefully. Finally he said, as if ticking them off on his fingers, "Junk food, movies, books. The holy trinity. Those are pretty much my interests. How about you, Milo? What floats your boat?"

Milo wanted to say, "You and your sexyass voice and long fuzzy legs, which I'd really like to feel wrapped around my head," but didn't. He wasn't a complete jerk. Usually. "Junk food, movies, books, and booze basically covers it for me too. Of course, no one can reach their full potential without the love of a good pet to come home to every night. Dog, cat, aardvark, hellbender salamander, whatever. The love of a good man would be nice too, but those are harder to come by."

Logan laughed. "Don't hold back. Tell me exactly how you feel."

"I am. Oh, and long walks. I really love long walks. Around the city, out in the high country, on the beach traipsing barefoot through the surf, off in the desert somewhere exploring the dunes and dodging rattlesnakes. Any and all locations acceptable. And surfing. And writing. No, I hate writing. Forget that one. And naps in the afternoon. And Spanky when he smiles. That's about it."

"Dogs smile?"

Milo sighed. "Boy, you really *don't* know anything about pets, do you?"

"One of my many flaws," Logan said, the unseen smile in his voice back again in full force. "And by the way, I like naps too."

"Well, that's a start." It was indeed, offering Milo a whole new range of fantasies to choose from. Morning snuggles, afternoon cuddles, snoring in each other's arms on the couch while the six o'clock news played unheeded on the TV and fingers began wandering over toasty soft skin.

A joking growl rumbled in Logan's throat, wresting Milo from his merry reveries. "Maybe someday you'll tutor me in correcting all my shortcomings. Show me everything I'm missing in life. I mean, within limits."

"Sorry," Milo teased, thinking he had never in his life heard anything as sexy as Logan's playful growl stuttering through the phone. "I don't do *anything* within limits. It's far too constricting."

"Wow. You *really* are an ass."

"Why thank you," Milo sweetly cooed, and they both laughed.

A comfortable silence settled in. After a few seconds, Logan said, "I'm probably interrupting your writing."

"Or maybe I'm interrupting your reviewing," Milo countered.

After a couple of heartbeats, they both said, "No, you're not," in perfect unison.

The extra few seconds of silence that followed *those* comments were even more comfortable. Milo found himself smiling again. He wondered if Logan was.

"I'd like to show you the city if you'll let me, Logan. After I see your new apartment and after I've rearranged all your furniture, because I'm just that kind of guy and because for some reason you impress me as being far too butch to be a disciple of feng shui and probably parked your TV in front of the toilet stool…. Wait, what was I saying? Oh yes. After all that we could walk straight down the hill from your place to the bay. Have a bite to eat by the water, or maybe a couple of drinks. Or both. You really must be exhausted after your move. A relaxing night off will do you good."

"I'm not even going to mention your lack of faith in my ability to arrange furniture."

"Probably for the best."

"Appreciate the 'butch' remark, though."

"Anytime."

"And what about your writing?"

"A night off will do me good too. Today I advanced my Work in Progress by a grand total of three words. That's right, three. And tomorrow I'll probably delete *them*."

Milo listened intently to dead silence on the line. Logan was hesitating. Or maybe he was just thinking things through. Milo had no way of knowing. He waited for what was probably six or seven seconds—in his head it was an hour and a half—and was about to start chewing on his bottom lip and go dig out his worry beads from the hall closet when Logan said, "Great!"

Milo breathed a happy sigh. "Great you'll let me rearrange your furniture? Or great you'll let me show you the bay?"

"Both," Logan said.

"And when would you like me to come by?" Milo asked, more than aware that his heart had started doing an excited little cha-cha underneath his pajama pocket.

"How about this evening? Around five? Would that work?" Logan asked. He sounded shy again, and for some reason Milo thought that was the sweetest thing he had ever heard.

"This evening at five is perfect. I'll look forward to it."

After jotting down Logan's address, Milo said a polite goodbye and ended the call. He stared down at Spanky, who was standing at the side of his chair looking up as if wondering what all the hubbub was about.

Being the loving mutt he was, Spanky rested his chin on Milo's leg and squinted his face into an obsequious grin.

Wow, you really do smile.

Spanky's big, soulful eyes burrowed straight into Milo's, shining with devotion. Broadening his doggy smile, he showed a few more teeth in a friendly manner, probably waiting for either an explanation or a butt rub. His long fluffy tail whapped back and forth in perfect unison to Milo's banging heart, and he cocked his head so far to the side that one ear flopped over his forehead and stayed there.

Finally Milo offered up an astounded laugh. "Holy shit, boy! I've got a date!"

"HOLY SHIT!" Logan sputtered, suddenly filled with terror. "I've got a date!"

He turned doubtful eyes onto his newly arranged apartment. Milo was probably right. Logan knew as much about feng shui as he knew about quantum physics. And he knew dick about quantum physics. Consequently, he probably *did* have all the furniture in the wrong place. This was California, after all. People worried about stuff like that.

He stood there with his hands on his hips, picking apart everything he had already done to make the place feel like home. He tried to imagine how the apartment would look if he moved his sofa *there* and turned his end tables around *that* way. And how the dining area might look kind of cool if he pulled the table a little closer to the window and stuck a potted plant on it. And how his overflowing bookcases might go better in the second bedroom, which he had turned into an office, than they did in the hallway, where they sort of blocked traffic.

The mere thought of going through all that work again made him want to crawl back into bed and cry himself to sleep. Besides, he had a sneaky suspicion that nothing would make Milo happier than to roll up his sleeves and set about redecorating Logan's apartment, with or without Logan's permission. Like he'd said, he was that kind of guy. And frankly, Logan didn't mind at all. The apartment probably *would* look better after Milo finished with it.

Logan heaved a sigh and, hating himself for it, started rearranging the furniture anyway.

Two hours later, sweating bullets, he yanked a beer from the fridge and dropped flat on his back on the couch. The couch was still sitting catty-corner in the middle of the living room because after moving everything else around six times, he couldn't find a place for the sofa that didn't block either the entrance to the kitchen or the front fucking door.

He lay there dabbing the sweat from his face with his shirttail and gulping down a beer, with his feet hanging over the end of the couch because it was only a six-footer and he was longer than that. It was during that miserable moment when he was draining the last refreshing drops from the bottle that he came to the soul-crushing realization he would have to put all the furniture back where it was when he started.

Jesus.

AT FIVE o'clock on the button, Logan's doorbell chimed. He hastily kicked a pair of dirty socks under the bed—where the hell had *those* come from?—before running to answer the door. Yanking the door open and finding Milo on his doorstep as he'd hoped he would, he offered a shy, "Hello, it's good to see you again."

"Is it?" Milo asked, catching Logan off guard.

"Y-yes," he said. "Why? Do I look like it's not?"

Milo laughed. "Sorry. Couldn't resist." He offered his hand. "It's good to see you again too, Logan. Thanks for asking me over."

Logan took the hand and simply held it, not bothering to shake, while Milo tipped his head back and stared up at the facade of the forties-era apartment complex. It was a rambling three-story jumble of offset bricks and leaded windows, most of it painted bloodred, with a slew of crooked chimneys poking up here and there across the roofline, along with winding masonry staircases shooting off in a dozen different directions. In Logan's opinion, the whole building, with its cupolas and spires and keystones over every aperture and funny little cast-iron balustrades, looked like it would have been perfectly at home on Diagon Alley, with witches and wizards popping in and out at all hours of the day and night. The building was tucked neatly among overgrown bowers of bougainvillea and a spray of towering palm trees, the fronds of which were creaking in the wind high above their heads. Logan's unit was on the ground floor, set well back off the street. It was almost hidden in a shadowy alcove beneath a sprawling jacaranda tree.

"I've always loved this old building," Milo said. "I've never been in it before. It's great that all the units open to the outside. I also love the fact that no two apartment entrances are in sight of each other. I have a thing about communal entrances. Hate 'em with a passion."

"Actually, so do I," Logan said, and since Milo's hand was in his already and he didn't know what else to do with it, he gently tugged Milo through the front door. "Come on in."

Milo followed along, and while Logan closed the door behind them, he stared into the apartment with a look of wonder on his face. "Wow," Milo breathed. "This is beautiful. Built-in cabinets and bookshelves, fireplace, overhead fans, broad ceiling beams in—what is that, polished teak?—and flagstone floors. The rent must be astronomical."

"Not as high as you might think," Logan answered. "And it's locked in for two years, so I don't have to worry about it going up for a while."

"Cool." Milo stared at Logan's leather sofa, then at the high-backed wing chairs and heavy wooden accent tables. He looked around the room, tapping his finger to his chin as if trying to figure out if he was pleased with the arrangement or not. He shot a mischievous glance at Logan's worried countenance and grinned. "You did good. You've put everything in exactly the right place."

Logan breathed an exaggerated sigh of relief. "Thank God. Since your call, I rearranged it three times and finally ended up putting everything back where it started."

Milo gave a gleeful snort. "Boy, I must scare you to death."

Logan's ears began to burn, but for some reason he didn't much care. He realized suddenly that Milo hadn't been in his apartment more than a minute and a half, and he was already having a great time. Hopefully Milo was too.

"Let me get you a beer," he said and rushed off into the kitchen. To his amusement, Milo followed along right behind him, exclaiming happily about everything he saw: the prints on the walls, the roomy dining area with a second tiny fireplace in the corner, the rounded ceilings, the vertical wooden blinds on the windows. The setting sun drenched the kitchen in orange light through a floor-to-ceiling window facing another jacaranda tree outside in the complex's inner courtyard. Another ceiling fan hung above a cozy kitchen breakfast nook. A small pantry, like a back porch, led away from the kitchen to the rear.

"Is that a back door?" Milo asked in amazement.

Logan laughed. "Yeah. I don't remember ever seeing an apartment with a back door before. Seems kind of homey, don't you think?"

"I do indeed." Milo smiled as he took the offered beer from Logan's hand.

"And check this out," Logan said, grinning. He pointed to a tiny oblong opening in the wall with a metal flap over it that stood beside the back door about a foot off the floor. "Ever see one of those?"

Milo stared at it, as if trying to figure out what it was. He finally gave up. "No. What is it?"

Proudly, Logan exclaimed, "That's where the milkman used to deliver the milk!"

Both men laughed. "Wow!" Milo said. "This building is older than I thought it was."

A companionable silence settled in while Milo continued to gaze around, taking everything in.

Logan pointed to the sofa in the other room. "Sit. Make yourself comfortable."

Milo did as directed, patting the sofa cushion beside him as he sat. Still blushing, but hopefully not as much, Logan accepted the invitation. He dropped onto the sofa at Milo's side and stretched his long legs out in front of him. Both men relaxed and sipped at their beers straight from the bottle.

After a short span of silence that Logan didn't find unsettling at all, much to his surprise, he turned to Milo and said, "I really do appreciate you coming over. I haven't done much socializing since, well, since everything happened with Jerry and all. If I start seeming awkward with my social interactions, don't think it's you. Just chalk it up to disuse."

Milo smiled. "Don't worry. I have a bad habit of interacting enough for everybody. I probably won't even notice you're there at all."

Logan laughed. "Well, that makes me feel special. I'm more comfortable already."

Milo barked out a chortle while his green eyes settled on Logan. "Good," he said, still teasing, but a little more gently this time. Tucking his beer bottle between his legs, he looked away to gaze about the room again. "This really is a terrific apartment. I can't imagine anybody in their right mind not being happy here."

Logan shrugged, trying not to seem evasive but knowing he probably came off that way. "I guess we'll see." He cleared his throat and not so deftly changed the subject. "Are you ready to go walking?"

Milo gave him a lingering look that seemed to indicate he knew exactly what Logan was doing. Still, he dutifully poured the last of his beer down his throat and hopped to his feet. Reaching down, he took Logan's hand and pulled him to his feet as well. They stood close, each man smiling at the other, Milo's head tilted back, Logan's tilted down.

Suddenly embarrassed, Logan pried his eyes away and plucked the empty bottle from Milo's fingers. Downing the last of his own beer, he set both bottles on the coffee table.

"Let's go, then," he said. "I'll let you lead the way."

"Slob," Milo chided, and scooping up the empty bottles, he carried them to the kitchen where, after a quick search, he dropped them into a trash can he found under the sink.

"Uh-oh," Logan said. "You've got me pegged already."

IT WAS a pleasant thirty-minute stroll from Logan's front door to Seaport Village, a touristy shopping mecca situated on the southwestern rim of the city at land's end, snugly abutting the San Diego Bay. With more than seventy freestanding shops, built in varying styles of architecture from Victorian to Mexican to Tudor, it offered a panoramic view of the waterfront. Milo and Logan weaved in and out among the storefronts, window-shopping here, stopping for an ice cream cone there, eyeing the easy blend of tourists and locals, each looking just as contentedly at home as the other. Not too far in the distance they could see the Coronado Bridge arching over the water, connecting the mainland to the city of Coronado, where Logan and Milo had first met.

They ambled along the cobblestone path at the water's edge and stared out as a Navy destroyer rumbled past, heading into port, the flume in its wake churning up orange sparks as the setting sun painted the water fiery red. Stopping to watch the ship sail majestically by, the sound of its great engines thrumming across the water, Milo was more than aware of Logan's physical presence beside him. His height. The way his hands moved when he talked. The easy way he strode along, the relaxed way he rested a hip on the concrete railing as he lost himself in the beauty before him. When he muttered, "Wow," under his breath as he stared out at the water, Milo was pleased.

"Gorgeous, isn't it?" Milo asked, feeling proud and more than a little proprietary, since this was one of his favorite spots in the city.

Logan nodded, clearly impressed with the broad bay laid out before him, drenched with the flaming light of sunset, and the cawing of seagulls swooping overhead, their wings burnished gold by the dying sun. He lifted his hand as if in greeting to the sailors in their dress blues neatly manning the destroyer's railing off in the distance, standing at parade rest, their crisp uniforms flapping in the wind as they floated past. If they saw him, they didn't show it.

Even Milo found himself wondering about the sailors. Were they as enamored of their calling as they appeared, or was it all just a job to them, this pomp and circumstance of returning to port after God knows how long at sea? A day, two months, a year? Were they as proud of their ship as they appeared, or were they simply eager to get their feet on solid ground again and hustle off to get laid, or drunk, or spend time with the people who had hopefully missed them while they were deployed, off sailing the seven seas for God and country?

Logan spoke softly while his hair thrashed around in the gusting wind rolling in off the water. "In New York, the beauty of the bay gets lost in the bustle and filth and chaos of the city. Barges, tugboats, gray skies, dirty water, floating trash, sirens forever screaming in the distance. Here the water is peaceful and blue, the way it should be. You can hear the terns. The air is clear." He turned his eyes to Milo and smiled. "You have a beautiful city here. I've never seen anything like it."

Milo fought the urge to get lost in Logan's dreamy hazel eyes. "So you think an uprooted New Yorker can be happy here?"

Without hesitation, Logan nodded. "Yes. I think I can. After all, there was really nothing for me back in New York. Not anymore.

I needed a change. And if a person wants to change, this looks like a perfect place to do it. Now that I've actually seen it, I know I've chosen wisely. Somehow San Diego feels like home already."

"I'm glad," Milo said. He companionably rested a hand on Logan's shoulder, and silently they both stared out at the water. The destroyer was almost out of sight now, ducking beneath the vast, arching bridge that connected the mainland to Coronado, headed for the Navy moorings deeper in the harbor. In the gray of dusk, as the setting sun dipped below the horizon, the ship's fiery wake turned back to white. Around them, darkness at last began to fall and streetlights sprang to life, chasing away the shadows.

On any other day, and in the company of anyone else, Milo might have regretted seeing those shadows flee. He might have enjoyed the anonymity they offered. Although he fought back continually at the ever-present social anxiety that had plagued his life since high school, somehow with Logan it didn't bother him much. Turning now to Logan in the harsh yellow glare of the streetlight over their heads, and with everything laid bare in the unforgiving light, Milo decided he was content. He didn't miss the shadows at all. Perhaps it was the ease he felt in Logan's company and the fact that there was something about Logan Hunter that he instinctively trusted. It wasn't only that Logan was handsome and tall and sexy as hell. There was also a generosity about him that Milo liked. He was generous with his time, with his gentilesse. And above it all was an inherent kindness in Logan that Milo admired greatly. The fact that Logan appeared to genuinely like him back didn't hurt. That perhaps more than anything made it possible for Milo to relax in Logan's presence.

Of course, when he was at peace and when his neuroses were kept at bay, Milo could also be intractably nosy. He let the cool evening breeze blow over him for a moment, and in his enjoyment of the ocean scents that flooded his senses, Milo's inquisitiveness blossomed. Damn. He was afraid it would do that.

"I've been reading some of your past reviews," he said, casually enough. "You have a good eye for fiction. What makes it work and what doesn't."

Logan eyed him suspiciously but with a smirk tweaking the corner of his mouth. "Is this going somewhere? Are you about to tell me I really don't know anything about reviewing books? It wouldn't be the first time, you know." As he uttered the last sentence, his smirk stretched into a grin.

"No!" Milo made the effort to look properly appalled. "No, you seem to really love what you do, and I was wondering how you keep your energy and optimism up. One lousy book can put me in a funk for days. I love to read too, but only what I choose. It seems to me a reviewer has to read everything, whether they particularly like the genre or not. Isn't that right?"

Logan laughed. "Okay, then. You win. Let's talk shop. There's nothing I love more." As if he couldn't engage in such discourse without being completely comfortable, he tugged his shirttail out of his pants and let it fan out around him. With that out of the way, he folded his arms across his chest and settled his ass against the railing at the edge of the cobblestone path. "There. I don't have to hold in my belly any longer."

Milo looked dubious. "The last thing you have to do is hold in your belly. I get the feeling there's a pretty good six-pack under there."

Logan flapped his hand through the air. "Oh please." He beetled his brows. "Now where were we? Oh yes. You were wondering if I really like my job or not."

Milo blinked. "No, that wasn't what I—"

Logan tutted him to silence. "The answer is no. I don't like it. I love it. And yes, I'll admit there are certain genres I prefer over others, but it's the craft of the writing I concentrate on when I review a book. That's what I base my opinions on. Not my own personal likes and dislikes. You have to be fair as a reviewer. You can't let your own preferences get in the way."

"I wish all reviewers felt that way."

For the first time since Milo had knocked on Logan's door, Logan frowned. "Yes," he said. "So do I. A lot of reviewers out there are, shall we say, less than kind. Being a critic gives some people the mistaken notion they can be vicious beyond the parameters of civilized behavior. What they wouldn't dream of saying to your face, they'll turn around and blabber to the world on any forum they feel protects them. I suppose we have the internet to thank for that."

"Still," Milo said, practically arguing with himself, "if a book sucks, the reviewer should say so, right?"

"Yes," Logan said. "But they don't have to be cruel about it. Someone put a lot of effort into writing the book they are trashing, and there's no sense in ripping the author's heart out just because a reviewer doesn't like the way it was written. There is also the point to be made that just because you're a reviewer, it doesn't mean you're always right. Leave a little leeway in your assessment. Give the writer the benefit of the doubt, and don't bash him by trying to turn off future readers. Put simply, be kind."

Milo jumped. "Exactly! Be kind! I'm glad to hear somebody else say that about reviewers besides a writer. We're not all overly sensitive weenies, although we sound like it sometimes. Some of us can accept horrific reviews if they don't go for the jugular, or if the reviewer isn't simply trying to toot his own horn by being catty and clever and snippily Truman Capote-ish with his insults."

Logan settled himself more comfortably against the railing, studying Milo's face. "I can't imagine you get too many horrific reviews."

Milo grunted. "I've had my share. We all have. It goes with the territory. I've never seen you give one, though. Not to play the devil's advocate or anything, but do you think that's fair? There really are some pretty rotten books out there."

Logan shrugged. "True, but I have a rule. I don't give one-star reviews unless I can legitimately explain what went wrong with the writing. Even then, I won't take a harsh, belittling tone. I love writers. Even the not-so-talented ones. The best of writers sometimes publish works that might better have been left buried under a pile of Macy's fliers on their desk than be thrust into the light of day. I also know that for someone to sit down and write a book, which is no small endeavor—"

"No kidding."

"—then that book, no matter how poorly it is presented, probably means a lot to them. Why should I try to spoil that? It would be mean-spirited and petty."

"Not all reviewers would agree with you."

"Of course not. That's why we're not the most popular people on the planet." Still smiling, Logan stretched out a huge fist and chucked Milo delicately on the chin. "I'm thirsty," he said. "Let's have a drink, and while we're drinking you can tell me about the book you're working on."

Milo peered around, his eyes following the arc of the cobblestoned path as if trying to remember what lay ahead. "There," he said. "Around the corner. There's a seafood restaurant and bar perched over the water. We can have a drink there. Dinner too, if you're hungry. I'm buying."

"I won't say no to that." Logan smiled. "Lead the way."

While they strode toward the building Milo had pointed to, Logan laid his hand on Milo's back, obediently following along. The hand was broad and warm, and as they walked, Logan caressed Milo's shoulder blade gently.

By the time they reached the restaurant, Milo was harboring serious thoughts of jumping Logan's bones. If not all of them, then most certainly one of them. Not that he hadn't been ready to jump it anyway.

IT WAS the best seafood Logan had ever eaten. Seared scallops and lobster mashed potatoes, topped off by lemon sherbet and several rounds of a delicious IPA brewed not a mile and a half up the street, or so Milo told him. They had both finished dining and settled back in their seats, nearly comatose from all they'd consumed.

"You look stuffed," Milo said, grinning from across the table. He was sitting with his back to the wall of glass that looked out over the water. Not five feet from Milo's head, on a piling outside, a fat pelican sat preening its feathers with its spoonlike beak. The fact that Milo had given up the view so Logan could face the water was not lost on Logan one little bit.

Logan gazed down at the empty plate before him. It couldn't have been any more spotless if he had picked it up and licked it clean.

"It doesn't seem fair," he said, surreptitiously loosening his belt under the table. "I bought you a cheeseburger, you buy me drinks and a feast with a view."

Milo eyed him with amusement. There was a white smudge of beer foam on Milo's upper lip that Logan thought might be fun to kiss away. Then he wondered where the hell *that* thought had come from.

"Maybe it's an investment," Milo said around a sneaky grin.

Logan grinned back. "Investment in what?"

"Investment in you. I have a feeling I've made a new friend. To keep you in my life, I'll have to keep you fed and happy."

There was a teasing light in Milo's eyes, and Logan became a little lost staring into them. He wondered if he was getting drunk. The IPAs were pretty strong. He decided to do a little teasing back.

"Are you sure it's a friend you want, or are you more intent on ensuring a good review for your next book when it comes out?"

"Why, I *never!*" Milo exclaimed, slapping his hand to his chest as if pierced through the heart by such a suggestion. "I hold far too much respect for the noble art of book reviewing to ever attempt such a despicable act!" Elbows on the table, he leaned in closer and added, deadpan, "But if you feel you absolutely *have* to give me five stars, don't let me hold you back."

"Oh believe me, I won't." Logan laughed, and after a couple of beats, Milo laughed along with him. Simultaneously, the pelican flapped his great wings and sailed off into the darkness as if even *he* were appalled by the very idea of buying a good review with a meal and a couple of beers.

Their laughter waned, and the two sat quietly for a minute, still stuffed, lethargically eyeing the other diners around them, absorbing the restaurant's tranquil ambience. In the midst of their easy silence, Logan discreetly waved for the waiter to bring two more ales. After they were served and the empty glasses taken away, Logan was surprised when Milo stretched his arm across the table and laid his hand over his.

He sat speechless, waiting to hear what Milo would say. When Milo finally spoke, Logan knew he had been carefully choosing his words. He spoke them so softly, Logan had to lean in to hear.

"You've been on your own for a year, then," Milo said, his eyes gentle. "That must have been a hard adjustment for you."

"You lost a lover too," Logan said. "You know how it feels."

"No," Milo said. "My lover left because we both wanted out of the relationship, not because he died. There's a big difference."

It took Logan a moment to decide if this was a subject he wished to discuss. After all, he barely knew Milo. They had just met. But still, there was such an open, caring look in Milo's gaze, Logan knew it wasn't for any of the wrong reasons that Milo had broached the subject. He wasn't prying. He was truly interested.

Logan sipped at his beer, then wiped a splash of foam from his lip with his thumb. "Do you really want to talk about this?"

Milo shrugged, looking a little guilty, but determined too. "I'd like to know how you survived. It couldn't have been easy. I—I was just wondering how you came out of it still maintaining your core of goodness."

Logan stared in amused amazement. "My core of goodness? Is that what you said?"

A lazy smile twisted Milo's mouth, but the stubborn tilt of his head told Logan he wasn't going to be deterred. "Yes. You have one, you know. It's like an aura that shimmers around you. I'm not sure I've ever met anyone whose goodness defines them as much as yours does."

"Jesus." Logan laughed. "Maybe you shouldn't drink."

Milo snickered, but his gaze remained obdurate. "If you don't want to talk about it, tell me. But I think maybe you do. I think maybe you *need* to talk about it."

"Why?" Logan asked. "Why do you think that?"

"Because *I* would," Milo said simply.

Logan stared at the open expression on Milo's face, at the plump line of his lips, moistened with beer, at his blondish curly streaks still tousled by the wind. He noticed for the first time that Milo's earlobe was pierced, but he wore no earring. Logan wondered why.

Logan heard himself speaking before he knew the words were coming. Before he heard them tumbling out. "The first few months were terrible," he said. "But people can survive anything when they have to."

"Can they?" Milo asked kindly.

"Yes," Logan answered without hesitation. "If you want to survive at all. After a while, time begins to heal you. I'm all right now, but like I said, the first few months were… tough. I'd never lost anyone I had been involved with before. I'd never lost… a lover."

"I'd like to see a picture of him. You must have one on you."

Logan blinked in surprise, as if wondering how Milo could know such a thing. In a daze, Logan reached into his back pocket and pulled out his wallet. Flipping through it, he extracted a small snapshot, a little beat-up and wrinkled around the edges. He handed it over.

Logan watched as Milo held the photo close to the candle burning on the table so he could see it in the restaurant's dim light. It was Logan's favorite picture of Jerry, taken on their first Christmas together. He was sitting at the foot of their Christmas tree in a white terry cloth robe, holding a cup of coffee, smiling up at the camera, his cheeks still rosy because they had only made love moments before. On pins and needles, Logan waited at the edge of his seat to see what Milo would say about it. But when he finished, he handed the photo back to Logan and sat back in his chair to take another sip of beer.

Only after he had patted his lips dry with his napkin did Milo say, "He was beautiful."

And those three simple words stung Logan so deeply that he felt tears rising in his eyes.

"He was," he said, looking at the picture himself while his vision blurred and that old familiar ache settled in his chest. "It's a funny thing," he said, lifting his eyes to Milo's yet again. "No one has ever loved me as much as Jerry did. I don't think anyone ever will again."

Milo kindly shook his head. "You can't know that."

"No," Logan said. "But I feel it. Sometimes true happiness only comes along once in a lifetime. I think Jerry was mine. In fact, I know he was."

For the second time that night, Milo reached across the table and rested his fingertips on the back of Logan's hand. "Sometimes we don't know everything we think we know," Milo softly said.

To which Logan dragged a smile to his lips. "That sentence sucked. Thank God you write better than you talk."

Milo laughed, withdrawing his hand. He studied Logan's face for a long moment. "You must be exhausted," he said. "Would you like to walk home, or would you rather I flag a cab?"

"I'd like to walk," Logan said.

Five minutes later, the bill paid and the evening breeze once again blowing through their hair, they strolled along the cobblestone path beside the water, going back the way they had come, heading for the city streets.

The silence that followed them along was an undemanding one. It held no embarrassments or accusations; it seemed to fit with the stars overhead and the lazy way their arms sometimes brushed together as they walked.

They strode along up the hill away from downtown toward Hillcrest where Logan's apartment was located and where Milo had parked his car. When they broke the silence to speak, they only spoke of inconsequential things. About the trill of a bird they passed, singing a night song from the bushes at the edge of the sidewalk. About the way the air had cooled as the night deepened. About the delicate shape of the fingernail moon.

When Logan's apartment building came into sight and Milo led him up the walk to his front door, Milo said, "We're friends now, Logan. I expect us to keep in touch."

"Yes," Logan said, moved by the simplicity of Milo's words. "So do I."

On Logan's stoop, Milo turned and asked softly, "Can I kiss you good night?"

Not trusting himself to speak, Logan simply nodded.

Raising up on tiptoe, Milo laid his hands at Logan's hips and gently touched his lips to Logan's mouth. Logan closed his eyes at the sweetness of it, his own hands moving, unbidden by him, to draw Milo close.

Slowly easing away from the kiss, Milo lowered himself from tiptoe and gazed up into Logan's face.

"Thank you," he said softly, and he turned and walked away.

Logan stood on his doorstep watching Milo go, not bothering to fish in his pocket for his key until Milo had turned the corner and disappeared from view.

Only then did Logan quietly say, "Thank *you*."

Chapter Five

WHAT A shithole.

The motel stood at the side of a blacktopped road in the middle of nowhere. The road had once been an honest-to-God state-sanctioned two-lane highway with a designated number and everything. Thanks to an eight-lane interstate constructed several miles over and about twenty years back, it was now reduced to little more than a nameless, potholed macadam cow path meandering through the winter-seared Indiana backcountry.

The Gateway Inn, once a popular low-budget stopover for travelers hastening between Ohio and Illinois, had only survived the transition by becoming even more low-budget. The single renovation that heralded the motel's transition downward from semirespectable to downright dodgy came when the word Gateway on the sign had been painted over with a bold streak of black paint. Now the place was simply known as the Blackslash Inn. It was the preferred go-to joint among the local high schoolers for a long tradition of first fucks, a venue for extramarital affairs perpetrated by their parents, an option for gay hookups between two farmers where they could blow each other in an actual bed instead of a hayloft without their wives wandering in to spoil the moment, and a cozy place where addicts could relax and gobble up the latest designer drugs without conking out and freezing to death on some back road in a parked car.

The person in unit 6 knew all about the Blackslash Inn, having researched the establishment thoroughly. But no amount of research could have prepared anyone for just how seedy the place really was. For one thing, it would have been physically impossible to find a square inch of flat space anywhere in the tiny room that hadn't been scorched by a burning cigarette. Toilet seat, dresser top, nightstand, fake bathroom marble encircling a rust-stained sink—they were all scarred at one time or another by a forgotten Lucky Strike or a hand-rolled joint left to smolder on the furnishings.

The carpet was so threadbare as to be worn through in places all the way down to the concrete. The single window was painted shut. The wall heater barely worked. A hint of long-forgotten vomit scented the air. On the grungy floor behind the commode, the traveler spotted a used condom. In the nightstand drawer beside the Bible, which was the only thing in the room that looked like it hadn't been touched since the day it rolled off the press, a discarded syringe rested. The bedspread boasted stains even a serial killer—and who should know better?—would find disgusting. The traveler, on the one night spent in the place, slept sitting up in a chair to avoid either bedbugs or scabies—or quite possibly some Hoosier-borne strain of flesh-eating bacteria that would nibble the meat off one's bones before the sun rose in the morning. Although truthfully, the sun had been absent for days. Maybe in winter it avoided Indiana like the plague. If so, it certainly couldn't be blamed.

Yes, it was easy to conclude that this little section of Indiana was the asshole of the world. And nothing had happened to the traveler in the last twenty-four hours to alter that opinion.

All this made it much more amazing that a fairly well-established book reviewer actually resided in the area. Only in the age of the World Wide Web could a rube who had a basic understanding of English and was literate enough to read a book now and then find it possible to carve out a name for himself as a literary critic. The ramshackle farmhouse this so-called critic lived in was twenty miles down a blacktop road, set back at the end of a rutted dirt lane that wove its way through a century-old forest of chestnuts and oaks and spindly little sassafras trees, the sweet scent of which one could smell on the brittle air even in the dead of winter. Those woods were currently barren and leafless, and as the locals might say while they chewed on a stick of hay and spit tobaccy juice into the wind, colder than the balls on a brass monkey. The traveler had scoped the farmhouse out the day before. Already wearing a woolen ski mask donned for the upcoming adventure, the guest in unit 6 gathered a few belongings from the crappy motel room and prepared to depart. A quick stop at the book reviewer's homestead to sort a few things out, and then back to the real world. Thank Christ.

The traveler peered through the motel room's filthy front window. The unit was on the ground floor because *all* the units at the Blackslash Inn were on the ground floor. Sort of like the Bates Motel, if one could make a literary reference. Well, no. Actually the Bates Motel was the

Waldorf compared to this dump. There were no other cars in the gravel lot. Apparently the weather was too cold even for the lowest of the low to come out and indulge their fantasies among the fleas and bedbugs. It was starting to snow again too, the traveler noticed, so it might be wise to get this show on the road. If a blizzard whipped through, it might make that winding, rutted lane leading up to the old farmhouse impassable. And wouldn't that be a bummer. Ruin the whole trip, it would. Yes, indeedy. For a moment, while leaning to toss a bag into the back of a rented Taurus, the traveler was tempted to duck into the motel office and stick an ice pick in the proprietor's neck, just for shits and giggles. But no. This was a mission. Important stuff needed doing. The serious act of righting wrongs should not be belittled by a recreational tangent, no matter how enjoyable it might be. If fun were required, one could go to Disneyland and visit Mickey.

Besides, the traveler had another use planned for the ice pick currently resting in a coat pocket.

After ducking out of the wind and quickly slamming the car door shut, the driver, with fingers already numbed by the cold, twisted the key in the ignition. If there was one thing to be said for this rental car, which reeked of exhaust fumes and pinged rather alarmingly when it topped sixty miles an hour, it did appear to be acclimated to cold weather. Tonight, even with the temperature dipping to eight degrees above zero, it started right up, just as it had the first time the traveler had turned the key at the Avis lot back at Indy International. Once the heater was set to high, the driver tucked frozen fingers into leather gloves and then adjusted the eye holes in the ski mask to offer a clear line of sight. With those things out of the way, the driver slipped the Taurus into Drive, and the car began crunching its way across the gravel parking lot. As the tires met blacktop, the traveler turned and headed east.

The road was empty. Humming an ABBA tune—being fond of the oldies—the driver steered with one hand and dipped into a bag of candy corn with the other. Almost immediately the snow began to fall with a little more determination. The flakes got fat and fluffy and were really quite pretty as they came spinning out of the darkness to ricochet off the windshield. When the flakes began to accumulate, the driver activated the wipers to sweep them back out into the night and send them on their way.

The road beneath the Taurus's wheels began to whiten too, but the car came with a good set of snow tires, so there was no need to worry about it. The Avis agent had said there were snow chains in the trunk as well, although they had yet to be needed.

While nibbling on the candy corn, the driver's mind meandered where it chose. That was the good thing about being alone. No one barged into your headspace, interrupting your thoughts.

It would be good when winter moved into spring. These cold-weather jobs were frankly uncomfortable. To put it literally, this "winter of my discontent" bullshit was a wearying endeavor. It would be nice to feel the sun again, to hear the drone of insects, smell the scent of green grass and warm ocean breezes, hear a fucking bird tweet now and then.

Thank God the traveler would soon be heading for the West Coast. It was familiar territory, the West Coast. San Francisco, LA, San Diego. All of them felt like home, and one of them actually was. Already a string of calls needed to be made there. Oh yes, a multitude of wrongs waited to be righted under the California sun. It seemed that cruelty positively flourished there. The traveler wondered why. Was it the very air of creativity that pervaded the California mindset, convincing everyone of their own artistic superiority? Hollywood might have something to do with that. The Dream Factory, Oscars, countless publishing houses, recording empires, the endless competition to be the greatest, the boldest, the most talented, the most popular, the most beautiful, the biggest seller.

For every movie or song or book, a story must be told, words must be written. And for every story, a critic must step forward to either praise it or rip it to shreds. The process was inescapable. Among the critics, there were always those who tore at the heart of the one with the real talent, the one with the creative spark to string the words together to begin with. Did they do it out of jealousy? Did they do it because they had failed at the very thing they were now ridiculing? What was their guiding principal? Was it simply to belittle what they themselves were incapable of accomplishing?

The more the lean traveler thought about it, the more tightly gloved fingers gripped the steering wheel. Humming faded away to silence, and eyes burned through the ski mask into the headlight-pierced darkness ahead. The driver's grip on the steering wheel relaxed to relieve aching arms. Blinking back to the present, the traveler saw that the snow had increased, as had the icy wind. It buffeted the car now. The heater was going full blast, trying desperately to keep ahead of the cold. Swaths of white flakes slapped the windshield like countless little suicide bombers, smashing themselves to death on the glass, only to be swept aside by the wipers to make room for the next volley.

The blacktop road was no longer black. Under the glare of headlights, it shone a startling white. The new snow was a couple of inches deep already. Pristine, with nary an automobile track to mar its alabaster perfection. Clearly this car was the first to travel on it since the latest flurries began.

The driver leaned closer to the windshield, peering out now more intently, searching for the cutoff to the lane that veered off into the trees where the prey sat waiting without the vaguest idea what was about to happen to him. Perhaps he was at his desk, penning another steely review, smiling to himself at how artfully his cruel words fell across the page, how clever his readers would think him to see how adeptly he could mock. How remorselessly he could demean. The traveler wondered what the man would look like. An exhaustive online search had yielded his address, but there had been no photographs available. Merely a long string of biting reviews on his own personal blog and scattered through Amazon's book section, where the damage could be even more devastating to writers' sales. It seemed BooksOnWheels—for that was what he called himself—had a true gift for being cruel. He had made a name for himself by being snarky and actually pretty amusing with his biting, crushing wit, assuming of course that *you* weren't the one it was aimed at.

The reviewer's real name was Edgar Price, the lean figure had learned. It was a nice name. It would look good on a tombstone. And at *that* thought, the traveler finally smiled.

Just past the rise of a low hill, the turnoff appeared. Flashing by as suddenly as it did in the beam of headlights, it surprised the driver into applying the brakes a bit too hard, which sent the Taurus skidding. Successfully spinning the steering wheel in the opposite direction to correct the slide, the traveler breathed a sigh of relief when the car bumped to a stop with its back wheels off the macadam. Since the ground was frozen solid, and since there was no other traffic coming in either direction, the tires gripped the verge at a tap of the gas pedal. It carried the car safely across the empty road and onto the long potholed lane leading into the trees. The traveler drove slowly and carefully because the frozen potholes on the rutted path were really quite atrocious. The last thing the driver needed was to puncture the oil pan or break an axle. Especially as the car entered a forest of winter-stripped trees, which could easily send the cold plunging another ten degrees. Some of the old trees stretched their naked arms across the rustic lane from either side as if to hold hands overhead. In a warmer month, with greenery involved, it might be quite pretty. Of course, one would still have those fucking potholes to contend with.

A glimpse of yellow light up ahead caught the driver's attention. Responding to a more careful tap of the brakes, the car crunched to a stop on the frozen earth. The headlights died, and in the sudden darkness, other lights appeared. They were house lights, and they came from up ahead, around a bend in the lane. The lights, filtered through the trees, looked warm and homey and welcoming, like a Walton Christmas special.

The traveler, nibbling on a final handful of candy corn, quietly eased the car door open while listening for the sound of a dog, maybe, or the bang of a screen door in the distance. But the night was muffled to silence by the snow. The only sound to be heard was the tick and click of the Taurus's engine, cooling down after the ignition was switched off.

The air that slipped into the cab when the car door opened made the traveler shiver. Jesus, even with the ski mask and gloves on it was cold. When a long leg swung out to set a foot on the ground, the snow tumbled over the top of the shoe all the way up to the ankle.

Stepping from the car, the driver lifted a collar against the wind. Having checked out the property the day before, the traveler anticipated no surprises concerning the layout. At the time, the biggest surprise was what a dump the place was. *A book critic lives here?* the traveler had thought. *Unthinkable!* But of course, the book critic did live here. And that, of course, went a long way to explaining why he was the miserable son of a bitch he was. After all, poverty and jealousy go hand in hand, do they not?

The man was probably a failed writer, like so many of them were. *Well*, the lean traveler thought, *if it's publicity he craves, let's see what I can do to get his name in the public eye one last time.*

The car was out of sight of the house as planned. There were no other sounds or lights for miles around. It was time to proceed. From the back seat, the traveler retrieved an old pair of coveralls, stolen from a clothesline on the drive down from Indianapolis, and put them on, along with a pair of buckled rubber boots picked up in an Army Navy surplus store on the outskirts of Mooresville. It was the same place the ski mask came from. The clothes would be discarded later, miles from here at some as-yet-unchosen location, where they would lay undiscovered until spring melted the snow, if they were ever found at all.

Ready now and squinting into the wind, with icy flakes brushing eyelids through the mask, the traveler set off up the winding lane. Sinking ankle-deep again and again, booted feet *chuffed* through the snow, and spurts of breath sent puffs of fog through chattering teeth and eagerly smiling lips. Considering the weather, the snow, and the stupid flapping galoshes, the traveler's step had a jaunty spring to it.

Show time.

THE TRAVELER didn't hear the dog yapping from inside the house until setting foot on the first step leading up to the porch. There was no porch light, so the only way to navigate was by the yellow glow of some interior illumination filtering through a limp, gauzy curtain. The curtain was made of what looked like age-yellowed lace, tattered and raveled around the edges.

By the time the traveler had reached the top step and clomped across the wooden porch, the dog was clawing at the front door and yapping like crazy. It sounded like a little fucker, maybe a shih tzu, or a dachshund, so that was encouraging. Hard to get mauled to death by a dachshund. The porch light came on overhead, and a face peered out through the curtained window on the front door before the traveler could lift a gloved hand to rap on the door.

The face was older than expected. Older and uglier. Surprisingly, the wizened old face peeked through the curtain at about waist level. The guy must be a munchkin.

The traveler smiled through the cold and waved a friendly hand at the old man peering out. The curtain fell closed, and the man could be heard mumbling something on the other side of the door, after which the yapping little dog finally shut the hell up. A moment later, the doorknob rattled and the door swung open to reveal a man, crippled up with either arthritis or some other horrendous ailment of decrepitude, sitting crookedly in a battered wheelchair like a starving old crow perched precariously on a limb.

"BooksOnWheels," the visitor mumbled near silently. "Of course."

The man was eighty if he was a day. He was huddled in a chrome wheelchair that had seen better times. A food-stained tartan spread lay draped over his knobby matchstick legs, and a little Chihuahua sat parked in his crotch, growling at the intruder standing at the door.

The old man was clearly surprised by his late guest but gathered his wits about him quickly enough. "Yes?" he asked. "May I help you?"

The visitor offered a reassuring smile, which was barely visible through the mouth hole in the mask. "My car broke down. I saw your lights through the trees. I was wondering if I could use your phone."

The old man leaned sideways and gazed out at the falling snow. "It's really coming down, isn't it?" He stared back up at his visitor and took a moment to analyze what he was seeing. The visitor got the impression it was more the cold air blowing through the door than any sense of reassurance the old man gleaned by his caller's appearance that prompted his next words. "You'd best get inside before you freeze to death. Yes. Yes, of course I have a phone. Come inside." He looked once again out into the night. "Are you alone?"

"All by my onesies." The traveler smiled around a shrug and, without waiting for a second invitation, stepped across the threshold. Ignoring the growling little mutt, the traveler stepped around the wheelchair into the room.

The old man closed the door and awkwardly pivoted the chair around to face his guest. "You must be cold, walking around in those coveralls without so much as a winter coat on your back." He pointed to a gas fireplace burning in the corner. "Go get yourself warmed up," he said.

"Thanks," the visitor mumbled, stepping toward the fire. With the gloves stripped off and stuffed into the coverall's icy pockets, standing in front of the fireplace with hands spread wide and shoved up close to the flames was delightful. The heat felt good.

"Mask too," the old man said. "You'll be more comfortable."

"No. I'd rather not."

"Oh. All right," the old man said in surprise, then hurriedly shushed himself as if not to be rude.

Mask still in place, the traveler turned and gazed down at the old gnome and his nasty little dog. Beneath the tartan lap robe, the old dude was wearing a ratty bathrobe with a woolen scarf tucked in around his neck to keep out the cold. The face above the scarf was cadaverous, yet oddly sweet. Just by looking at him, one would never suspect how many writing careers he had destroyed, how many creative hearts he had maimed and mocked beyond repair.

The visitor's gaze traveled around the room. There was an ancient Dell computer on a desk in the corner. The desk looked oddly incomplete without a desk chair, but of course the old guy on wheels didn't need one, did he? Bookcases lined the walls, each and every shelf stacked to overflowing. More books were piled here and there like stalagmites rising up off the floor. Everything in the room was coated with dust and pet hair.

"Are you out here all by yourself?" the traveler asked.

"Well, I have my friends," the old fart said, scratching the Chihuahua's ears and pointing to a corner.

The visitor turned to see what he was pointing at and saw a ratty cat lurking under a chair. It looked like it had mange. Another cat appeared perched atop an old chifforobe standing against the wall, and yet another cat was parked in a doorway leading off to some other part of the house. Only then did the ammonia reek of uncleaned cat boxes and pet urine become noticeable. Beneath an old sofa lay a tiny pile of Chihuahua turds. They must have been there for months. They were as dry as dust.

"Your friends," the traveler said wryly. "So I see." And with that, cold eyes came back to settle on the man in the wheelchair, who was still sitting there staring at his unexpected guest. He looked more and more nervous as the minutes passed.

Seeming confused by the intensity of his visitor's gaze, the old man asked, "Can I get you some coffee?"

"No."

"Would you care to use the facilities?"

"Fuck no."

The abruptness of the answer addled the old fart. "Oh," he said. "Then I guess you want the phone."

"No," the traveler said again. This time a hand dipped into the pocket containing the ice pick. Its slender blade felt cold on fingers now warmed from the fire. Cold and sharp. A chill stuttered through the traveler's body. It was a pleasant chill. An expectant chill. It had nothing to do with winter nights or falling snow or arctic gusts of frigid air, and everything to do with sheer unbridled anticipation.

"I've read your reviews, Mr. Price. You have quite a way with words."

The old man blinked in surprise. "How do you know what I do? And how do you know my name? I thought your car had—"

"Please be quiet," the traveler said. "Your voice is really most aggravating."

The old man tensed in his chair. "What? What did you say?"

"My car is fine. I just stopped by to right a few wrongs."

"I don't understand." But perhaps he did, for suddenly the first flash of fear showed on Price's wrinkled face. His rheumy old eyes flicked to a table in the corner. The visitor followed his gaze to an old rotary-dial phone—in designer black, straight out of the forties—parked on the table like an antique on display at the Smithsonian.

"Don't even think about it," the traveler lazily said through a smile.

Casually, as if enjoying the chat, the traveler leaned against a gigantic Mediterranean-style console TV sitting in the corner of the room. With crossed ankles, the visitor stared about the seedy room while speaking conversationally, "You're like the head lemming, you know."

"What?" the old man asked. "What did you say?"

But the visitor ignored him. "When you write a scathing review, other lemmings follow along. And other lemming reviewers follow along after that, each of you plagiarizing the other just to sound as if you have coincidentally come to the same conclusions, which in its own odd way adds verisimilitude to your original lies. By the time the prospective book buyer finishes reading your conglomerate of cruel comments and poorly-arrived-at criticisms, the unfortunate writer has no hope of making a sale, or advancing his numbers on Amazon, or seeing his beloved book delivered into the hands of people who might actually appreciate it for what it is. The book, the novel, the *story*, has been irretrievably sullied. And *you're* the one who started it."

The old man didn't seem to be listening. His eyes had settled on his visitor's hand—the one inside the coverall pocket—the one he couldn't see.

"What's that in your pocket?" Price asked, his voice reedier now with a dawning dread, all pretense of conviviality gone. His old Adam's apple bobbed up and down inside his wattled neck as he swallowed hard. His gaze at last refocused on his visitor's cool, emotionless eyes.

The traveler's smile broadened through the mouth hole in the mask. "Fine, then. If you don't want to have a reasonable conversation, we won't." Pulling the ice pick from the coverall pocket, the guest held it up for the man to consider. "Is this what you wanted to see?"

"No…," the old man sighed in a trembling exhalation of fear. "No."

The traveler held the ice pick up to better study the sharp simplicity of it and tapped the pointed end with a fingertip. The visitor's voice took on a dreamy quality. "Are you sure? It's really quite beautiful, don't you think?" Cold eyes turned back to the man in the wheelchair. "Sharp as a motherfucker, though. Wanna see?"

The man shook his head, terror dragging his already drooping face farther downward as he seemed to shrink into the chair.

The dog in the old man's lap began to growl again. The old man lifted him and held the wiggling mutt to the side of his face as if seeking comfort. His eyes were as big as chestnuts, rounded with fear. The dog's eyes weren't any smaller.

"Please don't hurt me," Price pleaded.

"Sorry," the traveler said, that ingratiating smile spreading wide. "It's time for the head lemming to take his final swan dive over the fucking cliff."

Without warning, the visitor took two long strides toward the old man and, standing directly in front of him, slipped the ice pick through the wrinkled skin beneath the quivering chin. With a gentle push upward, the ice pick pierced tongue and palate, then traveled onward and inward into the old fart's brain. Price's eyes remained open, but in the time frame between one heartbeat and the one that failed to come next, the light of fear in them departed. His visitor was rather sorry to see it go so quickly.

The old man's talonlike fingers relaxed around the Chihuahua, and before the dog could fall, the visitor scooped him up and set him on the floor. As if nothing untoward had happened at all, the little dog pranced off into the shadows of another room. Probably to poop.

Turning back to the corpse in the wheelchair, clearly unmourned by even his own dog, the traveler slipped the gloves back on and gripped the handle of the ice pick still protruding from beneath the motionless chin. It felt as solidly attached to the old man's head as a protuberance of bone. But for a trickle of blood from the corner of his mouth, the dead man's wound was almost bloodless. Gripping the ice pick lightly, the visitor wiped all fingerprints from the handle, but left the implement of murder where it was, thinking it made a rather forceful statement.

Taking a last look around the house and enjoying its peaceful silence, the traveler, humming softly, moved toward the front door, unlatched it, and stepped calmly out into the freezing night.

As a final stroke of malice, the door was left open to swing idly in the icy wind.

Chapter Six

MILO STARED down at the newspaper clipping Lillian Damons had mailed him. The clipping, taken from the *Indianapolis Star*, was dated three days previous and took up a mere two inches of column space. It told about a recent murder committed in an Indiana farming community just east of Terre Haute, close to the Illinois border. The article mentioned, rather offhandedly, that the victim, an aged man confined to a wheelchair and living alone in a secluded farmhouse, was a blogger and a book reviewer by avocation.

What the article failed to mention, and what Milo came to realize after a minimum of research, was that the victim, one Edgar Price, aka BooksOnWheels.com, was well-known on Amazon and several online bookselling sites for leaving a long string of one- or two-star reviews for practically everything he read. Mr. Price, it seemed, had never found a book he didn't hate. And his followers apparently loved him for it.

The simple one-line note that Lillian included with the clipping read, "What the hell is going on?"

Clearly, there was nothing offhanded about the conclusion Lillian had drawn concerning the importance of the victim's trade, nor in the way the rest of the writing community accepted the news of another book reviewer's murder. It did not escape Lillian's attention that both victims had been known for their irascible approach to reviewing. That little tidbit wasn't lost on the writing community either.

Having read reviews by both victims, Milo had to agree. Apparently so did everyone else he knew. Rumors began to spread like wildfire. Book blogs lit up across the internet with theories and suppositions and a few downright accusations—blaming authors, blaming the police, blaming the current political climate. Reviewers wrote pieces filled with outrage, claiming they were being victimized—victimized, hell, they were being *slaughtered*—for exercising their freedoms of speech and press.

Milo had no idea how the police were investigating the crimes, but in the public eye, in the world of writers and reviewers at least, the killings had been connected immediately. The term *serial killer* was being bandied about now, and the fact that *this* serial killer happened to be coming after their own seemed obvious to many. Milo wasn't convinced they were wrong.

While poor Grace's killing had barely roiled the surface of the literary waters, the second death of a book reviewer created a tsunami of buzz in Milo's world of writers, reviewers, and readers. With two reviewers down for the count—quite literally—the situation was getting rather salacious, according to a few who merrily rubbed their hands together in glee, waiting to see what would happen next. The fact that the victims were two of the most feared and roundly hated reviewers in the business ratcheted up their glee.

It must be said, however, that there were others, many of them reviewers themselves, who failed to find anything merry about it at all. And while some writers were screaming that revenge was sweet, most were disgusted and horrified by what had happened. Milo Cook was one of them. Having known Grace Connor in life brought a certain earthy reality to the proceedings that might not have been present had Milo simply seen her name on a byline now and then while reading her reviews and cringing at the heavy-handed way she dealt with those authors she found less than worthy of praise. The fact that he didn't particularly like the woman didn't factor in. He did like Grace's wife, and that was enough to bring home to Milo the tragedy of what had happened.

At the most basic level, Milo was ashamed by the reaction of some in the business. He thought it despicable that anyone should find entertainment value in the death of a fellow human being, no matter who the victim was. It was also a sad commentary that he could think of twenty people off the top of his head who themselves wouldn't have minded taking a potshot at the two victims.

Reading some of the vindictive comments on different blogs concerning the two murder victims and how they might have deserved everything they got, made Milo fear for the very future of humanity. Had we really grown so petty and heartless as to enjoy the suffering of others? Had it really come to that?

The new victim, Edgar Price, aka BooksOnWheels, was a name not unfamiliar to Milo, although he didn't follow his reviews as some who enjoyed seeing writers castigated in public did. Milo believed a reviewer had the right to say anything he wanted. It was Milo's opinion that once a book was released, it was on its own, to either sink or swim by its own merits. At the same time, he believed a writer had the right to tell a story the way he wanted, without being dragged over the coals for the editorial choices he made in the writing. Even when true technical missteps were exposed—missteps such as mundane plot devices, banal writing, flawed grammar, and incompetent editing—Milo saw no reason for a reviewer to ever chastise a writer to the point of humiliation. The sole exception was plagiarism. In Milo's eyes, that was an author's one unforgivable sin, and the offender *should* be keelhauled for it.

For plagiarists, Milo had no sympathy at all. Still, he didn't wish them dead. Exactly.

On this Monday morning, Milo sat at his desk with his Work in Progress scrolled out on the computer screen in front of him. He had written a few paragraphs, but his attention kept wandering. Between the murders and the evening he had spent with Logan Hunter, his thoughts were swirling dizzily in a sort of vortex. Revenge or karma. Right or wrong. And the more pressing question that kept invading his senses—romance or friendship? Which should he shoot for?

Where Logan Hunter was concerned, that was the $64,000 question, and Milo knew it.

Milo gave his head a shake and glanced at the calendar on his office wall. After the delightful evening they spent in Seaport Village getting to know each other, Milo had received a call from Logan explaining he would be out of town for a couple of days on business, but wondered if Milo would like to get together again on his return. Milo had said yes, hastily, emphatically. He hadn't even needed to think about it. Logan seemed to enjoy Milo's unhesitating response. Even his voice had mellowed when he said, "I really enjoyed spending time with you, Milo."

"And I with you," Milo answered, a little breathlessly. And it was true. He had. Even if the evening had ended with only a good-night kiss at Logan's door, it was still a hell of a night.

Logan cleared his throat, as if unsure of what he was about to say. "It's been a long time since I...."

Milo waited for the end of the sentence, but it never came. Finally he asked, "Yes? It's been a long time since you what, Logan?"

"Nothing," Logan sighed. Then he gave a chuckle as if laughing at himself, which confused Milo even more. "I'll see you when I get back."

"Good enough," Milo said and softly ended the call.

Now, three days later, feeling lonesome and forgotten, Milo stared back at the newspaper clipping lying on his desk. He wasn't sure where Logan had gone on his business trip, but he hoped he was keeping a weather eye out for serial killers. Not that Logan wrote the sort of reviews that led—that *might* have led—to the murder of Grace Connor and poor old Edgar Price. Logan treated writers and their works with respect. As an added bonus, Logan was neither an overweight woman with heart disease nor a wheelchair-bound octogenarian. In fact, of all the people Milo knew in the community, Logan Hunter was probably the least likely to attract the fury of a killer and the most physically capable of defending himself if he did.

Milo's gaze slid to the phone for the twentieth time. Jesus, he wished Logan would call.

At that moment, much to Milo's surprise, the phone rang. It was the landline, not his cell. Spanky gave a soft growl under the desk. The ringer had woken him up. Old dogs can be a wee bit protective of their naps.

Startled both by the dog and the call—Milo almost never used his landline—he dug his bare toes into Spanky's coat to calm him down and picked up the phone. "Hello?"

A booming, raspy voice came over the line with an unmistakable New York accent. *Queens? Brooklyn? The Bronx?* "Is this Milo Cook?"

"Speaking," Milo said, more confused than ever. "How can I help you?"

"This is Detective Robert Carlisle of the New York City Police Department. I'd like to take a couple of minutes of your time, if you don't mind. Can you speak freely with me?"

Milo assumed the detective was asking if he was alone and could talk. "Yes, sir. I'm free to talk." He thought he heard chewing sounds and the squeak of a desk chair. Maybe the detective was propping his feet up on his desk and scarfing down a donut? Could life really be that clichéd?

There followed an unmistakable slurp of what was presumably coffee, then another squeak and a thump. Apparently the detective had decided to forgo his sugar fix so he could sit up straight and concentrate on the call.

"I understand, sir, that you were friends with Grace Connor."

"Yes," Milo said, suddenly not so confused by the call. This had to do with Grace. He should have known. "I knew her. We weren't exactly friends, but she *was* married to a friend of mine. Lillian Damons."

"Yes, that's why I'm calling. Miss Damons gave your name as a contact."

"Have you discovered who killed her?" Milo asked.

"Uh, no. And I think this will go faster if I'm the one who asks the questions. Would that be all right with you?"

Milo grunted. He didn't appreciate the sarcasm, but he supposed the guy had a point. "Sorry, sir. Yes. Please go ahead."

"When was the last time you saw Miss Connor?"

Milo thought about it. "Lord, it must be almost a year. I did a book show in Kansas City, where Grace and Lillian lived. Still do, in fact. Well, Lillian does," Milo awkwardly amended.

The detective mumbled something to himself, then cleared his throat and said, "I understand Grace Connor wasn't exactly popular in her field."

Milo sighed. "If that's a question, I guess I'd have to say you're right. Her reviews could be harsh. Still, she had a substantial following of readers who thought she told it like it was."

"And you?"

"I try never to read reviews. Mine or anyone else's." Milo knew this wasn't exactly true. All writers read reviews whether they admit it or not. Sometimes the damn things were inescapable.

"But you were aware of her reputation," the detective prodded.

Reluctantly, Milo admitted, "Yes. I was aware of her reputation."

"Have you heard anyone make threats against her person for the things she wrote in her reviews?"

"No. Of course not. Like I said, I'm a close friend of Lillian's. I would never have let anyone say anything bad about her wife in front of me."

"Would you have reported it if you had?"

Milo considered this. He was also beginning to get a little mad. "Detective, if you mean would I have reported a threat against Grace after learning Grace had been murdered, of course I would. While I might not have been in love with the woman, I do love and respect her partner."

"I see. One more question and we'll be finished. Did you know or had you heard of Edgar Price? On his book blog he called himself

BooksOnWheels, a reference to being stuck in a wheelchair, I presume. He was a book reviewer who worked and resided in Indiana."

"No, sir, I didn't know him. Yes, sir, I had heard of him. Like Grace, among my fellow writers he wasn't the most popular of reviewers, if you really want to call him a reviewer. He was more of a troll, in my opinion. Cruising around the internet, spouting angry diatribes, hiding behind the anonymity the internet offers. And no, before you ask, I heard no one make threats against his person, nor do I know anyone who might have wanted him dead." Milo hesitated before asking, "Do you really think the murders are connected? That the killer is a wounded author who had an axe to grind because he didn't like the reviews he was getting from these two reviewers?"

For the first time, Detective Carlisle chuckled. "You sound skeptical. You don't think that's possible?"

"Well, it seems kind of far-fetched. I don't think I'd use it as a plot device in a book. Nor do I think most authors are quite as sensitive as that would seem to imply."

The detective's chuckle died as quickly as it came. "I hate to tell you this, Mr. Cook, but real life isn't a novel. I've seen far more ridiculous motives for murder. And yes, to answer your question. Going through a backlog of both victims' reviews, I think there's a pretty good argument for blaming those reviews for their killings. Neither Miss Connor nor Mr. Price was particularly subtle with their criticisms. I'll bet they wounded a great many egos over the years. They may even have ruined more than a few writing careers while they were at it."

The detective gave a rattling cough that sounded like it came all the way up from the soles of his feet. Milo imagined a cigarette dangling from his lips and a dried-up pair of diseased lungs withering away inside his chest. "Now then, I'm sorry I took up so much of your time, and I'm sorry if I offended you, but this is a homicide investigation. Uncomfortable questions need to be asked. If you think of anything, my number here in Manhattan is 212-555-1952. You can call me day or night. By the way, young man. I enjoyed your last book."

Milo couldn't have been more surprised if the detective had blown him a kiss over the phone. "Really? You mean you read it? Well, uh, thanks. I hope you find the killer, sir."

Detective Carlisle offered up a rather uncharitable grunt, which didn't sound particularly hopeful. "Yeah. So do I."

And with that, he was gone.

Milo hung up the phone, thinking the NYPD must really be stuck if they'd taken to calling acquaintances of their murder victims all the way across country.

For the first time, Milo feared Grace's murder—and maybe even that of Edgar Price—would never be solved at all.

Rather than getting mired down in that depressing possibility, Milo turned his attention back to Logan Hunter. That was a far, far happier place for his thoughts to dwell.

An hour later his phone rang again, and this time the call had nothing to do with murder.

Milo froze in his chair at the sound of a familiar voice competing with a loudspeaker announcing arrivals at Gate 12A, and even farther in the background, the roar of a jetliner climbing into the sky.

"I'm back in town. When can I see you?"

"When did you get in?" Milo asked, all too aware that his surprised heart had just done a somersault.

With a laugh, Logan said, "About twenty-seven seconds ago."

With a grunt of impatience, Milo asked, "How come you waited so long to call?"

"I LOVE your house," Logan said. He was standing on Milo's doorstep, still pulling his finger back from the doorbell since Milo had answered the door before Logan even finished ringing.

Milo stared out at him. His capacity for forming sentences in his brain and shooting them down a string of neurons to his mouth, where they could be uttered out loud like those of a normal human being, seemed to have taken a holiday. All he could do was ogle Logan standing there in front of him, looking as handsome and towering and fine as any man he had ever seen in his life. He could feel a flush rising to his cheeks and a slight tremor in his knees. What was he, fifteen?

"Thanks," Milo finally managed to mumble. He stepped aside to usher Logan inside. As he walked past, Milo caught the clean scents of Sea Breeze and Ivory soap. He thought he had never smelled anything more alluring.

He closed the door behind them and turned to find Logan facing him. Without thinking, Milo walked into Logan's arms. A tremor stamped through him when Logan wrapped Milo in a gentle embrace. Milo felt Logan's breath stirring his hair, and that sent a second shiver shuddering through him. For the briefest of moments, while he rested his cheek against Logan's shoulder and laid his hands across Logan's broad back to return the embrace, he thought he heard the gentle thunder of Logan's heart, but he wasn't sure. It might have been his own.

They pulled apart as quickly as they had come together. Once again Milo was surprised to find himself totally at ease in Logan's presence. Not so much as a whiff of shyness darkened his thoughts or dimmed his perceptions, as so often happened when he was in the presence of someone who was knockout gorgeous. Or worse yet, someone he was beginning to care about.

Stepping back, he smiled, and Logan returned it with a cryptic little smile of his own. "I've missed you," Milo said, before he could stop himself.

Logan glanced down at his own feet for a second before lifting his eyes back to Milo's face. "Thanks," he said. "I've missed you too."

"Was your trip all right? Make good connections? Didn't get snowed in in Buffalo Balls, Idaho, or some equally horrible third-world cesspool?"

Logan's smile widened. "Nope. Everything went like clockwork. And Buffalo Balls is actually quite lovely."

"No kidding. I'll have to remember it next time I book a vacation."

"Do."

Milo laughed. "Where were you *really*?"

"New York City. An employees' seminar for the ad company I told you I worked for. A total waste of time, as it turned out. Could have been handled with a conference call and a couple of YouTube lectures. At least they paid for the airline tickets, so I'm not out anything."

"Well, I'm glad you're back."

"Me too. I hated the cold. California weather has spoiled me for life, I think. On the bright side, I did get a couple of Gray's Papaya kraut dogs, so the trip wasn't a total waste."

"Glad to hear it." Milo grinned. "Now hopefully you'll never leave again."

Surprised to hear the words he had just uttered, Milo clapped his mouth shut before he said anything else equally stupid. Or true.

Logan batted dark lashes. His hazel eyes, flecked with cinnamon, pored over Milo's face as if memorizing every feature, every nuance.

Not for the first time, Milo noticed that when Logan smiled a certain way, it formed a tiny dimple in one cheek. As if the guy wasn't sexy enough already.

"You're right," Logan said softly. "Hopefully I won't. Leave again, I mean."

Milo gave himself a shake. "Christ, where are my manners? Come on. I thought we'd sit by the pool."

"Wow. You have a pool?"

Milo shrugged. "Yeah, it came with the house."

He took Logan's hand and led him across the living room, through the dining room, and into the kitchen. He paused to snag a couple of beers from the fridge, then led Logan onward through a sliding glass door that opened up to the patio out back.

The patio wasn't large, but it was nicely laid out with a couple of short palm trees, a small oval pool with handrailed steps leading into the water at one end, and a couple of chaise lounges parked beside a brick fireplace used for cookouts, which Milo had never once fired up. He wasn't much on cooking, be it cooking out or cooking in. An eight-foot plank fence encircled the patio for privacy. Milo had hung succulents and orchids in mossy baskets along the fence, interspersed with occasional bright red hummingbird feeders. There were hummingbirds and butterflies everywhere.

Logan stood spellbound, clearly impressed. "This is gorgeous." He strode to the edge of the pool and knelt down to trail his fingers through the water. "It's warm," he said, and Milo nodded. Logan stood again, and Milo handed him one of the beers while motioning to a chair. They made themselves comfortable, splaying their legs out on the lounges and sipping contentedly at their drinks. Milo kicked off his shoes, so Logan did too.

"If you get hungry, we'll order a pizza," Milo offered.

Logan laughed. "Good enough. I don't cook much either."

"Do you swim?" Milo asked.

"Yeah, but I didn't bring my trunks."

Milo took a long pull from his beer while wiggling his eyebrows like Groucho Marx. "Well, there are two solutions to that problem. One, you can swim naked, or two, I can loan you a pair of Bryce's old swimming trunks. I think he left a couple behind when he split. He was about your size, so they'd probably fit."

Logan laughed. "Perhaps the second option would be best."

Milo gave a horrendously exaggerated pout and said, "I was afraid you'd say that." Then he hopped off the chaise and said with a wicked leer in his eye, "Come on. Let's get comfortable."

Logan spent about two seconds looking wary, then seemed to decide, fuck it, what do I have to lose? With a laugh, he followed Milo back into the house, peeling his socks off as he went.

Milo's first glimpse of Logan in nothing but Bryce's swimming trunks was enough to ratchet his blood pressure up about thirty points. The fact that the trunks were actually too large and barely clung to Logan's narrow hips, cranked it up even higher.

Bronze-skinned, with lean muscular legs peppered with dark hair, Logan was a knockout. Beneath broad shoulders, his finely sculpted chest was shadowed by a sprinkling of hair that meandered from one copper nipple to the other, then trailed downward in a narrow swath to Logan's belly button, where it flared out again. By the time the tangled mass reached the waistband of Bryce's swimming trunks, and disappeared beneath it, Milo was left all but brainless by a sudden infusion of endorphins that seemed to knock out his circuit boards left and right, like somebody had strafed them with a machine gun.

The healthy bulge pooching up the crotch of Bryce's old trunks didn't help his blood pressure much either.

"Wow," Milo muttered, before he could stop himself.

LOGAN STOOD there, cautiously accepting the eyes on him and appreciating Milo's reaction, whether he wanted to admit it or not.

And he was just as pleased by the man standing in front of *him*.

Milo Cook, dressed in trunks of his own, had the sort of body Logan Hunter found most attractive. Lean, golden-hued, lithe. His legs were brushed with blond hair, his chest perfectly delineated but smooth. His waist tapered down from shoulders that were obviously those of a swimmer. His navel was a delicate puncture. Milo sported an appendix scar that looked like it had been there a long time. Probably since childhood. That one pale imperfection was like an accent mark, underscoring the flawlessness of everything else.

Logan longed to step forward and lay a fingertip to that white strip of scarred flesh. Just to feel the texture of it. To gauge its heat. That longing, that *need*, all but floored him with its intensity.

By sheer will, he dragged his gaze up to Milo's face and was immediately lost in Milo's green eyes. He allowed himself to float there for a moment in their praise, then pulled himself together.

"Back to the pool?"

Milo smiled and nodded. "Sure. You go ahead. I'll get us another beer."

Logan had to squeeze past, since Milo was standing in the doorway. The first contact between his bare torso and Milo's arm when they brushed past each other sent a surge of hunger clattering through him. For the first time, it was a hunger that had nothing to do with missing Jerry, and everything to do with this man he was with now. With Milo. With Milo Cook.

"Sorry," he mumbled, before sucking in his breath and squeezing past.

Stepping out onto the apron of the pool, he groaned at his own stupidity. Sorry? What the hell was he sorry for? Did he sound like an idiot? Worse yet, *was* he an idiot?

For lack of a better idea, Logan closed his eyes and allowed himself to tip forward, body as stiff as a board, falling flat into the pool with a tremendous splash. The water, warmed by the sun, melted luxuriously over him, finding every nook and cranny, filling in the contours of his long body like the gentle caress of sleep-warm sheets.

When he popped his head out of the water and gave himself a shake to clear his vision, he saw Milo standing close-by, laughing at him.

"That's the worst dive I've ever seen in my life!" Milo laughed, placing two fresh beers at the edge of the pool.

Logan grinned. "Actually it was more of a faint." He reached over the lip of the pool and wrapped his fingers around Milo's ankle, then gave a yank and dragged Milo into the water, where he landed just as ungracefully as Logan had.

They wrestled below the surface, all arms and legs and bubbles, then shot out of the water, sputtering and laughing and gasping for air.

Getting his bearings, Logan spun in the pool and found Milo—the water lapping at his chin, his sun-streaked hair dragged down over his eyes and plastered flat, his white teeth shimmering—staring right back at him. Before he knew what was happening, Milo leaped on him, and they both submerged again, playfully wrapped in each other's arms.

This time Logan had the presence of mind to concentrate on the feel of Milo next to him, the brushing of their legs together, the warm touch of soft bellies, and for a brief moment, the caress of Milo's laughing lips over the skin of his forearm when they fought for supremacy under the water.

When he felt his cock begin to lengthen in the trunks, he pulled back. Slipping gently free from Milo's tangled limbs, he draped his elbows over the edge of the pool and grabbed one of the beers. He took a long drink while hovering there in the water, his back to the pool. Milo swam up beside him and snatched up his own beer, tilting it back for a long swallow.

As they drank, elbows touching, they eyed each other, smiling. Logan couldn't help wondering if Milo knew why he had so quickly pulled away. By the sexy gleam in those incredibly green eyes, Logan suspected Milo knew quite well.

Logan turned back to look out over the edge of the pool to the beautiful grounds, when he suddenly found a long pink tongue taking a swipe at his nose. Logan jerked back in surprise, only to find a rather large dog standing there in front of him. Must be Spanky. Appearing out of nowhere, the dog now stood at the edge of the pool, his tail going a mile a minute, a doggy grin spread across his happy face. He stepped closer and resumed giving Logan's face a bath.

Logan sputtered and laughed, trying to twist his head away from the encroaching tongue.

Milo giggled beside him and reached out to grip Spanky's collar, gently dragging the dog in his direction. Wrapping his wet arms around Spanky's neck, he let the dog bathe him for a while with that worshiping tongue, so as to give his houseguest a break.

"Where's he been?" Logan asked, still laughing.

"He was asleep under my desk. See all the gray on his muzzle? He's old. He sleeps more than he's awake."

"How many years have you had him?"

"Quite a few, and he was almost old when I adopted him. It's not just puppies that need good homes."

"Well, he's friendly." Logan grinned, still wiping the dog spit off his face.

"He likes you," Milo said proudly. "He doesn't deign to lick just anybody, you know."

Logan gave Milo a sidelong glance. He wasn't buying it. "Yeah, right. He probably licks the mailman, the bug man, Jehovah's Witnesses, burglars, Girl Scouts schlepping cookies, the guy that reads the meter."

Laughing, Milo gave Spanky a kiss between the eyes. "Actually, you're right. He does." After giving the dog another smooch and a final hug, he pointed to the chaise lounge over by the fence. "Go take a nap, boy. Go on."

Spanky blessed Milo with one more swipe of his adoring tongue, then padded off toward the fence with a slightly arthritic limp, shaking the water from his coat as he went. With a last glance backward, he tucked himself under the chaise out of the sun, gave a broad yawn, and promptly fell fast asleep with his chin on his paws.

Logan studied him for a minute, then said, "I like him. He doesn't hold back."

"Nope." Milo grinned. "What you see is what you get."

"It was nice of you to adopt an older dog."

"Thanks."

Logan watched as Milo opened his mouth as if to expound on that, then take another long pull from his beer instead.

Logan found himself interested in certain other aspects of Milo's life, and he thought this might be a pretty good time to do some snooping. He wasn't sure why he wanted to know. He just did.

"Were you in this house when you lived with Bryce?" he asked.

Milo nodded. "Yeah, I had bought it just before we met. When we first moved in together, it was in this house. It was new to both of us, just like we were new to each other."

"Do you miss him?" Logan asked.

Milo shook his head. "No. Bryce was sexy as hell, and he could have his kind moments. But overall, he was a bit of a dick. For one thing, he couldn't open his mouth without lying. Even if it was something inconsequential, he seemed to feel he had to lie about it. Make it more interesting. Make it more grand. I never quite understood why he couldn't be the writer he wanted to be. God knows he had the imagination for it."

Logan watched as Milo's eyes grew pensive.

"Still, like I said, he had his good qualities. He was terrific in bed, for one thing. That's a pretty good quality to have."

Logan smiled. "Indubitably."

"Unfortunately, he was good in bed with a lot of people, not just me. When I found out, I dumped him."

"I'm sorry."

Milo shrugged. "Now for loyalty, I have Spanky. Aside from licking the occasional houseguest, he's never cheated on me once."

Logan grinned and made a kissy face at the dog. "What a good boy," he cooed. Spanky opened one eye, then promptly closed it again, while Milo laughed.

An evening breeze slipped through the palm trees, dove over the fence, and skimmed the water, ruffling their wet heads.

Milo shivered. "Damn, it's getting cold."

Logan snorted. "It must be sixty-five degrees."

"Yeah. Like I said. Cold."

Logan rolled his eyes, bopped Milo gently on the shoulder with a balled-up fist, and squinted his way into a mocking grin. "It's funny. You don't *look* like a weenie."

Milo narrowed his eyes. "Oh, really."

Carefully placing his beer on the concrete out of the way, he dove headfirst at Logan, dragging him under the water yet again while Logan's beer bottle flew out into the middle of the pool and sank like a rock. After they rolled around in the water for a minute, gagging and choking, Milo slipped out of Logan's clenches and dove deep to retrieve the bottle. Happily it hadn't broken when it settled to the bottom.

While Milo was underwater, Logan pulled himself out of the pool and raced to the kitchen to grab two more beers from the fridge. Might as well make himself at home. And seeing as he was, he also took a minute to grab a fistful of paper towels off the counter and wipe up the trail of pool water he'd dribbled across Milo's kitchen floor.

When he went back outside, Milo was once again hanging by his elbows at the edge of the pool, watching him.

"Don't be shy," Milo said. "Help yourself to a beer."

Logan smirked and waved the bottles in front of him, then placed them carefully before Milo on the concrete. "I did. Mind if I cannonball?"

"No, I—"

Logan sprang over Milo's head, hugging his knees. He landed with a horrific splash that all but swept Milo out of the pool. Even Spanky lifted his head to see what the hell was going on.

When Logan emerged, blowing water out of his nose and giggling like a kid, Milo groaned. "And here I thought you were an adult."

Not to be outdone, Milo climbed out of the pool, hitched up his shorts, and spun around to launch himself out over the water just as Logan had. He landed flat on his back with a smack that sounded like it hurt. Still, he came up sputtering with laughter.

Logan swam over and spun Milo around as he treaded water. He ran his hands over Milo's back, which was bright red from the impact. He found himself gently brushing the red skin with his fingertips and saying quietly, "That must have stung."

Milo paddled in the water, propelling himself around until he faced Logan. They floated there so close together their chests were almost touching. Logan's hands still reached around to Milo's back, holding him in place.

"Sorry," Milo said, his gaze suddenly soft and thoughtful. "I can't resist." Still treading water, Milo paddled closer and laid a gentle kiss on Logan's lips.

Logan's eyes opened wide in surprise; then he felt them closing of their own accord, blocking out the world completely as he let himself be drawn into the kiss.

When Milo eased away and spread his hand across Logan's chest, his thumb came to rest on Logan's nipple as if by accident. Logan stared wordlessly into the face before him. Milo's lips were still moist, either from the pool or the kiss. Logan couldn't be sure which. He licked his own lips and tasted Milo yet again. A flame seemed to kindle in Milo's eyes as he floated there, still in Logan's arms, staring back. His breath brushed over Logan's face, smelling warmly of beer.

Before he could stop himself, Logan asked, "Do you think we're rushing things?"

Milo frowned, but his hand never left Logan's chest. "It doesn't feel that way to me."

Logan lifted his hand and caressed Milo's cheek. Milo pulled back and looked at it.

"Didn't you use to wear a ring on this hand?"

Logan nodded. "Yes. I... I didn't want to wear it tonight."

Milo's eyes bore deep into his. "It was a wedding ring, wasn't it? You and Jerry were married."

Logan glanced at the pale band of flesh that the ring had left behind. His fingers were starting to prune from being in the pool so long. "Yes." He gazed back into Milo's green eyes. "Were you and Bryce?"

Milo jumped. "What, *married*? God no. Sometimes I think we were barely *lovers*." His eyes grew serious, as if he suddenly understood something. "I'm sorry, Logan. Being here with me, please tell me you're, you know, *comfortable*. That you don't feel like you're cheating on Jerry's memory."

The question shocked Logan, but only because he was asking himself the same thing. "No, I…. Maybe. I don't know."

"I'm not rushing you. Please don't think that."

Logan nodded, lost in wonder as he stared yet again into Milo's eyes. There was something about the color of them that drew him in. He had never in his life seen eyes quite so green. "I don't think that," he said, resurrecting a smile.

Milo lifted his hand from Logan's chest and laid it across his own. A teasing grin twisted his mouth. "Uh-oh. I can't stand it when you look at me like that with those gorgeous hazel eyes. I think I'm going into arrhythmic shock. I could die from that, you know."

"You can die from a lot of things," Logan said quietly, eyes bright, still stroking Milo's cheek.

Milo lifted his hand to Logan's face and caressed it in return.

"Spend the night," Milo whispered. "Please."

Logan was touched by the way Milo spoke the words. Touched and turned on. Once again he felt his cock lengthening, growing erect. Logan hesitated, but his eyes never left Milo's face. "It's been a long time since I've been with anyone. Not since Jerry… left."

"It's like riding a bicycle. It'll come back to you."

Logan offered a tiny smile. "So I've heard."

"I can do all the pedaling, if you like."

Logan grinned. "No, I think I can hold my own."

A drop of water gathered at the end of Milo's nose, and Logan laid his thumb to it, wiping it away before it could fall.

Beneath the pool's surface, Milo's other hand stroked Logan's waist. Their legs brushed together as they lazily paddled to stay afloat in the crystal-blue water. Lingeringly, Milo's hand slid across Logan's stomach and dipped beneath the waistband of his trunks. When Milo's fingers circled Logan's iron cock, Logan closed his eyes and tilted his head back with a groan.

Milo drew closer and pressed his mouth to Logan's throat, causing Logan to buck against him, pulling him closer.

"I've never slept with a reviewer before," Milo gasped, his tongue doing a taste test on Logan's Adam's apple. "No matter how badly I bungle this, I'll expect four stars at least."

"I'll try to be generous with my critique."

"Wiseass."

Logan's lips parted as he pulled Milo closer, lifting him in the water at the same time. He dipped his head into the crook of Milo's neck and laid his lips there, tasting the man for the first time in what was other than a kiss. Discounting the chlorine, Milo's flesh was a delicious mixture of sweet and salty. Logan squeezed his eyes shut, savoring the flavor, the scent, the heat. The satin softness of Milo's skin. His own hand slid down the back of Milo's trunks and dipped into the warm crevice of flesh he found there beneath the fabric. It was Milo's turn to arch against him at the touch. His legs came up and wrapped around Logan's waist. Milo's erect cock, trapped inside his trunks, pressed against Logan's belly.

Logan felt an old familiar fire burning inside him. It was a fire that had been absent far too long from his life. "My God, you're beautiful," he whispered, his lips on Milo's throat now, a lone fingertip resting lightly on Milo's opening as he cradled him in the water. "Take me to your bed, Milo. Please."

Milo's mouth found Logan's and kissed away the words. "Yes," he gasped. "Yes."

Together, they climbed from the pool. Beers forgotten, Milo snatched up a humongous beach towel from one of the chaise lounges and wrapped it around them. Their fingers woven together, their hearts pounding, Milo led Logan silently into the house.

Spanky opened his eyes and watched them go, then slowly sank back into dreamless sleep.

Chapter Seven

HOURS LATER, with the house steeped in darkness, Logan opened his eyes. The first sensation he experienced was the taste of Milo's sweet juices still sleeping on his tongue. The second sensation was the mingled scent of their two bodies, as if a residue had been left on the air from their lovemaking that yet permeated Milo's lightless bedroom.

Logan turned his head to gaze down through the shadows at Milo, who lay snuggled against his side, one hand resting lightly atop Logan's stomach, his face pressed into Logan's armpit where his breathing tickled the hair there. It was that tickling breath that had woken Logan. That and Milo's grumbly, leonine snore.

The sudden awareness of Milo's sleek naked body pressed against him sent a surge of contentment rushing through Logan that was so powerful it almost stopped his breath. Milo's leg lay draped over his own, Milo's leg hair bristling softly against his skin. Against his hip, Logan could feel Milo's cock, it too sleeping now. Spent. At rest.

Logan's arm was asleep because he had it twisted up behind his head in lieu of a pillow, which Logan remembered tossing to the floor earlier in the night because it was getting in the way as the two of them made love. Stifling a groan, trying to ignore the pins and needles as blood rushed back into his starving arteries, he straightened his arm out enough to carefully drape it around Milo's head. Resting his hand lightly against the smooth skin of Milo's back, he relished the silky texture of it beneath his fingertips. Somehow it was thrilling, and a little bit erotic, to know Milo was unaware of Logan's touch as he lay there at his side lost in sleep.

Logan smiled and, tilting his head down a little more, lightly pressed his lips into Milo's tousled hair. The scents he encountered there sent a dozen other memories clamoring through his sleep-addled brain. Milo's delicious cock, pulsing with desire, spilling come between Logan's lips. Milo's warm mouth teasing the come from his own at the same time. Logan crying out at their moment of simultaneous release.

Not just because it was perfect, but because it had been so very, very long since he had shared that experience with anyone.

Mostly Logan remembered the moments that followed. When, with Milo's mouth still tasting him, still capturing his cock inside that worshiping well of moist heat, still drawing the last drops of liquid from Logan as if he simply could not get enough, Milo uttered a little purring sound deep in his throat. It was a sound that said Milo was content having Logan near, drinking from him, fulfilling Logan's need and letting Logan fulfill his own.

Carefully, Logan cuddled closer, still savoring the feel of Milo's body against his, holding him as tightly as he dared without waking him up. He looked far too peaceful to disturb. And far too beautiful.

Lying alongside Milo's small frame, Logan felt clumsily large. As if he was taking up all the space in the bed, all the air in the room. Milo was more ethereal, more gently *present*. If this were an artist's studio, Milo would be a soft swath of muted color on a pristine canvas, Logan a big fucking glob of thick paint on the artist's shoe. Logan grinned at the analogy. Then his grin faded as he remembered how, when they were standing, the top of Milo's head was at the perfect height to tuck neatly under Logan's chin. Logan liked that. He liked it a lot.

But what Logan liked even more was Milo's way of seemingly absorbing what he wanted from Logan even while he slept. That touched a place in Logan's heart that had not been touched since Jerry left. Logan *enjoyed* Milo snuggling close to him like this. He *enjoyed* Milo holding on to Logan as he snored softly against him. He *enjoyed* knowing there was something in Logan that Milo felt was worthy of claiming even when Milo lay lost inside his own contented sleep. There was a giving nature and a *goodness* in Milo that Logan had not sensed in any other person since Jerry left. There was also clearly something in himself that Milo felt a need to lay claim to. And that, perhaps, was what Logan enjoyed most of all.

Then there was the way Milo had taken control the night before, the way he had led Logan through pleasures Logan had all but forgotten existed. And how it had all left Logan a little in awe of this man beside him.

Milo had surprised Logan last night. Surprised the pants off him. No pun intended, Logan smirked quietly to himself as he lay there in the dark. After all, Logan had expected sex. Had expected it and longed for it. But what he'd received was far more. There was a sweetness in Milo's lovemaking that had taken Logan's breath away a dozen times during their coupling, and still pulled at him now, at this very moment, just thinking back on it. The oh-so-gentle but confident stroke of Milo's hands. The kneading of his fingertips. The tender way Milo had cooed softly while happily exploring the terrain of Logan's body, and the way he freely and unashamedly allowed Logan to explore his own. Offering everything, fearing nothing, never holding back.

Logan had never known a first time with someone to be so faultless and utterly trustful. Even with Jerry there had been a good deal of stumbling at the beginning. They had needed to learn what pleased the other. They had needed a few trial runs on certain more invasive acts of love. They might have laughed their way through those exploratory runs, but they had still been awkward.

With Milo there had been no awkwardness at all.

Logan closed his eyes again, willing sleep to reclaim him. Yet he didn't really want to sleep either. He was so content lying there with Milo's hand resting lightly on his belly, Milo's slim, warm fingertips nestled entwined in Logan's pubic hair, brushing lightly against the base of his sleeping dick. Logan fought against the arousal he knew was only a breath away. He didn't want to lose this moment. It was too precious to be wasted on hungers of the flesh.

Once more, he lightly pressed his lips into Milo's sun-streaked hair and breathed in the scent of the young man cuddled next to him. When Milo mumbled in his sleep and his lips pushed harder into Logan's armpit as if the hair there were beginning to tickle him too, Logan smiled. God, the guy was just so damned *cute*.

And without warning, Logan's mind was suddenly filled with Jerry's face. It was as if Jerry had reared up at the foot of the bed and stood there now in the shadows, watching him. Watching *them.*

Logan opened his eyes wide and stared out at his own memories, hovering there in the darkness before him. Jerry. But he wasn't really there, of course. He couldn't be. His still, breathless body was penned inside that horrible concrete box in the wall of the mausoleum in Calumet City, two thousand miles away. Could Jerry really know where Logan was at this very moment? Did he know that Logan had finally shaken himself free of all the guilt and loyalty and love that once bound him to Jerry and given himself, at least physically, to another man for the very first time since Jerry left? And if he did know, was it all right? A year had passed. A year to Logan at least. God knows how many lifetimes a year is to someone no longer here, no longer on this plane. To Jerry, did that passing of time feel like a century, or did it feel like an instant? Or did it feel like anything at all?

Was death simply dark, timeless nothing? Could the closing of life really be that empty?

Milo's fingers twitched over Logan's stomach, a reflexive act, perhaps, as if he relished Logan's feel even in his sleep. Just as quickly, Milo's hand fell still again, his fingers lay motionless, unknowingly cradling Logan's cock in a protective fist now. Logan squeezed his eyes shut, loving the way that warm, caressing hand felt around him, loving the way Milo's hot breath flowed across his ribs as he continued to snore like a buffalo. Despite his best efforts, Logan's blood began to flow, and he felt his cock harden and lengthen inside Milo's gentle, sleeping grip.

God, it had been so long since he had felt like this with anyone.

Without warning, a blade of guilt stabbed through him, as sharp as a sliver of glass. Jerry's sweet face appeared yet again in the darkness at the foot of the bed. Jerry neither smiled down at him nor frowned. His handsome face, which Logan knew by heart, merely floated there watching, emotionless, unaccusing, unmoved. All the accusations were in Logan's head, not Jerry's eyes.

Stifling a cry, Logan eased himself away, sliding free of Milo's hand, cradling Milo's head before it fell, lowering it lightly onto the bed. As if suddenly finding himself untouched, his connection to Logan broken, Milo curled into a fetal position and snuggled into the tangled sheets, still sound asleep.

Logan unfolded his long legs and rose slowly. Standing naked in the darkness, his cock still hard and pulsing, he stared down at Milo on the bed before him. Milo was silent now; his snoring had stopped. A sliver of moonlight lay along his pale hip, where his golden tan didn't reach. Logan longed to touch it, to stroke that swath of moonlight-blue skin. To make it his own once again, just as he had done last night. To lay his lips to it and taste it. To ease Milo onto his back and take his hardness into his mouth and coax him into another explosive climax. To savor the juices that spilled from him, and have his own juices savored in return.

Gnawing at his lower lip, suddenly desperate to get away, Logan turned from the bed. Trying to be quiet because he didn't want a confrontation, didn't want to have to explain why he was leaving, he carefully maneuvered his way through the shadows in the unfamiliar room. He found his clothes where he had left them the night before when he dressed for swimming. Gathering them in a bundle and snugging them to his chest, he padded softly outside to the patio, aglow with moonlight and the green shimmer of the underwater pool lights. There he stood barefoot on the cold concrete and slipped them on. He found his shoes beside the chaise where he'd kicked them off earlier. Turning, he spotted Spanky, standing at the edge of the pool watching him. Logan knelt, and Spanky walked up to him, tail wagging. The old dog rested his gray snout on Logan's leg while Logan twiddled his ears and whispered quiet words.

When Logan turned to leave, the dog followed, his toenails tapping along behind him across the kitchen floor, then falling silent as he trailed him through the rest of the carpeted house.

Logan slipped outside and quietly pulled the front door shut, leaving Spanky safely locked inside. He tried the knob to assure himself the lock had clicked. When the knob didn't turn, he walked slowly along the street to his car. Ducking inside and closing the car door behind him, Logan breathed in the familiar scent of his own belongings. Funky gym clothes in the back seat. A hamburger wrapper with secret sauce balled up on the back floorboard. Years-old cigarette butts moldering in the ash tray from when he used to smoke. God, he really should clean that thing out one of these days.

The smells were mundane, and somehow emptily lonesome, compared to those he had just left.

Logan lifted his forearm to his face and sniffed. Wonder of wonders, there it was. Milo's scent. It still lay on his skin. He breathed it deeply in, thinking back over the night behind him. He dropped his arm and, with a sigh, stared out through the windshield at the empty street. After a while, he turned the key in the ignition and slipped the car into gear.

But still he didn't want to go back to his apartment. Not yet. So he simply began driving, not thinking of a destination at all.

An odd sadness, and an equally odd elation, followed Logan as he explored the abandoned streets in this unfamiliar city he now called home. It was after four in the morning. He slid the car windows down so the cool night air would rush through the cab. There was almost no traffic at all. He shuffled through the untidy stack of CDs on the passenger seat, but just as quickly pulled his hand away, leaving them where they lay. He didn't feel like sharing his headspace with Adele or Katy or Usher. He didn't want them steering the route his thoughts would take. He wanted to steer his own thoughts.

Thoughts of Milo Cook.

He smiled remembering how Milo had thought it was cold when the wind whipped over them as they treaded water in the pool. He closed his eyes and stupidly blocked out even the street he was driving down when he recalled the sound of Milo crying out when the semen gushed from his body. And the way he had cried out too at that same moment. Letting himself go. Sharing with Milo as Milo was sharing with him.

Logan wasn't sure he could *ever* remember a climax quite like that one. Even with Jerry. There was something about Milo that had set Logan's inhibitions free last night. It wasn't the beer. Hell, he'd only had three or four. No, it was Milo.

And suddenly Logan was furious with himself for leaving. His foot rose off the gas pedal, and for a second he thought he'd just turn around and go back. Knock on the door, pound on it if he had to, until Milo answered. Plead with Milo to let him back in. Lead Milo back to bed and gather him in his arms.

But just as quickly, Logan knew he couldn't do that either. It would be too… crazy. Too miserably, pathetically desperate.

He fed the car a little gas and traveled on. Tired of driving aimlessly around, he turned at the next street corner and headed for home. Before he got there, he found his brain teeming again with thoughts of Milo. Milo clothed. Milo naked. Milo laughing at a joke. The curve of Milo's ass as he cannonballed into the pool. Milo arching his back in orgasm. Milo stooping to pet the dog.

Milo just being Milo.

As Logan drove, the roar of the wind rushing through the open windows was the only music he needed to hear. In fact, he barely noticed the absence of music at all, which was strange. Logan *always* had music blasting in the background. It kept him company. It helped him think. It helped him *not* think. It made him feel less alone.

But not this time. This time, it wasn't the silences in his life that made him lonely. It was Milo not being there that did it. Suddenly, he knew, his life was no longer empty at all. Nor did he want it to be.

And just what the hell was he going to do about *that*?

MILO AWOKE the next morning feeling like he had spent the night with his head attached to one of those clattering machines they use at Home Depot to stir paint. He wasn't hungover. He wasn't sick. On the contrary, he was flat-out euphoric. It was just that his brain seemed a little scrambled. And why wouldn't it?

Holy cow, what a night!

Milo thought back to everything he and Logan had done together. The roughhousing in the pool, the talking over beers as they floated in the water, the way Logan had looked damned near naked in those droopy swimming trunks Milo had loaned him.

And the hours they really did spend naked, wrapped in each other's arms in the bed. Jesus.

Milo had woken up starving because in the excitement of their being together, neither he nor Logan had thought to eat dinner.

He sat now at his computer, trying to will himself to write. He had an industrial-sized bag of potato chips beside him—breakfast of champions—and as hungry as he was, he hadn't touched them. Staring at the words on the screen he had written only minutes before, he realized with dawning horror that they made no sense whatsoever. They might as well have been typed in Swahili. Maybe they made no sense because all his little gray cells were taken up with a far more important problem.

Trying to figure out why Logan had slipped away in the middle of the night. That was the problem. Another problem was why Milo, waking alone in his bed with the scent of Logan on the sheets beside him, felt so crushed that Logan had gone.

Milo's hand reached out for the phone, but he quickly pulled it back. Would he sound desperate if he called Logan so soon? Would he sound accusatory if he demanded to know why Logan had left? And if he did, would it *matter* that he sounded desperate and accusatory? Well, yeah, it would. Milo didn't want to come off as some lovesick dipshit who falls for a trick after one blow job and a cuddle.

Still staring at the phone, he squeezed his fingers into a fist and frowned. Somehow, he didn't like thinking of Logan as a trick. Christ, it had been more than that, hadn't it?

More confused than ever, he glanced at the meaningless words on his computer screen, then shifted to stare through the window that looked out over the pool. God, he longed to see Logan again. Standing there. Right now. Right this minute. In Bryce's old swimming trunks, maybe, his beautiful tall body glistening with pool water, the dark hair on his strong sexy legs slicked down by the water sluicing off him, eyes laughing, one perfect dimple etched into his cheek. Or in the bed, flat on his back, his long muscular arms wrapped around Milo's hips, drinking from Milo at the moment of climax. Just as Milo was drinking from him.

Milo remembered it all. Everything about last night was seared into his brain. Just recalling all he and Logan had done together—talking, laughing, making love, wrestling in the pool, all of it—made Milo's heart start to hammer against his ribs. Even his breath quickened when he remembered how Logan's skin felt beneath his hands, how Logan responded to his touch, and how his own body responded to Logan's touch.

As if sensing his feelings, Spanky rose from the floor and rested his chin on Milo's leg, staring up lovingly into Milo's face with his soulful golden eyes. Milo gazed down with a sad smile and stroked his snout.

"I'm in trouble now, aren't I, boy?" Milo quietly asked, already knowing the answer.

His worried eyes wandered to the telephone again. At that moment, he heard a tentative knock on his front door.

Milo and Spanky both jumped. Spanky howled like a banshee and took off running for the door with Milo right behind him. Hope swelled in Milo's heart, and maybe in Spanky's too, considering how excited he was. Or was that just a figment of Milo's imagination?

Milo licked his lips and tried to run a few fingers through his sleep-tangled hair. Gazing down forlornly at his crappy pajamas and wishing he had donned something a little more presentable in case it was Logan on his front porch waiting to be let in. And really, who else *could* it be?

Without giving himself any more time to fret or freak out about it, he yanked the door wide open.

And there stood Bryce.

Chapter Eight

BRYCE GAVE a rather uncharitable grunt. "Well, you look like shit."

Milo just stared. Finally he was able to bury his disappointment that it wasn't Logan and mutter, "Bryce. It's been a while." *Not long enough, of course.* "I thought you moved away."

"Well, now I'm back. I've been back for a while, actually."

Bryce smiled wide, showing off those handsome teeth he had always been so fond of flashing when he wanted to get his way. "It's good to see you, Milo. Are you going to ask me in?"

Milo blinked, then reluctantly stepped back, holding the door open. "Oh, yeah, sure. Come on in."

Even after all this time, Bryce strolled inside as if he had never been gone at all. Milo watched in consternation as Spanky pranced around at Bryce's feet, tail wagging, showing off that gray-muzzled smile of *his* and giving Bryce a far more convincing welcome than Milo had. The traitor.

Bryce dropped to his knees and gave Spanky a hug and a backrub, which sent Spanky's ass trembling in ecstasy. "Wow," he said. "He remembers me."

Milo fought valiantly not to roll his eyes. "Imagine that."

Still occupied with Spanky, Bryce gazed up at Milo standing by the door.

"I guess I interrupted your writing. I seem to recall you always did look like death warmed over when you're in the middle of one of your books."

Milo tried to drag out a smile, and he did finally manage it, but he doubted it was very convincing. "You know me too well," he said, his voice sounding flat even to his own ears. Never taking his eyes from Bryce's face, he reached out to close the front door behind him with a faint click.

Bryce looked good, Milo had to admit. Of course, Bryce always looked good. He was the only man Milo ever knew who could jump out of bed in the morning looking like he had not been asleep at all. Hair reasonably neat, eyes clear, body limber. Milo inevitably woke up groaning and bitching, looking like he'd been run over by a garbage truck and dragged ten blocks through rush-hour traffic.

Milo noticed Bryce had not arrived on his doorstep empty-handed. He carried a white manuscript box tucked casually under his arm. Just looking at that manuscript box gave Milo a sinking feeling in the pit of his gut.

While their breakup hadn't been anything like World War III, it hadn't been particularly cordial either. Between Bryce's jealousy of Milo's writing successes and Milo's jealousy of Bryce's tricks and how toward the end Bryce hardly even bothered lying about his infidelities, Milo had always been amazed they had parted as amicably as they had. Well, perhaps not amicably, but at least no shots had been fired and no SWAT teams called in.

There was something about Bryce that always reminded Milo of thinly plated brass—glittery and polished at first glance, but weak and easily tarnished underneath. Even with the brash and arrogant facade he presented to the world, there was an undefined facet of melancholy indolence that followed Bryce around like a little dark cloud. Since Milo was always known to root for the underdog, perhaps that was what drew him to Bryce in the beginning. In the end, of course, it had been far from enough to keep them together.

Today Bryce wore a white knitted sweater over brown chinos. Green canvas shoes graced his sockless feet. As he squatted in front of Spanky, Milo could see the beginning brush of dark hair above Bryce's tanned ankles, which carried Milo's memories onward to how Bryce used to roam around the house naked.

There was no two ways around it, Bryce was hot—what with his long, lean hairy legs, hairy chest, hairy ass, and a dick that went on for days. Milo hadn't lied to Logan when he told him Bryce was impressive in bed. And why the hell shouldn't he be? God knows he had racked up enough hours of on-the-job training by jumping into *other* people's beds. Looking back at the time they had spent together, over a year of Milo's life wasted on a cheater, Milo felt some of the old resentment flooding back. He wasn't proud of it, but there was no denying it was still there.

"Got any coffee?" Bryce asked, clearly oblivious to what Milo was thinking, or not caring.

"No," Milo said. "I haven't made any." It was a lie, of course. The whole house reeked of the Hawaiian Gold Kona blend Milo enjoyed so much and brewed endless pots of every single day he was working. But if Bryce took notice of the smell, or the fact that Milo was lying through his teeth, he at least had the good grace not to call Milo on it.

"Seeing anybody?" Bryce asked. There was a hint of a smirk on his face when he asked it, which Milo didn't like. He also didn't like the fact that it sent his thoughts straight to Logan. Not that there was anything wrong with that. But for some reason, thinking about the perfection of Logan while Bryce was standing in the room was a lot like eating an ice cream cone while sitting in a dirty toilet stall at the bus station with your pants down around your ankles. In other words, it was totally unacceptable, with a sleaze factor of ten. Maybe eleven.

"Yes" was all Milo said. And after saying it, he immediately wondered if Logan was of the opinion he was seeing someone as well. Namely Milo. God, Milo certainly hoped so.

Before Bryce had a chance to press him for more information, Milo asked point-blank and none too graciously, "Why are you here?"

Bryce gave one of his patent pouts. Phony, but handsome as hell. At least it used to be. With a final pat to Spanky's head, Bryce unfurled his long body—he was almost as tall as Logan—and stood up. Straightening his back, he swept a thick bank of black hair out of his eyes and flashed a few more teeth. "I have news," he said. "I wanted to share it with you, since I know it's something you've always wanted for me."

"You mean your dick fell off?"

Bryce laughed, but there wasn't a lot of humor in it. "Funny. You always were a chuckle a minute."

"I'm charming. What can I say?" It took all Milo's willpower not to glance at the box under Bryce's arm. "So what's your news?"

Just as Milo suspected he would, Bryce held the box out at arm's length. Since he really had no choice, Milo took it and asked, "What's this, then?"

"My second book," Bryce said proudly.

"Your second book? What was the first?"

Milo knew in an instant he had finally struck a nerve. A furrow appeared between Bryce's eyebrows. His eyes darkened. "I thought you would have known."

Milo stared down at the box in his hands, then back to Bryce's face. "Known what?"

"About my book. It was published last year."

And for the first time since this unwanted reunion began, Milo felt an honest-to-God smile blossoming across his face. He gazed down at the box again and slipped the cover open. Inside lay a hardback novel written by someone named Thomas Giles, and beneath that, a typed manuscript with a title page declaring it also to be the work of one Thomas Giles.

Milo lifted his gaze to Bryce. "I don't understand. Who's Thomas Giles?"

"Pen name," Bryce said with a mysterious glint in his eyes.

"My God," Milo breathed, setting the box with the typed-up manuscript on the coffee table and taking up the book to open the flyleaf. "Horizon Home Press," he said, glancing at the spine. "Very respectable house." He ruffled through the pages and then flipped the book closed again to study the cover. "Bryce, it's beautiful."

Bryce stood beaming. "Thank you. The manuscript is my second offering. I haven't submitted it yet."

"Why not? If they loved the first book enough to publish it, they must be receptive to a second. Or is the first book not doing too well? If so, you have to understand sometimes that happens. It doesn't mean the book's bad. It just means...."

Bryce's eyes narrowed again. "I know what it means, Milo. I lived with a writer once. Remember? And I've had my own experiences since we parted. So please don't lecture me. I just want...." Bryce's words trailed away. For the first time, maybe *ever*, he looked uncertain, even a little bit uneasy.

"You just want *what*?" Milo asked. But he already knew. He knew beyond a shadow of a doubt.

"I want you to proof the second book. Tell me if you think it's ready."

Milo hated reading other writers' Works in Progress. It never ended well. If you hated it, the writer was crushed. If you liked it, you never liked it *enough*. He fumbled for a way out. "Bryce, you're published now. You don't need me to okay your words. Have faith in yourself. If you think the book's ready, then mail the fucker off."

Without being asked, Bryce stared around the room and finally chose a wing chair in the corner. He strode over and dropped himself into it. His eyes never left Milo's face. "You're right. The first book isn't doing that well."

"I'm sorry," Milo said, and he was instantly surprised to realize he meant it. He knew what it was like to put your heart and soul into a book and then watch it languish after being released—unbought, unheralded, maybe even unreviewed, and usually ending up in a dollar book bin somewhere, if it even got that far.

He stared down at the book again and back to Bryce. To stall his answer more than anything else, he asked, "Why the pen name? I would have thought—"

"I know what you would have thought. Of course, I'd rather have published under my own name, but one of the publishers I sent the first book to told me I was getting a reputation among certain of her colleagues. I may have sent off a couple of pissed-off responses to rejection letters. Apparently with publishers, word gets around."

Milo frowned. So like it always had, Bryce's big mouth and bigger ego had gotten him in trouble again. "That publisher was right, Bryce. You can't do that. This business has a long memory and a short fuse."

Bryce's jaws clenched. "So I learned. But anyway, now I want your help with the new manuscript. Please, Milo. I value your opinion. I care what you think."

It took most of Milo's willpower not to laugh. He would have given his next royalty check to say, *If you cared what I think, you wouldn't have cheated on me with every swinging dick that crossed your path.* But he didn't. Because frankly, Milo knew, and he knew it immediately after they had broken up, that losing Bryce was the best thing that could have happened to him.

Bryce wasn't finished asking favors yet. "If you like it, and if it's published, I'd also like you to write a blurb, a testimonial for the cover, recommending it. You have a big following, Milo. Your support for this book could mean a lot to the sales. Horizon Home is already probably regretting they put their trust in the first book. You could help me get over the hump with the second."

Milo looked down at the cover again. "How were the reviews?"

Bryce's eyes darkened. "Some of them were pretty good."

Milo offered a heartening smile. "Then you don't need me. Word-of-mouth will carry you through. I don't usually put my name on other people's works, Bryce. I think you probably already know that."

"I thought for me you might make an exception."

Milo heaved a sigh as he gazed down at the manuscript box on the table. He knew his decision had been made the moment he opened his door and saw that box tucked under Bryce's arm.

"I'm sorry," he said. "I can't do it."

Bryce scowled. His usually lush mouth became an angry slit in his face. "Why not? It's not like I'm a stranger. We have a past. We're friends."

It tore at Milo's heart to say the words, but he said them anyway. "We're not friends, Bryce. We're ex-lovers. And everything that *made* us ex-lovers left me not caring for you very much. You need to follow the same path all other writers follow. Produce the best manuscript you can produce, and by all means find some beta readers, if you think it will help. Just don't expect me to be one. You're already a step up from the poor guy on the corner who's never been published at all. You got your foot in the door with the first book. Take advantage of what you have, what you've learned, and apply it to the second. I'm sorry, but my decision is final. And frankly, Bryce, the advice I've just given you is probably worth more than any technical help I can give you with your manuscript. Hell, I barely know how I write my own books, let alone have the skills to tell anyone else how to write theirs. Writing a book is like masturbation. It's an enterprise best practiced alone."

Bryce flicked a speck of lint from his pant leg. His hand was trembling, and his eyes were as cold as Milo remembered them ever being, even after a few of their knock-down, drag-out fights. "So that's it, then," he said. "That's your answer."

Milo nodded. "I'm afraid so."

A nasty smile flicked at the corners of Bryce's mouth as he eyed Milo up and down. "Fancy a fuck for old time's sake? I could have those pajamas off you in no time at all."

Milo offered a cool grin and shook his head with disbelief. "You never change."

"That's not an answer."

"You want an answer, Bryce? Well, here it is. I'd rather fuck a rhino."

Bryce threw his head back and laughed, yet somehow Milo knew there was a great deal of anger hidden in the middle of it. Bryce had never liked being turned down for anything. Especially sex.

As Milo watched, Bryce unfolded himself from the chair, strode casually across the room, and plucked the book from Milo's hands. He tossed it into the box atop the unpublished manuscript and closed the lid. Tucking the box under his arm, as it had been when he'd arrived, he doffed an imaginary hat in Milo's direction and headed toward the door.

"Good luck with your books," Milo said, and he actually meant it.

But perhaps Bryce didn't see it that way. "Fuck you, Milo," he said and, gazing down at Spanky, added, "You too, mutt."

When Milo moved to get the door, Bryce held up his hand. "Don't bother. I'll see myself out."

After a mumbled curse, which Milo didn't quite catch, Bryce did exactly that, not quite slamming the door shut behind him as he left.

Milo stared at the closed door for perhaps five seconds, grateful as hell to be alone again. Turning to Spanky, he casually asked, "Ready for breakfast, you traitorous little shit?"

And as he and the pooch headed back to the den and his industrial-sized bag of potato chips, he found his mind already returning to Logan and the night they had shared together.

Then he thought back to the visitor who'd just left.

"Fancy a fuck?" he mumbled to himself, chuckling. "Did he really say, 'Fancy a fuck'?"

What a putz.

LOGAN DIDN'T see the car parked at the curb or the handsome dude with the scowl on his face sitting inside. He was so caught up in what he was about to do, he walked right past without turning his head at all.

He had parked around the corner because he needed a few minutes to build up his nerve. Having accomplished that to a degree, he now strode up Milo's front walk on wobbly legs puffing nervously on the cigarette he held in his hand. The cigarette tasted like crap. It also tasted like failure and broken promises to himself, especially since he had worked so hard to quit smoking four years earlier at Jerry's insistence and had stoically not lit one up from that day to this. At least until he stopped at the liquor store on the way over to Milo's house and bought a pack.

A million things were going through Logan's head. Some of them not so good, such as being mad at himself for smoking again. Some of the other things whirling around inside his noggin were scary as hell, such as his reason for walking up Milo's sidewalk not more than eight hours after climbing out of the guy's bed and sneaking off in the middle of the night.

He gave his head a shake, thinking that might calm his thoughts and lower his blood pressure a little, not to mention quiet the strange pounding in his chest, which didn't seem to want to go away no matter how much he tried to ignore it.

All those pureed feelings and doubts and worries whirling in his brain had everything in the world to do with Milo, of course. Logan knew he hadn't felt like this since he met Jerry, all those many years ago. He hadn't fallen in love with Jerry on the spot back then, and he hadn't fallen in love with Milo last night either. But he was hooked. That much he knew. Hooked, fascinated, lost in lust. Just as Jerry had nailed him four years back, Milo had nailed him last night.

The plain and simple fact was that Logan wanted to see Milo again. He wanted to see him a lot. And the only way he knew to go about it was to just come right out and tell him. That's why he was here.

It occurred to Logan that perhaps he was a little too much of a romantic. I mean, why else would he let himself get into this situation? Twice. Of course, what was happening to him now was Jerry's fault too. If he hadn't died, Logan wouldn't be here standing on Milo's sidewalk sweating and *smoking*. But then, he couldn't really blame Jerry for dying, could he? After all, it was an accident.

Logan stopped dead in his tracks. What the hell was wrong with him? He wasn't making any sense at all, and he knew it. He ground the cigarette butt out under the toe of his shoe and immediately lit up another one, even though the first one was making him want to puke.

With a satisfying and somehow comforting cloud of carcinogens hovering once again around his head, he took a deep breath, which damn near gagged him. Girding his loins, as the ancients used to say, he climbed Milo's front steps as quickly as he could so he wouldn't have time to think about what he was doing.

With the reeking cigarette dangling from his lips and almost blinding him with the smoke, he tapped on Milo's door. It opened so quickly, and Milo looked so mad and impatient when he yanked it open, that Logan almost fell backward off the porch. Still, seeing Milo for the first time since he held him in his arms the night before sent a jolt of affection through Logan that was so sharp it almost hurt.

Logan watched Milo take soundings and realize it wasn't who he had expected to be knocking on his door, and Logan had to admit Milo looked considerably relieved when the truth dawned on him. So Logan was relieved too.

"It's you!" Milo sang out as a welcoming smile crept across his face.

Logan just stood there. He tried nodding, but it made the smoke from the cigarette in his mouth drift straight into his eyes, so he merely squinted a returning smile and tried not to look like an idiot.

"I didn't know you smoked," Milo said.

Logan peeled the cigarette off his lower lip and tossed it into the grass. "Up until last night," he said, "I didn't."

Milo squinted in mock belligerence. "Really? Am I supposed to take that as a compliment? Or does it mean you woke up in the middle of the night thinking you'd had your fun so you thought you'd sneak out of the house like some lameass burglar and run out and buy a pack of cigarettes because that's what guys do after they get their rocks off. On the other hand, maybe you were feeling trapped thinking you had let me weasel my way into your life, so you snuck out of the house because you didn't know how the hell else to get away from me." Milo stomped his foot. "So which was it?"

Logan grinned even though he wasn't entirely sure if Milo was kidding or not. "The second one. The weaseling thing. Only without the feeling trapped part."

"You don't feel trapped?"

Logan's grin broadened. "Far from it."

"In that case, I'm tempted to kiss you," Milo said, returning a smile as he stepped out onto the porch.

"When will you be tempted enough to know whether you're going to actually do it or not?"

"Now, I think." And taking that final step forward, he walked into Logan's arms. Rising up on tiptoe, he laid his lips to Logan's mouth.

Logan hoisted him a little higher while holding him in his arms. "Hmm," he moaned, savoring the kiss. "What about your neighbors?"

Still holding the kiss, Milo mumbled, "Fuck 'em." Then he pulled back. "Yuck. Blech. Gag. You taste like an ashtray. And not just any old ashtray either. A really stinky *disgusting* ashtray."

"Enough with the sound effects and the adjectives."

Logan still clutched Milo's arms, not letting him back away. He was happy to see that Milo didn't seem to mind, even if he did stink.

"Did you really start smoking because of me?" Milo asked, his eyes wide, his head tilted back since Logan hadn't shrunk in the last eight hours and consequently was still a head taller.

Logan gave an embarrassed shrug. "Yeah."

"Why?"

"I was nervous about asking if I could see you again."

"Is that what you're doing here?"

"Yeah."

"You want to see me again?"

"Yeah."

"Why did you leave last night?"

"Guilt."

"Guilt because of Jerry?"

Logan blinked, obviously touched Milo had figured it out so easily. "Yes."

"And now you're not feeling guilty anymore?"

"Well… I'm trying not to."

"Just so you know, Logan, I enjoyed last night."

"So did I."

"You have a beautiful body."

"So do you."

"Your mind isn't too annoying either. A little scattered maybe. A little harebrained."

"There you go with the adjectives again."

"If you step inside, I'll take you back to bed."

Logan's heart started pounding. Really loud. "Do you promise?"

Milo smiled. They were still standing on Milo's front porch in broad daylight wrapped in each other's arms. Since that clearly wasn't enough for Milo, he started pulling Logan's shirttail out of his pants. "Yes, I promise. I'll take you to bed as soon as I flush your cigarettes down the toilet and you spend a few intimate moments with my toothbrush and a gallon of Scope to scrub away the stench of tobacco."

"Borrowing toothbrushes is unhygienic. What if you have a gum disease?"

"After last night, if I have a gum disease, then you've already got it."

"Oh, yeah. Just so you know, Milo. I'm not in love with you or anything."

"Of course not. We barely just met."

"I just want us to fool around some more. I mean, you know, maybe even on a regular basis."

"A regular basis sounds good to me."

"No kidding?"

"Yeah. No kidding."

They both turned toward the street when the sound of a car peeling rubber jolted them out of their moment. The car sped past Milo's front yard, tires screaming as it rounded the corner and disappeared.

"Who was that?" Logan asked.

Milo shook his head and sighed. "Just my ex. He seems to be jealous. Isn't that a hoot?"

"You mean he's jealous of *me*?"

"Could be. Or maybe he's just being a dick as usual. Who knows? Who cares? Let's go back to talking about us."

Logan didn't quite know how to feel about Milo's ex being jealous, or what he was doing on Milo's street in front of Milo's house either, since they had broken up years ago, but he wasn't going to waste any time worrying about it. He felt his heart accelerate when Milo reached up and rubbed Logan's earlobe. The gentleness of that touch made Logan's eyes drift blissfully shut.

"Come inside now," Milo said softly. "My toothbrush is waiting."

Logan could only nod. With that gentle, sexy timbre in Milo's voice and that glimmer of naughty fire burning in his eyes, Logan would have followed him anywhere.

Chapter Nine

DURING THE ensuing weeks, which positively flew by and were a wonder to Milo, he and Logan developed a routine. The routine was quite simple. They spent as much time as they could together. They talked. They made love. They walked the city with Spanky in tow. They ate out. They caught movies. They browsed bookstores. They made love some more.

Mostly they got to know each other.

The high point of their new routine, aside from making love and eating out, because nothing could top *those*, was lying naked in bed on Sunday mornings—either at Milo's house or at Logan's apartment—drinking mimosas and reading out loud to each other. Sometimes they read new installments of Milo's WIP—which was finally moving along nicely—and sometimes they read Logan's latest reviews or new additions to his blog. At other times they simply read whatever novel caught their fancy. Although it was not a genre Milo wrote in, or a genre Logan usually reviewed, gay romances quickly became a favorite. With the steamier ones, sometimes they didn't finish reading at all.

Such as today.

A patina of sweat covered them both. The book Logan had been narrating lay forgotten on the floor at the side of the bed, right where it landed after Milo decided they had read enough for one morning. With a well-placed kiss or two in strategic places, he coaxed Logan into finding another pastime to help while away the morning. Now, exhausted and sexually sated, Milo lay in his favorite position at Logan's side, his lips pressed to Logan's ribs, his right leg flung over Logan's left, trapping him in place, his hand splayed softly against the scruff on Logan's cheek. While his thumb explored Logan's lower lip, still moist from kisses and other exertions, Milo mumbled into the fragrant flesh before him.

"I love the way you smell," he mumbled.

Logan twisted to the side and pulled Milo into his arms. He pressed his lips into Milo's hair. Maybe he figured that was answer enough. And for Milo it was. He spent a long, joyous minute relishing the feel of Logan's warm strong arms wrapped tightly around him.

"Logan?" Milo whispered, this time into the hair on Logan's chest, which was another one of his favorite destinations.

"Hmm?"

"Do you still feel guilty about being with me?"

Logan hooked a finger under Milo's chin and pulled his face up to where he could see it. When their gazes connected, he smiled. "No. I haven't felt guilty about that for a long time."

Milo offered a lazy smile in return. He could still remember the feel of Logan's cock buried deep inside him. He didn't think he had ever been so contentedly fucked in his life.

"Good," he softly uttered, slipping from Logan's line of sight and scooting inward to press his mouth into the warmth of Logan's throat. He loved the scrubby feel of his beard in the morning before Logan shaved. He thought it was one of the most erotic sensations he had ever experienced. Especially after sex, when all his nerve endings were buzzing anyway.

"Do you want me to read some more?" Logan asked, his voice as lazy and contented as Milo's.

"Only if you want."

"Or maybe I could just hold you for a while."

"Goody," Milo muttered, and once again he buried his face in the hair on Logan's chest. From there, he could hear the echoing thud of Logan's heart. It was a sound he was growing dangerously fond of hearing.

Idly, Milo asked, "Who do you hold when I'm not around?"

"No one. I don't like hugging more than one person at a time."

"And I'm that person for now?"

"You're that person."

"You could get a dog for a little variety in your hugging. Nothing underhanded about a person hugging their dog if they, you know, have a rule about hugging only one person at a time."

"I'll think about it."

"Do. Dog owners are more trustworthy. I really like dog owners."

"Do you?"

"Yeah."

"I read Bryce's book," Logan said. He was smiling now. Milo could hear it in his voice. He also wondered if Logan was trying to change the subject, since he didn't own a dog, and as far as Milo knew, didn't plan on *ever* owning a dog.

Milo lifted his head and propped himself on one elbow so he could stare into Logan's eyes. It was funny, but they were always a softer, warmer color after sex. "Really? What made you decide to read Bryce's book?"

Logan killed a minute picking a loose eyelash from the corner of Milo's eye. When he finished, he said, "I guess I was curious."

"So how was it?" Milo asked, not really caring one way or the other. He was too comfortable to care about much of anything.

LOGAN HESITATED before answering. He let his eyes skid to the window and the cloudy sky outside. San Diego was having its first rain since Logan had moved into town almost two months before. He thought it odd that everyone here thought a rainstorm was such an event, such a treat, when back home it would have been nothing but an inconvenience. Weather-wise, Californians were like children, easily impressed, innocently awed. Still, it *was* kind of nice to see rain again. Logan hadn't realized how much he missed it until it suddenly rolled in off the Pacific and began to rinse the city clean and freshen the air. When a gentle clamor of thunder grumbled overhead, he almost smiled. It was like hearing the long-forgotten voice of a grumpy old friend.

His gaze slipped back to Milo's face. "His book wasn't bad."

"But?"

"But it had its faults."

"It's a first novel," Milo said, surprising himself to be taking Bryce's side. "You have to cut the guy some slack, don't you think?"

Logan shrugged. "I suppose. But still, the faults were fairly serious. I almost didn't finish it."

"Ouch. Poor Bryce. Are you going to post a review?"

"I haven't decided."

Logan lost himself in Milo's green eyes for a second. They were so beautiful he almost forgot what they were talking about.

"Well?" Milo urged. "If you do decide to write a review, how many stars are we talking about?"

"I don't know. I'm assuming you haven't read it."

Milo gently nibbled at Logan's nipple. "No." He looked up with a guilty expression on his face. "But I googled it. Checked out some of the other reviews."

Logan grinned. "Professional envy is such an ugly brute."

"Fuck you."

"I thought I just did."

Milo stretched up and laid a kiss to Logan's chin. "And you did it spectacularly."

Logan couldn't believe it, but he could actually feel himself blush. "Thanks."

Milo eyed him for a minute, clearly charmed by seeing a blush on the man who only twenty minutes earlier had his cock buried in Milo's thrummingly eager ass and was pounding him like a jackhammer. And *that* thought made Logan blush even more. It also sort of turned him on.

"Well?" Logan asked, pulling Milo close, savoring Milo's heat. "How were they? The reviews?"

Milo purred in Logan's arms. When he answered, he spoke with his lips pressed to Logan's chest, which turned Logan on even more. "They weren't that great. A few comments spring to mind. 'A lackluster first outing.' 'Too bad the book wasn't as good as the blurb.' 'A promising but ultimately unsatisfying debut.'" Milo looked up, suddenly frowning. "And now there's you about to add to the chorus. Poor Bryce," he said again.

"If you don't want me to review it, I won't."

"No," Milo said, breaking eye contact and once again resting his forehead on Logan's chest. "Do what you want. It's okay. I know that whatever you say, it'll be fair. Bryce has to learn to take his punches like the rest of us. Writing's a tough business. Hard on the ego sometimes. But we all have to learn to deal with it."

Logan lay there considering what Milo had said. While he thought about it, he stroked lazy circles on the velvet skin of Milo's back. Shuffling around to get more comfortable in the bed, he groaned happily and pulled Milo more firmly into his arms. Soon Bryce's book was forgotten.

"I've been enjoying our time together," he said softly, Milo's hair tickling his lips.

Milo nodded and snuggled closer. When he spoke, his words came so softly Logan could barely hear them. "Me too."

"I never want it to stop."

"Neither do I."

As if on cue, they each pulled back. Milo looked up into Logan's face just as Logan gazed down into his. Even to Logan's own ears, his voice sounded broken, weak, bruised somehow, when he said, "We're not just friends anymore, Milo. I think it's gone beyond that. For me, anyway."

Milo nodded. "I know. For me too."

Again Logan folded his arms around Milo to hold him close. They lay quietly then, listening to the wind and rain rattle the windowpane at the side of the bed, enjoying the rare sound of thunder rumbling high in the sky. They clung to each other, thinking their own thoughts. Milo's warm breath wakened the nerve endings on Logan's skin as he continued to gently stroke Milo's back.

Soon Milo dozed. With a wondrous smile, lost in wondrous thoughts, Logan tucked Milo's head under his chin. Burying his fingers in Milo's hair, he held him there while he slept. Safe. Protected. Needed.

In the blink of an eye everything had changed, and Logan knew it.

He was pretty sure Milo knew it too.

LATELY, LOGAN had taken to spending more time in Milo's house than he did in his own apartment. He was continually astounded by the way his life had changed since he moved to California. It was as if fate had dragged him all the way across the country and, without hemming and hawing around about it for one little minute, immediately dumped him in front of Milo Cook and then stepped back to let their chemistry finish the job.

And lord, how it had.

Looking around at his apartment now, he realized he still didn't feel at home in it. He was more at home with Milo and Spanky. Here he was a stranger even to himself. Even his possessions seemed alien, as if they belonged to someone else.

When his phone rang, he picked it up, hoping it was Milo, for truthfully, that's where every thought carried him. To Milo.

To his surprise, it was Kathy, Jerry's sister. "Logan," she said, sounding breathless. "I've been trying to reach you for the last couple of weeks. Those two reviewers that were murdered. I've been so worried."

Suddenly Logan was swamped with guilt. He had played her messages. He knew she had called. But somehow he had never been in the right frame of mind to deal with his past, with the memories she brought flooding back. The guilt came because Kathy had always been a friend and a staunch ally of his and Jerry's marriage. He knew how unfair it was of him to suddenly shut her out of his life.

"I'm sorry, Kath," he stammered lamely. "I've been meaning to call you back. And those murders were far away from here and had nothing to do with me."

"Are you sure?"

"Yes. I'm sure."

She didn't sound angry, just a teeny bit perturbed. "Fine, then. I'll be magnanimous about it. I forgive you for not calling me back. So have you gotten completely settled? Do you feel at home yet? Everyone here misses you, you know. Mom and Dad said to tell you hello."

Jerry's parents, while never allies, had always shown Logan a rather befuddled courtesy, as if they could never quite wrap their heads around the fact that their son had married a man. Still, they had tried their best to accept him into their family. For that, Logan knew, he had their love of Jerry to thank more than their acceptance of himself. But that wasn't their fault, and Logan always gave them credit for trying.

"Tell them I miss them too," Logan said. And then it happened. Without warning, the words came out of nowhere. "I've met someone, Kath."

His statement was greeted with absolute silence. Finally, a faint tinkle of laughter came through the receiver. "Well, it's about time," Kathy said. "It's been over a year since Jerry died. You've been alone long enough!"

Logan suddenly realized how what he said must have sounded. He immediately backtracked. "Don't get me wrong. We're not really together or anything. It's just that...."

"That what?"

He was sounding lame again, and he knew it. "It's just that I, well, I *like* him."

Again, Kathy laughed. "I remember when you hooked up with my brother. Jerry told me getting you to tell him you loved him was like pulling teeth. You almost lost him over it."

"I know."

"Please, Logan. Don't make the same mistake this time. It doesn't sound to me like you *like* the guy. It sounds to me like you're head over heels in love with him. And if you are, you should damn well tell him.

The poor guy probably doesn't read minds or have a crystal ball. You need to tell him how you feel. Bare your soul a little bit. Otherwise, how is he supposed to know?"

"Who are you, Dear Abby?"

Kathy huffed. Logan assumed it was for show, but he wasn't sure.

"No, asshole. I'm not Dear Abby. But I am the only person you currently have in your life who'll actually tell you the truth without fear of bruising your legendarily sensitive ego."

It was Logan's turn to laugh. "I'm not that insecure!" Then, less sure of himself, he asked, "Am I?"

Kathy huffed again, this time around a chuckle. "Okay, fine. You're not that insecure. So what's this guy's name? What does he do for a living? How much money does he make? How is he in bed? Is he a top or a bottom? For that matter, are *you* a top or a bottom? And while we're on the subject, what exactly *is* a top or a bottom? I've never been entirely sure."

Kathy only stopped talking after Logan took the phone and banged it several times against the wall to shut her up. Howling with laughter, he said, "I'll answer the first two questions and that's it! His name is Milo Cook, and he's a writer. So there."

Kathy sounded duly impressed. "Good lord, I think I've heard of him."

"This from the woman who only reads cookbooks and *Far Side* cartoons."

"Oh hush. So tell me the truth, Logan. Are you in love with him?"

"I—I think so."

"But you haven't told him."

"Well, no. Not yet. I keep hoping he'll figure it out on his own."

"Well, that's just plain stupid. You have to *tell* him!"

Logan nodded as if she were in the room. He caught himself at it and stopped. God, he was getting dumber by the minute. "Yes. I know. But…."

"But what?"

Logan swallowed hard. He hadn't really faced what it was that scared him so much about telling Milo how he felt until this very moment. Somehow Kathy had made him see it. And when he spoke the words out loud, he knew they were absolutely true.

"I'm afraid I'll scare him off."

"Baby," Kathy cooed, "let me ask you something. When you make love, does he cling to you afterward? Do you hold each other and talk about really stupid stuff for hours on end? And when he kisses you out of the blue, do you automatically close your eyes and lose yourself in the way he tastes?"

Logan grunted in exasperation. "What the hell are you talking about? That's the dumbest th—"

"Tell me. Do you?"

For some reason, Logan felt like he had a balled-up pair of socks stuck in his throat. He was sitting in his desk chair now, and he wasn't exactly sure how or when he'd arrived there. Nor was he sure when he had opened the desk drawer and taken out his old wedding ring and slipped it on. The ring whose mate was still resting on Jerry's poor cold finger, two thousand miles away.

He stared at the ring now. As always, he loved the way the unblemished silver glinted in the light. He loved the perfect symmetry of it and the familiar weight of it on his finger. On his hand. The way it caused memories to come flooding in. Happy memories. Memories of him and Jerry.

Kathy was waiting. He could feel her frustration radiating through the receiver like heat rolling off a potbellied stove. He could hear her softly breathing in little gasps, impatient as usual. He thought he could feel her smiling too, as if she already knew what he was going to say. And she was right. She probably did.

Logan gave an exasperated sigh, knowing he couldn't deny any of those things even if he wanted to. God, Kathy was a pain in the ass. "Yes," he admitted. "To *all* those questions, yes."

"And when I called you just now, you were hoping it was him, weren't you?"

"Y-yes."

"Then tell him, Logan. Tell him the next time you see him. Make it the very first thing that comes out of your mouth. Can you do that?"

"I—I think so."

"I'm happy for you, you know. I was happy for you and Jerry when you got together, and I'll be happy for you this time too. That's because I love you."

"I know," Logan said, his voice catching, his eyes misting up. "I love you too, Kath. I guess there was a reason Jerry thought you were the smartest woman on the planet."

She giggled at that. Finally. A lessening of tensions. Detente. "I'm glad he recognized my many talents."

Silence settled over the phone for a minute. It lasted until Logan asked in a breathless, desperate hush, "Do you think Jerry will understand?"

Logan heard a tiny intake of breath. Followed immediately by "Yes, baby. I think he'll understand. I *know* he'll understand. He wanted you to be happy when he was here, and now that he's gone, he still wants you to be happy. I know he does."

"You truly believe that, don't you?"

"I truly do."

Another short silence, this one less tortured, settled between them. Logan drew in a trembling breath. "Thank you, Kath. I think I finally believe it too."

With a smile in her voice, she said, "Good. And you're welcome. I'm happy for you, Logan. You're a good person. You deserve to be loved."

"Milo's a good person too."

"I'm sure he is."

"I'll be a blubbering mess if he says no."

"He won't say no."

"I love him to death."

"No," Kathy said. "Not to death. Not this time. Just love him *now*. Love him today and tomorrow. Love him during every minute that ticks by with the two of you in it."

Logan smiled. "You're a poet."

"Oh be quiet." And softly, oh so softly, she made a kissy sound and disconnected the call.

Five minutes later, scared to death, Logan was out the door and heading for his car.

He drove the city streets, barely watching where he was going, his mind a maelstrom. When he spotted the exit for Milo's street up ahead, he didn't turn. He didn't even slow down. He realized suddenly he had *another* destination in mind. He'd had it in mind all along; he just hadn't been smart enough to know it. When he admitted to himself what it really was, his worried face broke into a grin for the first time since Kathy's call.

"First things first," he muttered to the empty car and to all the disinterested people whizzing past him on either side, absorbed in their own little stupid pursuits. With a smile broad enough to squeeze his eyes into such squinty little lines he could barely see where he was going, he whispered under his breath, "Backup. Gotta have backup."

Goosing the accelerator, he shot past Milo's street and headed for the freeway.

Chapter Ten

SINCE IT was the tail end of winter, the mercury in the thermometer hovered between seventy-five and eighty. El Centro natives call that a cold snap. In summer months the temperature perpetually tops a hundred. Sometimes a hundred and ten. Every blessed day. The natives call that normal.

Miserable, dry, bleached out, and baked to within an inch of its life—thanks to 350 days of scorching sunshine a year—El Centro, California, sits forty feet below sea level at the northern edge of the Sonoran Desert like a chunk of bacon sizzling in a skillet. Located just above the Mexican border abutting Mexicali, El Centro is the winter home of the Blue Angels, the US Navy's elite precision flying team.

More importantly, as far as tonight's festivities were concerned, El Centro was also home to Evelyn Tomes, aka BookBlogger.com.

It took a mere thirty minutes of research, padding quietly across the internet like a cat burglar, to learn BookBlogger lived in a mobile home situated all by itself in the uglyass desert wasteland outside El Centro's city limits. There the ancient single-wide Fleetwood trailer sat propped up on crumbling concrete blocks, roasting and rotting among the dunes and sagebrush.

The whole place shimmered with neglect. Rust stains trailed down the corrugated walls, which on any given day of the year were too hot to touch with bare hands. Out front, a patio covered with lopsided, sun-warped latticework offered the only shade. Under the latticed rooftop, standing dead in their pots in the sweltering air, stood a few desiccated rosebushes that hadn't bloomed in years. Tucked in among the rosebushes stood a single thriving cactus, the only touch of green on the place. The cactus hadn't been watered in months, but that didn't seem to bother it one little bit. After all, with or without attention, cacti were the only things that could thrive in this miserably hot climate. Well… cacti, rattlesnakes, and sweat.

Looking as it did, it was a safe bet the Tomes homestead would not be featured in the Celebrity Style section of *Architectural Digest* anytime soon. Firstly, because the place was a fucking dump, and secondly, because Evelyn Tomes was no celebrity.

The fact that she was known anywhere at all outside her desert-baked hovel of a home was surprising enough. The fact that she was known to the fairly sophisticated world of writers and reviewers and those who cherished the written word was nothing short of amazing. However, to be known is not always to be loved. In fact, in literary circles, Evelyn Tomes, no matter how apropos her name might be to her occupation, was internationally recognized as a nasty, ill-tempered bitch. Especially after one read a few of the vicious book reviews that chased each other across her blog like rabid dogs, snapping and snarling at any unsuspecting author they could sink their malevolent teeth into. The traveler stood in the shadows, all but invisible, not more than fifty yards from Evelyn's crappy trailer. Overhead, the broad, star-specked desert sky spread its canopy endlessly and gloriously from one horizon to the other. At the moment, from those very same shadows, the sound of chuckling could be heard, and that chuckling resembled the sound of brittle leaves tumbling and dancing along an empty street, pushed by an arid wind. There was no humor in the sound. It was more a death rattle than a laugh. Bloodless and dry, yet oddly high-pitched. An omen of things to come, perhaps. And at that thought, the chuckle deepened.

The reasons for laughter were threefold. First, the traveler had been anticipating this night for a very long time. Second, it was amusing that Evelyn should live in such a fleapit when the home she displayed on her blog was a Tudor mansion parked majestically among a stand of towering ponderosa pines. With leaded windows and ivy-covered walls, the blog mansion sat regally upon a perfectly groomed lawn. The lawn sloped down to a lake and was spotted with topiaries, impeccably molded into the shape of whimsical forest creatures. The truth was far less whimsical. In fact, the only forest creature that might visit *this* dump was perhaps a scraggly, mange-riddled coyote, slouching in from the desert looking for a place to shit.

Lastly, the laughter derided the fact that in the photos on her review site, Evelyn portrayed herself as a beautiful young woman, prone to wearing caftans and saris draped across her luscious, lithe frame. She also sported caramel skin, almond eyes, and a long mane of lustrous black hair that hung fetchingly across her shoulders in deep billowing waves. Eyeing the crappy trailer and the dusty lot it sat on might lead one to entertain a sneaky suspicion that the woman's looks, like her residence, would be another broken promise. Not that our merry trespasser truly cared. It would be fun to kill the bitch no matter how she looked.

Tucked in among a stand of chaparral and tumbleweeds, the traveler stood watching the trailer for a while. A rental car was parked over a rise and well off the highway, hidden in a copse of teddy bear cholla—a cutesy-named indigenous tree with spines so deadly they would gleefully rip the meat from your bones if you were dumb enough to get tangled up in them. An endlessly beautiful sunset had provided a truly lovely viewing experience as the horizon turned from pink, to red, to puce, before the darkness finally claimed victory, erasing the colors from the sky completely. At one point, the *schkking* of a rattlesnake sounded in the bushes not far away, but the traveler remained motionless until the beastie finally slithered off. Two fellow predators nodding respectfully in passing, doffing their hats, then moving along to wreak their own individual havoc.

From this vantage point, the traveler could see an old station wagon, caked in dust, parked at the side of Evelyn's trailer. When darkness deepened, lights came on inside, illuminating the trailer's grimy windows. A shadow moved inside what was probably the kitchen, seen through a god-awful ugly calico curtain with sunflowers on it, rotted limp by the sun. Evelyn preparing dinner, perhaps, or puttering around at the sink. The shadow was huge and moved with the rolling gait of a sea lion.

The mysterious figure hiding in the bushes snickered mirthlessly. That settled it. BookBlogger had lied with her profile pic too.

On the desert air, overpowering the stench of sage and dust, wafted the heavy scent of lard frying, and shortly after, the unmistakable greasy reek of tortillas crisping.

There had been no sign of dogs or anyone other than the single occupant inside the trailer. No telephone rang. No canned laughter from TV shows blathered its forced camaraderie into the evening quiet. Even the highway was far enough away that the sound of passing automobiles barreling through the desert night could barely be heard.

Evelyn and her visitor were all alone, separated by only a rusted aluminum shell and a sun-bedraggled calico curtain.

This time the traveler wore a cheap pair of Walmart coveralls over street clothes and a new pair of Playtex gloves. Canary yellow. The sort a housewife might wear to clean her kitchen sink. From the coverall pockets the traveler fished out a pair of blue paper medical booties, then pulled them over dusty shoes. A taupe length of sheer nylon, cut from a pair of panty hose, and pulled snugly over head and face, formed a mask to cover the hair and mold what the traveler considered rather pleasant features into a melted horror.

Lastly, the shadowy figure in the chaparral extracted a plastic shopping bag from a back pocket. It was, in fact, the very bag the coveralls came in, and it crinkled in the darkness very prettily, the traveler thought. Very crisp. Very innocent. Very lethal.

Funny what you could transform into a murder weapon if you really set your mind to it.

With face well hidden, as always, and tools in place, the figure in the bushes was left with only pinpricks of starlight overhead and a square of dirty light spilling through BookBlogger's filthy kitchen window from which to take bearings. Stepping out of the bushes on long legs and quickly crossing the crusty ground, the shadowy figure ducked beneath the latticed patio that sheltered the trailer's front door.

The front steps tucked against the base of the trailer consisted of fat concrete blocks, stacked haphazardly atop each other. Uncemented and wobbly, they made a crunchy, grinding noise underfoot.

Not giving a shit about the noise, the visitor rapped merrily on the Fleetwood's ratty front door with a canary-yellow hand. A moment later the whole structure swayed as the gigantic shadow inside approached the sound.

"Coming!" a sweet, melodious voice called out. The voice spoke in an Australian accent, which was surprising but quickly forgotten. The traveler didn't care if BookBlogger enunciated like the Queen of England, sang like Julie Andrews, and scatted jazz like Ella Fitzgerald. It was the words she put in her blog that had decided her fate, not the manner in which she uttered them in real life.

Evelyn Tomes pulled open her squeaking front door and peered outside. Squinting into the darkness, she flicked a switch, and a naked 100-watt bulb hanging at the side of the door illuminated her visitor the same as it illuminated her. As expected, Evelyn looked absolutely nothing like the photo on her blog. She was huge. Her hair hung greasily around a circular, pallid face bedecked with far too much makeup, poorly applied. Nary a square inch of caramel skin or a single almond eye was in sight. A pudgy hand with a cheap ring on every finger rose to clutch at a string of dirty beads dangling down over a massive bosom. Obviously braless, that bosom swayed, unhindered, like great pendulous weights beneath the bodice of a gaudy floral muumuu. Evelyn's eyes rolled over her visitor in amazement. She took in the coveralls, the Playtex gloves, the blue paper booties. When her startled gaze settled on the nightmarish face sheathed in nylon, they widened in fear.

"No!" she exclaimed. But even as she cried out her nonsensical response to an unasked question, her eyes suddenly filled with a terrible understanding. A horrible, dawning terror bloomed in her gaze. Her mouth fell slack, and her gaze flitted to the side. Without warning, she reached out a heavy trembling hand to slam the door in her caller's face.

But her caller was quicker.

A foot shot out, and the flimsy metal door sprang back into the woman's face with a most satisfying crunch. She bellowed in pain and stumbled backward, rivulets of blood already sluicing down across her mouth, spattering red droplets across her bodice. Pinwheeling her arms, she tried unsuccessfully to regain her balance. Clutching at her injured face as a fresh wave of terror widened her eyes, she crashed against the opposite wall, then cowered there, trying to shrink as far away from her intruder as she could.

Which wasn't nearly far enough.

The traveler crossed the room in two long strides. As Evelyn raised her arms to ward off her attacker, a hand swept out to backhand her across the face. Flung sideways by the blow, she struck her head on the corner of an end table, sending a lamp crashing to the floor and opening a cut on her forehead that smeared another stream of blood across her face.

With the last injury, she released a pitiful mewling scream.

As her attacker approached yet again with a hand drawn back to strike once more, she wept with horror, "Please don't rape me!"

At that, her visitor froze. Even through the nightmarish stocking that warped the features beneath it, an expression of disgusted wonderment could be seen. The traveler stared down at the woman and burst into laughter. And while the laughter fairly bubbled out, a gloved hand reached down to where Evelyn Tomes lay sprawled across the floor like a beached whale and gently—and quite respectfully, it seemed—tugged down the hem of her muumuu to cover the fat, pale leg that had been exposed in her fall.

"Trust me," the traveler said, still quaking with high-pitched laughter. "Your virtue is safe with me."

Evelyn's eyes were skittering all over the place now. The lean visitor could see her trying to decide what to do. What she could use for a weapon. How she could get away. But it was all fantasy. In truth, there was nothing she could do at all. For all intents and purposes, she was as good as dead already.

Somehow the fact that she probably knew it pleased her attacker greatly.

Composed now, although a smile was still threatening to rear up any second through the nylon mask, the attacker regarded the bleeding face with cool, unpitying eyes.

"Do you know why I'm here?" the traveler asked.

Evelyn Tomes smeared a rivulet of blood away from her mouth with the back of her hand while a sprig of rebellion flashed in her eyes. "Yes. You're the one I've read about. You must be. It's—it's because you don't like my reviews."

The lean figure crossed arms over a narrow chest and stared down at the woman, stunned by the understatement of what she'd said and spoke gleefully even while the laughter threatened to bubble back up. "Oh, my dear, you have no idea *how much* I don't like your reviews. You have no idea *how much* I don't like *any* of your reviews." The attacker leaned down, speaking louder with every sentence, eyes flashing with fury, foam forming in the corners of the snarling mouth wet the stocking that covered it. Spittle flew. "I see you all over the web. Gladreads, Amazon, a dozen other review sites. Trashing books left and right. Laughing at the authors. Treating them like fools. Sometimes you trash and mock as many as five or six books a day." Leaning even closer, the voice broke into an infuriated scream. "*So what are you, a fucking speed-reader?*"

Evelyn's fat hands with all the rings on them clutched the beads at her throat. Even in the midst of fighting back a sob of panic, her eyes turned mean. "You can't do this. You can't just come into my home and…."

Her visitor shook a wondering head and plucked the wadded Walmart shopping bag from a back pocket. Smiling now, the anger once again under control, the traveler shook out the bag—taking extra care to smooth every wrinkle, iron out every twist in the plastic—and hooked it over one wrist for easy access.

"I see you haven't fully grasped the situation yet. I'm afraid your days of ruining people are about to end most precipitously and with a great deal of pain." Evelyn's cocksureness immediately faltered. "No, please...."

Ignoring her plea, ignoring the dread on her face, the attacker stepped forward and straddled her bloated body, pulled her hands gently from her face, and tenderly laid them on the floor at her sides. She stared up with a glimmer of hope. *My God*, the traveler realized, *she thinks it's an act of kindness, that she is about to be helped.* Quickly proving her wrong, the attacker planted a blue-bootied foot over each of the woman's hands and began grinding them into the cheap linoleum.

The screams that erupted were earsplitting. And just as they reached their highest point, the traveler slipped the shopping bag over the shrieking woman's head and tied it into a granny knot beneath her chin. The knot was so tight it all but disappeared into folds of fat.

Happily, since Evelyn had a really annoying voice, her screams were immediately muted by the knot at her throat and the plastic bag wrapped tightly about her head. Her great body thrashed back and forth, still pinned between the traveler's legs. Tiny bones in her fingers snapped and popped as they shattered like matchsticks beneath each grinding foot. She flailed her head from side to side, convulsing with the agony of her broken fingers, of the many rings tearing into her trampled hands. The plastic bag crackled, swelling and collapsing with each billowing, tortured breath. The bellows of fear and pain grew louder. As the air inside the bag thinned, her bare heels began to pound the floor in a merry tap dance. The staccato rapping echoed through the trailer.

Off in the kitchen, a haze of blue smoke built. Apparently the good woman had carelessly left a tortilla crisping on the stove. She should have known better. Kitchen fires are one of the leading causes of fatal household accidents. Of course, one can't die twice, so she wouldn't have to worry about it too much.

The swelling and shrinking of the plastic bag wrapped around Evelyn's head began to slow. Oxygen deprivation at long last began to do its job. The clattering tattoo of Evelyn's heels banging on the floor abated. With a retch, her body convulsed one last time as the Walmart bag filled with a great gout of vomit. After that, the noises coming from inside it were truly awful.

The masked intruder stepped back, lifting feet from Evelyn's ruined, bloody hands, and gazed on in fascination as Evelyn Tomes, aka BookBlogger.com, heaved and shuddered and gurgled, and slowly, oh so slowly, drowned in her own bile, her poor fat ruined fingers trembling crookedly at her sides.

Staring down as the body finally collapsed into silence, the visitor smiled and pulled off first the stocking mask, then the Playtex gloves. Prodding the corpse with a foot elicited no response. The massive bosom, still speckled with droplets of blood, no longer heaved. The stench of puke was only now beginning to seep through the bag and foul the air.

With a snort of disgust, the traveler turned and walked back out into the night. The shadowy figure was less than twenty feet away when the overheated skillet in Evelyn's kitchen caught fire with a *whoosh*. A moment later the ratty calico curtain on the kitchen window blossomed into flames.

The traveler stood watching with interest as the flames spread. The old Fleetwood trailer, each and every window now filled with cleansing, golden fire, resembled nothing less than a big fat jack-o'-lantern.

It was really quite festive.

Chapter Eleven

"Hi, Logan." Milo beamed, then immediately stared down at his front porch steps. "Hey! Who the heck is that?"

Logan followed his gaze to the tiny puppy staring up from the bottom step. The puppy was brown and gray and had about a gazillion cowlicks, making his coat look like it had exploded from within. Amid this chaos of hair, two black shiny eyes peered out, taking everything in. The puppy was tethered to a brand-new leash, which was clipped to a brand-new collar, and he had a brand-new stuffed duck, which was twice his size, clamped in his sharp little puppy teeth as if he refused to entrust it to anybody else. The leash was anchored securely to Logan's hand.

"That's Emerson," Logan said proudly. "As in Ralph Waldo."

"His name is bigger than he is."

"He'll grow into it."

"You think he'll grow into the duck?"

"Maybe."

Milo looked doubtful. "If you say so. Umm, I thought you didn't like dogs."

"I never said I didn't like dogs. I said I didn't *have* one. There's a difference."

By this time Milo was down the steps and on all fours, and the puppy had dropped the stuffed duck long enough to rise up on his back legs and go to town on Milo's face, his little tail whapping a mile a minute, his tongue going even faster. "He's so tiny," Milo sputtered around a shower of doggy kisses.

Logan smiled. "He's a Yorkie."

"I know. Humane Society?"

"Yeah."

"Is he a loaner? Did you get him on spec?"

"Nope. He's mine or...."

"Or what?"

"Or... ours."

Milo twisted his head up, and they stared at each other.

"What do you mean, ours?" Milo asked. "You mean like two humans with one dog 'ours'? You mean like community property 'ours'? You mean like 'Here, boy!' and he comes to whichever one of us looks the neediest because he loves us both equally? That kind of ours?"

Logan glanced up and down the street, then back at Milo. "Stand up. And can we go inside, please? I'm about to kneel down." Actually, he was about to pass out, but he didn't think he wanted to admit that.

Milo's eyes grew big as he groaned his way to his feet. "You are?"

Logan gulped. He suspected his eyes were bugging out too. "Yes, I am."

Milo looked worried. "Okay. Then come inside." He reached over and took Logan's hand, gently leading him through the doorway, pulling him away from the prying eyes of any neighbors who might be watching. Emerson reclaimed his duck and pattered along behind, his teeny toenails tapping merrily on the foyer floor, looking here and there and everywhere like this was quite an adventure for him. After a puppyhood spent at the Humane Society, Logan supposed it probably was.

Milo closed the door behind them and turned expectantly to Logan, still holding his hand, still gazing deep into Logan's bugged-out eyes.

"Why are you looking so nervous? And why are you about to kneel? Is it to play with your new dog?"

Logan frowned. This wasn't going as planned. "No."

"I didn't think that made any sense," Milo said. "You could have knelt down and played with him on the front porch like I did just as easily as you could kneel down and play with him in here. After all, it doesn't matter *where* you kneel down to play with the dog so long as—"

Logan rolled his eyes and tugged at his collar. "Could you shut up for a minute?"

Milo snapped his mouth shut like a mailbox.

Logan inhaled a deep, shuddering breath and dropped to one knee, still holding Milo's hand.

Milo looked momentarily horrified. "You're doing it. You're actually kneeling."

"I told you to shut up."

"Oh, yeah."

Logan gazed up into Milo's face while a trickle of ice-cold sweat slid down his rib cage. Another trickle of moisture seeped from his left eye. That trickle was warmer. He figured it was only a matter of time before the right eye started leaking too. "I want you to trust me," he said, swallowing hard. "I want it more than anything."

Milo blinked in surprise. "What makes you think I don't trust you already?"

"Because you said you could never trust anybody who didn't own a pet."

"I said that?"

"Yeah."

"Well, that's not exactly what I mea—"

"Hush."

A faint smile twisted the corner of Milo's mouth as he clapped it shut again and stared at Logan with those incredible green eyes, which always made Logan want to swoon a little bit when they were burrowing into him. Especially at moments like this. Not that Logan *had* many moments like this. Thank God. He didn't think his heart could stand it if he did.

"Why is it so important for me to trust you?" Milo asked.

Logan glanced down at the floor, but just as quickly raised his eyes back to Milo's face. "I want you to trust me because I'm a pet owner."

Logan knew he was losing him because Milo was starting to look confused.

"Okaaaaay," Milo drawled. He had the look of a man who was mentally flailing, clearly trying to understand just what the hell was going on but not succeeding very well.

"I don't want Emerson to be just mine, Milo. I want him to be ours."

"Ours?"

"Yeah. Like you said. Like community property."

Milo didn't look so confused anymore. In fact, he appeared to be growing more enlightened by the minute. "You mean, like if we were together?"

"Bingo!" Logan cried so sharply that Milo jumped like he'd been stabbed with a pin. "That's exactly it! Like we were together!"

"Aren't we together already?"

"Not officially," Logan said.

And finally, Milo understood it all. Everything.

"Is that what this is all about? You're asking me to make our relationship official?"

Logan almost fell over backward with relief. "Yes!"

"Why didn't you just say so? And I still don't understand why you felt you had to get a dog."

"I'm begging you, Milo. Please shut the fuck up."

Milo narrowed his eyes but dutifully dragged an invisible zipper across his mouth, went through the motions of locking it with an invisible key, then petulantly tossed the invisible key over his shoulder. As if that wasn't enough, he finished up with a three-fingered Boy Scout salute, then topped it all off by crossing himself like a good Catholic, which he sure as hell wasn't. "Shutting the fuck up now, boss. Yessiree, I is."

Still staring up into Milo's eyes from his vantage point on one knee, Logan pulled Milo's hand to his mouth and held it against his lips.

"I'm nuts about you, Milo."

"I know. I'm nuts about you too."

"I know," Logan said, savoring the hair on the back of Milo's hand as it tickled his nose.

Milo's voice sounded fractured. Not unlike his own. "You do? You know it?"

"Yes. At least I was hoping. And now I feel like I have to tell you how *I* feel."

"Why? How do you feel?"

"I feel like I'm in love."

Milo's hand tensed against Logan's lips. "With me?"

"No. With Spanky. Yes, of course with you!"

While Logan's lips played across the palm of his hand, Milo stretched out his thumb and slid it over Logan's cheek. "It must be going around, then," he said softly, "because I feel that way too."

Logan blinked. "You do?"

Milo nodded. "Uh-huh. I have for a while now."

"You mean like you're in love?"

"I mean *exactly* like I'm in love."

"With me?"

"No, with Vanna White. Yes, of course with you!"

Milo dragged his gaze from Logan's face and studied the little dog. "You know, you really didn't have to get a dog to make me trust you enough to get me to tell you I loved you back."

"Did you just say you loved me back?"

"Yeah. I think so. It wasn't a very good sentence. And I'm a writer too. You'd think I could do better."

They smiled at each other. The moment was oddly innocent.

Still on one knee, Logan pressed another kiss into Milo's hand. "Are you mine now?" he asked softly.

"I've been yours since the day we had hamburgers in Coronado."

"But we had just met."

Milo shrugged. "I know. But my book signing was a bust, and then you came along in those tennis shorts and asked for my autograph. You also bought two books. I guess that's what did it."

"Christ. What would have happened if I'd bought three?"

Milo's grin flickered. "I hate to think."

Logan saw Milo's face begin to swim in front of him as his eyes filled with tears. Another tear slid down Logan's cheek, and he didn't even bother to brush it away because he was pretty sure there would be others trailing along shortly. "So we're lovers, then?"

Milo nodded. Shyly, he asked, "Do you really love me, Logan?"

Logan nodded back. There was a twitch in his lip. He wasn't sure if the twitch meant he was about to smile or about to sob like a baby. "Milo Cook, I love you more than anything."

Milo laid his warm hand to the side of Logan's face. He stared down, his gaze gentle. "And you think Jerry will understand?"

"Yes," Logan said without a moment of hesitation. "I think Jerry will understand."

Dragging Milo closer, Logan wrapped his arms around Milo's legs and pressed his face into his belly, just kneeling there in front of Milo, holding him tight, clutching him close.

"I do love you too," Milo whispered, his fingers kneading Logan's hair.

Logan inhaled Milo's heavenly scent, absorbed his familiar heat. Milo's legs trembled in his arms. "I've wanted to hear you say that for so long."

Gazing up, Logan released his grip on Milo's legs and sat back on his haunches to brush the tears from his face. He smiled weakly but without shame. He was six foot five and blubbering like a baby. So what? Milo didn't seem to mind, so neither did he.

He reclaimed Milo's hand and pressed it once again to his lips. "This isn't all about us, you know. We should probably introduce Emerson to the rest of his newly adopted family."

Milo straightened his shoulders and wiped his eyes since he was leaking tears too. He gave himself a shake as if it was time to get down to business. "You're right," he said. Turning and directing his voice out toward the pool, he yelled, "Spanky! Get your ass in here. My lover and I want you to meet your new baby brother!"

THEY CELEBRATED with a couple of beers and a nude swim in the pool. Treading water, Logan wrapped his arms around Milo, their naked bodies pressed together in the sun-warmed water, as they watched the two dogs over by the fence get to know each other. Emerson, it seemed, was doing most of the work.

Spanky looked confused and vaguely appalled, as if he couldn't quite believe there was a guinea pig—or whatever that little ratty-looking thing was—chewing on his tail.

For his part, Emerson pranced, nibbled, teased, and finally scaled the long slope of Spanky's back like he was climbing a hill. Once he reached the crest, the area right behind Spanky's huge head, which was ten times bigger than his, Emerson collapsed into the big dog's fur, nestled comfortably in, and fell sound asleep. In response, Spanky shot a baleful glance in Milo's direction, as if asking, "What the hell did I do to deserve this?"

Logan and Milo laughed and turned to each other.

"They'll be okay now," Milo said.

"You think?"

Milo nodded. "Yeah. And I think we'll be okay too."

Logan smiled and tweaked Milo's chin. "So do I," he whispered softly as the water lapped at his lips, and he edged closer for a kiss.

Their erections rubbed together under the water, and Logan thought he had never had a happier moment in his life. He was about to duck his head beneath the shimmering ripples and try to snorkel with Milo's dick, when Milo's words snagged his attention first.

"Move in with me, Logan."

Logan pulled back just enough to study Milo's face. "What did you say?"

"I said move in with me. If we love each other, we should live together. We'll be sleeping in either my bed or your bed anyway. We might as well move in together." Milo's hand slid under the water and his fingers circled Logan's cock, causing Logan to close his eyes and emit a sexy groan. Milo moved closer and laid his mouth to Logan's throat. "If you're my lover, I want you with me. Here in this house. Please. Let's get your stuff and move you in. Today. Right now. Right this minute."

Logan was so lost in the feel of Milo's fingers and Milo's lips, not to mention Milo's words, he could almost ignore the pain of what he was about to say. Almost. He pulled Milo into his arms and rested his chin on Milo's shoulder. Sliding his hands over Milo's back to savor the feel of him, Logan sighed and laid his lips to Milo's ear.

He died a little just speaking the words. "I can't do it. I can't abandon the apartment. I have a lease."

Milo snuggled closer too. "We'll find someone to sublet it."

Logan froze, considering the possibilities. "Do you think we can?"

"Sure. Why not? It's a great apartment."

"But... but do you have room for me here?"

"We'll make room."

"What about Emerson?"

"Emerson weighs about eight ounces. How much room does he need?"

"I have furniture."

"What won't fit we'll put in storage. Or we'll put mine in storage and keep yours. I'm not picky."

Logan pressed his lips to Milo's cheek, still holding him close. Milo had released his dick and was now stroking Logan's back, just as Logan was stroking his. Their cocks were no longer erect. Other thoughts had momentarily pushed the hunger away, but Logan knew it wouldn't be gone long.

"You'll hate my music," Logan said. "And I play it really loud."

"I'll buy earplugs. If that doesn't work, I'll break all your CDs."

"I get up in the middle of the night and raid the fridge. In the morning there's crumbs and dirty spoons everywhere."

"I do the same thing."

"I'm a slob. I only moved to California so I wouldn't have to clean my bathroom back in New York."

"That's okay. There are days when I actually enjoy housecleaning."

"Really?"

"Fuck no. I'm babbling."

"I've never walked a dog or picked up doggy poop in my life."

"You'll get used to it."

Logan stared into Milo's eyes, racking his brain for something else to complain about. When nothing sprang to mind, he said, "I suppose I could pay you rent."

"The house is paid for. Do shut up."

"Then I'll help with expenses."

"Hell yes, you will. I'm too young to be a sugar daddy."

Logan guffawed.

They floated silently in the water, still hanging on to each other as the sun beat down on their heads and the sensation of their naked bodies pressed together once again began to fill their cocks with need.

Logan felt so deliciously comfy cradled in Milo's arms, as if he truly belonged there, that he began to feel his eyes misting up again. The tears were starting to embarrass him.

"I never knew I was such an emotional guy," he muttered, holding Milo close.

"Love changes us all," Milo whispered back, his embrace tightening, his fingers sliding up to caress the back of Logan's neck.

Logan let Milo's hands and the heavenly feel of Milo's sleek body cuddled snug against his own carry the next few seconds into a memory Logan knew he would cherish forever.

"It's the right thing to do, isn't it?" he finally said. "Us moving in together."

Milo nodded, his head tucked neatly under Logan's chin. "It's the *only* thing to do. We love each other. We have to be together. Please say you'll do it. I want you here. With me. Every single day."

"And the nights?"

"God yes. The nights too."

Logan splayed his broad hand across the back of Milo's head and gently held him close, rocking him as they lazily treaded water. When he squeezed his eyes shut, another tear slid down his cheek. As if somehow knowing it was there, Milo tilted his head up and kissed it away.

This time his tears didn't embarrass Logan. He smiled down, cupping both sides of Milo's face in his hands, his thumbs resting lightly at Milo's temples, their cocks once again thrumming like crazy under the water, their legs paddling gently to keep themselves afloat.

"Yes," Logan said. "Okay. I'll do it. I'll move in."

At that moment, a tiny ball of fur sailed out across the water, its four little feet flapping in midair. It landed with a splash right beside them. Emerson sank like a rock, then just as quickly bobbed up through the surface of the pool, sputtering and yipping in glee. He paddled closer with his little front paws and slathered each man with kisses and licks like he hadn't seen them in a week.

Laughing, Logan scooped him from the ripples and parked Emerson on his shoulder, where he sat up, shook the water from his coat, and looked around like a tourist.

Still cuddling close, Logan and Milo—and Emerson—turned as one to study Spanky under the chaise lounge over by the fence. Spanky eyed them in return with little or no interest, then yawned, flopped over onto his side, and drifted back to sleep.

"My lover," Milo muttered, pressing a kiss to Logan's chin.

"Your lover and his dog," Logan muttered back, as Emerson bathed them both in happy kisses.

Over by the fence, Spanky started to snore.

WITHIN A week, Logan had found a young Navy couple to sublet his apartment. Ten minutes after the new tenants cosigned the lease, Logan hired movers. As Milo had suggested, he put most of his furniture in storage, retaining only his desk, his TV for the bedroom, and his bookcases, along with all the books he knew he could never live without, which was every single one of them.

On the first evening after everything was neatly put away, Logan sat in front of the fireplace in their newly shared living room with Milo at his side. They were sipping martinis because Milo wanted to celebrate and because he thought the drinks were pretty and the stemmed glasses festive. Plus he liked olives. They spoke softly so as not to disturb Emerson, who was tucked into a tiny ball of fluff between Logan's legs, sound asleep. Spanky was sprawled out on the sofa where the humans *should* have been, but the old dog growled and grumbled so much when they tried to move him, they let him stay and parked themselves on the floor by the fire, which was more romantic anyway.

The house in South Park felt like home to Logan already. His desk sat across from Milo's in the den. His many bookcases were restocked with his vast collection of books and scattered around the house anywhere they would fit. Logan's flat-screen TV was mounted on the wall across from the bed in the master bedroom where they could watch the latest television shows when they had nothing else to do in bed, which was absolutely never.

At the moment, Milo's head rested lightly on Logan's shoulder as each of them sipped their drinks and stared contentedly into the fire. They had made love not thirty minutes before, right there in front of the fireplace with the dogs looking on.

Logan thought he had never been so contented in his life. But his contentment was quickly jarred by Milo's first words in ten minutes.

"There's been another murder," he said, his chin digging into Logan's shoulder as he tilted his head up, presumably to see what Logan's reaction might be to the news. "I heard it on the radio when I was showering."

Logan's heart sank, as if a sudden weariness had taken hold of him and stripped him of all energy. "Oh God. Who was it this time?"

"A woman named Evelyn Tomes. She lived in El Centro and reviewed under the name BookBlogger. They found her burned to a crisp in her charred trailer somewhere out in the desert. The cause of death was suffocation. A plastic bag had been tied around her head. She had apparently been tortured before she died. Every one of her fingers was shattered. The killings are getting more vicious."

"They are getting closer to home too," Logan said on a sigh. "El Centro's only a hundred miles away."

"I know."

They sat silent. Each took a sip from his drink and listened to the fire crack and pop in front of them. It was really too warm for a fire, but it was so romantic neither wanted to let it die. Logan leaned over and pressed a kiss to the tip of Milo's nose just because he wanted to. "Had you heard of her?" he asked softly.

Milo shook his head. He was chewing on an olive, which he had just speared from his glass and poked into his mouth. He edged closer. "No. But I looked her up after I heard the news. She wasn't really a reviewer. She was like the other victims. More of a troll. True reviewers don't trash five books in a single day, one-starring everything in sight."

"Is that what she did?"

"Yeah. On Gladreads she had over two thousand books on her list of reviewed books, and of those two thousand, a mere handful had more than two stars. All those books had been listed there in the last six months. Her comments were cutting and belittling, and she seemed to really enjoy striking out at authors. I have a theory about people like that."

"What theory is that?"

"I think they are miserable in their own lives, so they take it out on anyone they perceive as having even a modicum of happiness or success in their own. I also think sometimes these trolls are failed writers. Jealous, spiteful, and remorselessly petty. They are lashing out at anyone who accomplished what they themselves could not."

Logan nodded, and when he did he enjoyed the way Milo's ginger hair slid softly across his cheek. "I've always thought that too. But it doesn't make it any easier for the writer who's being mauled."

"No," Milo said. "It doesn't. It also doesn't help him recoup the sales he might lose by readers who steer clear of his books thinking the bad reviews and the abysmal ratings might be justified, even if they aren't."

"So that's three deaths," Logan said quietly, staring once again into the flames.

"Three that we know about anyway."

"You think there are more?"

"I hope not."

Milo set his empty martini glass aside. "Me too," he said, sprawling out on the floor and resting his head on Logan's leg. He gazed up into Logan's eyes. "I love you so much. Don't be trashing any books when you do your reviews. It's not conducive to long life, and long life is exactly what I want from you. Promise me."

Logan grinned. "No one-star reviews. I swear." He stroked Milo's cheek with a fingertip, loving the feel of a smile forming beneath his touch.

But loving the man even more.

MILO SNUGGLED close. "I hope you're happy here," he whispered, trying not to disturb Emerson, still quietly snoring on the floor, the orange light from the fire dancing in his coat.

"I'm as happy as I've ever been in my life," Logan purred, planting a kiss in Milo's hair.

Milo sighed, reassured by the words, by the loving gentleness in Logan's voice. "Good." He tipped his head to gaze at the fire for a moment before turning back to study Logan's face. "Come with me tomorrow. The neighborhood book club is meeting again. If you're there with me and we make a big enough show of being madly in love, maybe they won't grill me about the murders like they did the last time."

"Do they know you're gay?"

"Do I care if they know I'm gay?"

Logan chuckled softly. "Apparently not."

"So you'll go?"

"Yes. I'll go."

A sneaky gleam lit Milo's eyes. "You'll be in for a treat. My ex is on the guest list too."

"You mean the legendary Bryce? The same Bryce who peels rubber and speeds past in a huff when he spots another beau on his ex-lover's front porch?"

"That's the one. They sent me a program of the evening's events. Food, me, Bryce—although they have him listed under his pen name of Thomas Giles—and a couple of other local writers. Say, did you ever review Bryce's book?"

"No, I recused myself. Conflict of interest."

"*What* conflict of interest?"

Logan smiled. "You."

"Oh."

"Anyway, it must not be getting bad reviews if he's copped an invitation for schmoozing and free eats at the local writing club."

"I guess not."

"I saw a picture of him on your Facebook page," Logan said. "He really is a hunk."

Milo shrugged. "He's also a dick. Are you sure you want to go?"

Logan wiggled his ass around like an eager kid. "As long as I'm with you, I'll be happy. And free food appeals to me mightily. It means we won't have to cook. Like either one of us ever does. I can hardly wait."

"It'll be fun." Milo grinned as he rolled over on his side and lifted Logan's shirttail to plant a kiss on his belly button.

"Uh-oh," Logan breathed. "Somebody's getting frisky."

"Bedtime," Milo whispered, sitting up to brush Logan's lips with his own. "Please. I want your clothes off. Now."

"Pushy," Logan said, but he didn't appear too appalled, especially when Milo's hand gently cupped his balls in a most promising caress. "We just made love less than an hour ago, you know."

Milo batted innocent eyes. "And your point is?"

Logan snorted. "No point. Just making conversation."

A moment later, Emerson was on the sofa, tucked neatly between Spanky's front legs where Logan had deposited him. The fire was properly screened and left to die on its own.

Arm in arm, shedding clothes along the way, Milo dragged Logan toward the bed.

Once again, the flat-screen TV recently attached high on the bedroom wall was completely ignored as the two lost themselves in other pursuits. None of those pursuits had a single Neilson rating to recommend it, but they were most enjoyable anyway.

JUST AFTER the antique school clock in the den chimed three in the morning, Logan slipped out of bed and padded softly from the room, leaving Milo snoring in the bed. He quietly closed the bedroom door behind him. Standing naked in the hall, he heard a patter of toenails approaching. It was Emerson, scared to death he might be missing something. Logan bent, scooped him into his hand, and lifted him up to tuck the little pup safely under his chin. Together, they went into the den, and Logan closed that door behind them too.

He parked himself at his desk with Emerson in his lap and booted up his computer.

Since he couldn't sleep, and since the murders were preying heavily on his mind, he logged into Grace Connor's review site, or tried to. The website was shut down. After a few minutes of surfing, he found the BooksOnWheels website. It was still up and running, although no new posts had been added since the day of Edgar Price's murder. Nor had an announcement of his death been included on the website by either a friend or a gloating murderer.

Logan scrolled through the long list of Price's more than 3,000 book reviews and ratings and found exactly what he expected to find. Almost every book that came under the BooksOnWheels microscope was rated either one or two stars, rarely three. There were no four- or five-star reviews at all.

A quick scan of the author names produced a long list of writers Logan himself had reviewed. Most of their works were fine examples of the craft, although good old Edgar Price certainly didn't see it that way, nor was he reticent to say so.

Price's star ratings were bad enough, but his written reviews were far worse. Cutting, cruel, mocking, and unflinchingly unapologetic. There was a conceit about his reviews that inferred his was the only opinion that mattered, that he brooked no opposition, and that his was the final word on all things literary. By the time Logan finished skimming through a score or more of Price's reviews, he was ready to kill the man himself. Especially when he found all four of Milo's books targeted by BooksOnWheels as well. Milo's newest book had been given such a thrashing that Logan huffed in exasperation and immediately signed out of the website with a sputtered curse.

He tried Evelyn Tomes, aka BookBlogger, next. Her website too had no new postings since what he assumed to be the day of her murder, only a week or so before. Nor was there an announcement of her death. Logan supposed the website would continue on in stasis until her domain privileges were revoked for lack of payment. It seemed a fairly moribund way to end one's career. Of course, being murdered with a Walmart bag wasn't exactly a classy way to go either.

Studying BookBlogger's list of reviewed books was like rereading the ratings on BooksOnWheels's website. One and two stars abounded. Threes were rare. Fours and fives were nonexistent. Evelyn Tomes, however, had gone one better than Edgar Price. She had included one-star reviews on a few of the truly great classics, such as *To Kill a Mockingbird* and Tolkien's *The Lord of the Rings*. As if fearlessly carried away by her own sense of power and blithely assholing along, ignoring the possibility of eternal damnation, she even included a one-star rant against the St. James version of the Holy Bible itself, calling it "…pedantic, trite, annoyingly over-written, and begetting a treasure trove of pointless metaphor…."

Logan sat staring at the computer screen, trying to swallow down his laughter so he wouldn't wake either the puppy in his lap, the lover in the bedroom, or the old dog snoring away on the couch in the living room.

By panning God, Evelyn Tomes had taken being a bitch to the highest level possible. No wonder she was now a charcoal briquette.

Surfing over to the Gladreads review site, which every author knew was the equivalent of visiting the most murderous slum on the planet brainlessly unarmed, Logan tried to construct a mental spreadsheet on the writers most affected by the three reviewers who had been killed. So many common names came up under the reviews of all three victims, including Milo Cook's, Logan immediately abandoned his idea of maybe homing in on the killer by triangulating the names of those writers targeted with the most ferocity. Hell, the three reviewers had targeted *everybody*. Consequently, every writer in the world had a motive for wanting them dead.

For the first time since the murders began, Logan began to feel sorry for the cops in charge of the three cases. It must be rough when you are looking for a suspect with a motive to suddenly come up with a cast of thousands who fit the bill. On top of that, the murders had taken place thousands of miles apart from each other. New York, Indiana, and the Southern California desert. Anyone who read police procedurals knew the far-flung logistics of an investigation like that were daunting at best.

Offering the police a cluck of sympathy in absentia, he switched off the computer and simply sat there in the dark for a few minutes, his mind blank.

At the squeak of a door, he turned and saw Milo standing naked, peering into the room.

Milo's voice was scratchy with sleep. "I woke up and you were gone," he said. "Is anything wrong?"

Milo was so beautiful there in the shadows, brushed by moonlight, that Logan felt a smile creep across his face. "No, baby. Nothing's wrong."

Milo eased into the room on silent feet and swung Logan's desk chair around so he could kneel before it. On his knees, he wrapped warm arms around Logan's waist and laid his head next to Emerson's. The puppy woke and gave him a lazy kiss hello while Logan caressed them both from above. A moment later the pup was softly snoring again.

"I missed you," Milo whispered, his lips on Logan's thigh. "I don't like waking up alone anymore. Come back to bed."

"Okay," Logan said through a gentle smile. Leaving Emerson asleep on the chair, they slipped arm in arm through the darkened house and crawled back into bed, where they drew instinctively together.

"I can never get enough of you," Logan whispered in the shadows.

"Nor I you," Milo whispered back, strangely formal.

Without another word, Milo twisted around in the bed. Logan smiled, unsurprised as his lover obeyed that great urge downward that steers all gay men. Moments later, starving with desire, they were yet again making love.

This time their hunger for each other carried them into dawn. As the rays of a new sunrise lightened the room around them, they at long last cried out in unison when their bodies writhed, their juices spilled.

Afterward, trembling with exhaustion, they clung together. Eventually Logan fell asleep in Milo's arms, more in love than he had been before. Did Milo feel the same? Logan thought maybe he did.

And how astonishing was that.

Chapter Twelve

LOGAN AND Milo were tooling down Juniper Street, headed for the home of the host of tonight's South Park Reading Club extravaganza. Milo didn't really want to see Bryce, or anyone else for that matter, as he had explained to Logan earlier. He mostly hoped the cheese dip would be as good as last time. In spite of all that, he still looked forward to the evening. What he was most excited about, he said with a wicked gleam in his eye, was showing off Logan.

Logan had dutifully laughed, but the truth was he didn't care about anything except being with Milo, although he was starting to get a little worried. Especially after last night. He suspected if he fell any deeper in love, he might end up sprouting Cupid wings and burping little red hearts into the air every time he opened his mouth. He was six foot five, after all. Six foot five guys should be butch. Maybe even a little aloof. It was disconcerting when they started acting romantically goofy.

Riding along at Milo's side, Logan shook his head and chuckled at himself in the dark. When Milo's hand came across the console and claimed his, his chuckle died, and he turned to study Milo's profile in the dashboard lights. Logan's heart swelled just looking at him. Uh-oh. He was about to start acting goofy again.

"Does Bryce know you have a new lover?" he asked.

Milo tickled Logan's palm. "He knows I've been seeing someone."

"Good. So who are the writers who will be there?"

"Adrian Strange, who writes science fiction. Lois Knight, a gay romance author. Bryce, of course, who dabbles in thrillers and excels at pissing me off. And myself. You know what I do."

Logan clucked in agreement. "Intimately. So. It's a motley crew, then."

Milo squeezed Logan's fingers until one of them popped. "Thanks a lot."

Logan laughed, yanked his hand away, and flexed his fingers to get the blood moving again. As soon as they were tingling properly, he slid them back into Milo's grip.

After a pause, Milo said, "With all these reviewers being killed, I've been thinking maybe we should buy a gun."

Logan grinned. "How do you know I don't *own* a gun?"

"Well, do you?"

"No."

"Good. If I thought you were armed, I would have never bitten you on the balls last night."

"I sort of liked it."

"Yeah, well, I couldn't have known that, could I? Might have been shot, I might've."

Both men smiled broadly as they sat there holding hands, staring through the windshield, watching the city roll by.

"Did you really like it?" Milo asked, still smiling.

"Yeah, I really did."

"Then maybe I'll do it again tonight. But only if you're good."

"I can be good even when I'm bad."

"When you're bad, you're even *better* than when you're good."

"Wait. I'm confused...."

Logan laughed while Milo pointed to a house ahead. The house was all lit up, every light in the place burning. Several people were standing on the sidewalk outside, smoking and shooting the shit, and even more could be seen through the windows milling around inside. As they drove slowly past, Logan realized every parking space was taken for blocks around.

Milo groaned. "I've never seen so many people at one of these meetings before. My God, it's a full house. I wonder if the murders brought everybody out. This is going to be a nightmare."

"Just so they don't run out of food," Logan murmured in fake alarm.

Milo turned to him with a wry expression. "Leave it to you to dig through the chaff and unearth the one kernel of true horror in the situation."

"Thank you," Logan said, smiling shyly. "I do what I can."

FROM THE moment they walked into the house, Milo thought the hostess appeared a bit frazzled and glassy-eyed by the sheer number of guests who had showed up on her doorstep. Seeing her cast fretful glances at the food trays, he and Logan quickly filled their plates while they had a chance. By the time the meeting officially started, they had grazed their way through everything edible, and Milo was surreptitiously trying not to belch, even while he continued eating.

Milo caught more than one intrigued glance coming his way from Bryce, who seemed inordinately interested in who the long, tall drink of water stapled to Milo's side might be. Consequently, Milo laid claim to Logan even more enthusiastically than he would have ordinarily, offering whispered asides and fawning pats on the arm and leaving a forgotten hand resting on Logan's thigh now and then, just to piss Bryce off. God, he could be a dick.

Bryce, on the other hand, and quite possibly in retaliation, made a show of being chummy with Adrian Strange, the science fiction writer. Strange was clearly peacock-proud that such a handsome young man was showing him attention. Both men were almost as tall as Logan. Since Adrian Strange was not the most handsome man on the planet, Milo would never have thought he would be Bryce's type. But love is blind, they say, so Milo finally came to the conclusion that even though he didn't like Bryce anymore, which was putting it mildly, he was still happy Bryce had made a connection with someone. He also came to the conclusion he was glad that person was Adrian Strange, because Milo didn't like him either. In Milo's eyes, they deserved each other.

Logan leaned in and whispered, "You're plotting some sort of mayhem. Stop staring at your ex and his new boyfriend. Have an egg roll. They're really good."

Milo grunted in reply and snatched an egg roll off Logan's plate.

"Hey!" Logan cried. "I didn't mean mine!"

There must have been fifty or sixty people in attendance when the South Park Reading Club finally came to order. The hostess, looking considerably relieved now that the feeding frenzy was over, officiously clapped her hands to get everyone's attention.

The four authors in attendance were introduced, with Bryce, known to the hostess as Thomas Giles, lastly singled out as a welcome newcomer. To his credit, Bryce graciously accepted the acknowledgment and rose rather formally to offer a muted little bow of acceptance of her kind words. When he sat back down alongside Adrian Strange, Adrian beamed proudly and patted Bryce on the back, causing Milo to once again find it fascinating that the two should have become so close.

Last but not least, and much to Milo's delight, the hostess offered a final introduction to another new attendee. Logan Hunter, aka BookHunter, who she proudly stated was one of her favorite reviewers.

Then, simpering and with a mischievous glint in her eye, she stepped up to Logan and Milo and pulled them to their feet. "I would also like to announce," she said coquettishly, casting her gaze around the room while the blood positively poured into her cheeks, "that Milo Cook and Logan Hunter are now officially an item. Let's give them a round of applause and wish them all the luck in the world, shall we?"

Dutifully, her guests did as she asked. A rousing roar of approval rose up, and Milo was pleased to note that most everyone seemed to be truly happy for them. If there were any homophobes in the room, they were smart enough to keep their feelings hidden. Lois Knight, the gay romance writer, positively tittered with delight at the news. Milo had seen her often at the trade shows and knew her to be a San Diego native. She was a spinsterish woman with a plain face, tall and razor-thin, who was a health fanatic, known to run marathons and hike the high desert every chance she got. Always somewhat short on fashion sense, tonight she had enlisted a bizarre collection of barrettes to hold her curly hair back. As if that weren't enough, ten or fifteen additional barrettes, all different shapes and colors, were clamped in here and there with no discernable purpose whatsoever. For tonight's occasion, she had chosen to wear saddle shoes, a cashmere sweater with buttons on the sleeves, and a poodle skirt straight out of the '50s. One couldn't help but wonder if she had confused this get-together with a Halloween party she had promised to attend six months hence.

"Bravo!" Lois cried, leaping to her feet and leaking copious tears of joy, which Milo thought was a little over-the-top since they had barely spoken five words to each other in all the years he had known her. Still, she was being kind and enthusiastic about something very dear to Milo's heart, and for that, he loved her like a long-lost sister, even *with* those fucking barrettes in her hair.

Bryce and Adrian Strange, on the other hand, looked less than enthralled by the news. Milo wasn't sure if it was because Milo was Bryce's ex, or because Logan was a reviewer. And frankly, he didn't care. After he and Logan succeeded in wiggling out of the arms of their hostess and reclaiming their seats, Milo snatched a second egg roll off Logan's plate, which garnered him another homicidal look, and sat back waiting for the evening's festivities to continue. Logan relaxed beside him, no doubt glad at last to no longer be the center of attention, even if he had lost two egg rolls in the process. It wasn't the first time Milo noticed there was a touch of shyness in Logan. Somehow that teeny crack in Logan's armor made Milo love him all the more. Especially since Milo had the same crack of shyness in his own armor. He also realized he would have to be careful in the future in regards to snatching food off Logan's plate without permission. One might very easily lose a hand in such an enterprise.

After the introductions, Milo was called on first to do a short reading of whatever struck his fancy. He had brought along on his iPad a few pages of his Work in Progress, just in case, so now he dragged it out and, still seated at Logan's side, read to the crowd around them. During his recitation, Logan's hand never once left his side, tucked in as it was unobtrusively next to his pant leg, his finger occasionally stroking the fabric as if to let Milo know he was there and rooting for him.

When Milo finished, the crowd gave him a nice round of applause, praising his words, exclaiming how they couldn't wait to see the book in print, and swearing by all that was holy they would rush out and buy it the moment it hit the stores.

Lois Knight was called upon next. She had chosen an excerpt from one of her earlier novels to read. The excerpt was so packed with male-on-male sex (anal and otherwise), with copious amounts of seminal fluid spewing in every direction and some of the largest cocks Milo had ever heard referred to on the written page, that by the time she finished, more than one person in the crowd was cherry red and squirming in embarrassment. The fact that Lois Knight herself looked like someone's dotty maiden aunt who wouldn't recognize a dick if it walked up and poked her in the eye, made her reading about such matters all the more unsettling. When she was finished, Lois clapped her tablet closed with a finality that made everybody jump. She gazed around the room, looking pleased as punch by all the shocked expressions gawking back at her.

No one was more pleased than the hostess that Lois was finished. Flustered, she hurriedly introduced Bryce, or in this instance, Thomas Giles, who popped open his laptop and read a long section from a rough draft of his latest WIP, which he had titled *Sunset*.

As he recited in a proud, stentorian voice, leaving long pauses in the narrative as if pompously giving his audience time to appreciate the beauty of his language, the deft handling of his phrasing, Milo felt Logan stiffen beside him. When he glanced at him, Logan was staring into his own lap, his brow furrowed.

"What is it?" Milo whispered.

Logan shook his head. Not once did Logan raise his eyes to look at Bryce. Not once did he turn his gaze to Milo either. He merely sat there, as closed to the room around him as if he had locked himself behind a door, refusing even Milo entry.

Bryce's reading ended with an appreciative clamor from his audience, no doubt made even more appreciative by the fact that not once during the entire reading had there been a single orgasm described in horrendously minute detail nor one gram of seminal fluid wantonly splashed about the room.

With Bryce finished, Adrian Strange took the floor. His reading was a snippet from one of his earlier novels as well, probably because, as far as Milo knew, the man was living off past glories. He had written nothing new in several years. Still, he made the rounds at conventions, touting his old books. And in all fairness, he was still a fairly popular science fiction writer. Why he chose to publish no new books, Milo didn't know, and at the moment, he didn't care. He was more eager for the evening to end so he could get Logan alone and ask him what it was about Bryce's reading that had disturbed him so.

But that would have to wait. Once Adrian Strange ended his reading to an appreciative, if rather reserved, round of applause, the evening instantly took a turn for the macabre, just as Milo had suspected it would.

With all four writers finished with their readings, an older man in a tweed jacket with leather patches on the elbows, who couldn't have looked more pompously literary if he were packing a goose quill, parchment, and a bottle of india ink, ostentatiously cleared his throat and took the floor.

"What about the killings of all these reviewers?" he demanded, his voice booming through the room like a foghorn. "I'd like to hear what our guests have to say about *that*." Both Adrian and Bryce looked vaguely annoyed by the question, as if unhappy the conversation had turned to a subject other than themselves. Lois Knight merely scooped a huge glob of bean dip onto a chip and poked it in her mouth, as if she couldn't be bothered with murder as long as there was still free food lying about. More than one club member, including the hostess, perked up at the mention of murder, as all eyes eagerly turned to the panel of working writers assembled before them, eagerly awaiting a response.

But the foghorn wasn't finished quite yet. "First I'd like to hear what BookHunter has to say about it, since it's his profession that is being most horrendously targeted. Mr. Hunter? What are your thoughts, sir?"

If Logan was surprised to be singled out, he did a good job of hiding it. He simply stared back at the man, taking time to get his thoughts in order before answering.

Finally, he cleared his throat and spoke quietly, firmly. "First off, I'd like to address what I consider to be a misapprehension about these killings. Everyone talks about this murderer going after reviewers. But as far as I can see, these are not reviewers being targeted. They are trollers. Troublemakers. Under the *guise* of being reviewers, these are people who use the internet to seek out the lowest common denominator of humanity for the sole purpose of shaming and ridiculing authors while trying to advance their own brand, their own following, their own websites. These are bloggers whose sole purpose is to increase their readership, and consequently their popularity. They do this by presenting themselves as experts, when in truth they are merely agitators. They do not do what they do to further literature. They do not do what they do to enlighten readers. They do it because they crave attention. And because they enjoy damaging the brand of legitimate writers. They are the modern version of schoolyard bullies, hiding behind the anonymity offered by the internet. In other words, they are cowards."

Milo found himself staring at Logan's profile as he spoke, as proud of him as he had ever been. The room, too, he didn't fail to notice, was absolutely silent. Other than Logan's voice, not a sound could be heard. Every pair of eyes in the crowd was riveted to Logan's face, every ear to Logan's words. It wasn't lost on Milo that the words Logan spoke were almost identical to what Milo himself had told the detective from New York. These victims were not reviewers. They were far from it.

But Logan clearly had more to add, and Milo squelched his own thoughts so he could listen. He was getting a rare glimpse into the public persona of the man he loved, and he didn't want to miss it.

Logan looked blandly about the room, a sad smile accompanying his gaze, as if amazed people couldn't see the truth for themselves. "Two of the people killed trolled the internet without revealing their true identity. Nowhere on their websites could their real names be found.

One even claimed to reside in a mansion by a lake a thousand miles from where she actually lived. She also claimed to be beautiful, according to a few pirated photographs on her website. In reality neither assertion was true. An honest reviewer would have no need to hide behind lies such as that. An honest reviewer would have nothing to be ashamed of to begin with. Nor would a true reviewer implement a scorched-earth policy by posting ratings and reviews of numerous books in a single day, each and every review more insulting, more damaging to the author, than the review before it."

Milo was grateful to hear a murmur of agreement in the crowd. A few scattered heads bobbed up and down. Glances of approval were exchanged. If Logan noticed, he didn't let it show. He kept his head down as if studying his hands while he calmly spoke, loud enough to be heard in the farthest corners of the room, but not so loud as to sound like he was preaching. His voice was that of a kindly professor, languidly orating for his students a lesson plan he had memorized years before. Logan had obviously thought these murders through long before he came here on this night and was asked about them point-blank.

Finally, Logan lifted his head and peered around the room. Without groping for it, he reached over and grasped Milo's hand, as if he knew it would be exactly where he expected it to be. At the confident and possessive way he captured it in his own, Milo's heart swelled with pride. "This man is mine" Logan was saying by his actions, and he was proud to let everyone in the room know it. Milo had never loved Logan more than he did at that very moment.

But Logan still wasn't finished. "Grace Connor was the only victim who proudly—or foolishly, maybe—published her blog under her own name. She attended public events using her true identity and put herself recklessly out there for everyone to see. She was attending just such an event when she was murdered in New York." Logan paused, surveying the faces around him. Then he frowned. "But if you read a few of her reviews and see how cruel those reviews could sometimes be, you'll realize she probably should have been a little more circumspect in either releasing her true identity or making herself so accessible to the people she was attacking. It pains me to say it since she was a friend of Milo's, but it's still the truth."

Logan cast a glance in Milo's direction, but his gaze didn't linger. He did not ask for forgiveness for what he had said about Grace, as

Milo knew he wouldn't. As Milo knew he didn't need to. Logan quickly turned back to the room. "Having said all that, I still find the whole business appalling. Murder is kind of cool on the written page and makes for exciting books. In real life I have no stomach for it. It's terrible and cowardly that these killings have occurred, and it tarnishes our industry. It does. I feel empathy for the victims even while I abhor the things they did when they were alive. And I mourn the loss of innocence these killings have brought to the business we all love so much. The business that brought us all here tonight. The business of books."

A sudden fury rose to Logan's eyes. His free hand clenched in his lap. "I *hate* that so many people despise legitimate reviewers because of a handful of vicious lunatics who make us *all* look bad! Most reviewers are smart and caring. They understand writers. Many are even professional editors, and certainly all of them are lovers of books. Heck, many reviewers I know are writers themselves. They don't deserve this. *None* of them deserves this."

By the time he finished, Logan was so emotional his hands were shaking.

Milo touched his knee, as if to say, "Shush now. It'll be all right."

Logan nodded, then looked shyly around at all the faces once again before slowly rising to his feet. Milo stood with him.

"That's enough of that," he whispered humbly for Milo's ears alone. "Now I think I'll see if there are any more egg rolls to be had since you ate mine. Jabbering makes me hungry."

Milo reached up and touched Logan's cheek, signaling his support for everything Logan had said. At the same time a soft round of applause began to roll around the room.

"Yes!" Bryce exclaimed eagerly from his seat across the room. Several heads swiveled in his direction. Logan's was one of them. Milo also noted that Logan's eyes narrowed, and he realized, not for the first time that night, how much Logan disliked Bryce. Once again, he wondered why. With that one explosive cry of "Yes!" Bryce had grabbed the spotlight. And just as Milo remembered him always doing when he found himself to be the center of attention, he ran with it. Probably for the purpose of civility, he tried to ratchet down his own exuberance. Bryce's voice took on a calmer edge, a cooler tone. Still, a fire burned in his eyes, and the room fell silent before it. His words quieted the crowd even more.

"BookHunter is right," he declared, gazing from face to face, making sure he had everyone's undivided attention. "Grace Connor and all the other victims got exactly what they deserved."

"That's not what I said!" Logan roared, the muscles in his jaw clenched, his grip tightening around Milo's hand.

Bryce brushed away Logan's denial with a flip of his fingers as if shooing a fly from a bowl of potato salad. "Only because you're too polite to admit it," he said, offering Logan the briefest of glances. "But it's true nevertheless. Grace Connor and the others set out to anger people, and they succeeded beyond their wildest dreams. After all, you can't blindly attack people over the internet without ruffling a few feathers. And in this case, they apparently ruffled the *wrong* feathers. Unhappily for them, revenge was sought and exacted because of it. Basically what these so-called victims did was piss off the wrong madman. And they paid for it with their lives."

"That's awfully presumptuous of you!" Lois Knight sang out from her seat on the divan. She had stopped eating and was now following the conversation with interest.

Bryce whirled on her as if he had been verbally attacked, causing the woman to glare right back.

"Is it?" he asked, his eyes cold, the muscles in his jaws clenched. "And why should it bother you so much if it is?"

Lois Knight laughed, startling Milo, since it seemed to him to be the strangest reaction of the evening. But her next words startled him even more.

"I wasn't saying the victims didn't deserve it. My sales have been hurt by trolls too. No, what I am questioning is your assessment that the killer is a madman. If he's mad, he has a funny way of showing it. Seems to me he's handling the situation quite competently. Don't get me wrong. The deaths are appalling, of course, but still I sympathize with the murderer's motives."

The hostess gasped, and for a moment even Bryce appeared shocked. Then he pulled himself together and recommenced his tirade, ignoring Lois Knight like the plague from that point forward.

"The fact remains, these are not respected reviewers who are dying. They aren't. They are internet trolls, just like Hunter said. Instigators of ridicule whose sole purpose is that of sabotaging as many writing careers as they can. In the process they are belittling professionals like Logan Hunter who take pride in being civil and being fair with their reviews."

"Leave me out of it!" Logan flared.

But once again Bryce ignored him. "People like Logan Hunter, and a thousand other respectable reviewers out there who love books, who love authors, all do what they can to bring exceptional examples of literature to the world of readers, to bring talented new writers into the limelight where they can be most appreciated. If you ask me why these victims, these *agitators* as Mr. Hunter called them, really do what they do, I'd have to say I don't know. They're just assholes, I guess. But if you ask me why they are being killed, I'd have to say I *do* know. And like Lois Knight, I understand it completely. What happened to them, happened as a direct result of their actions. God forgive me for saying it, but every one of them asked for it!"

A chorus of agreements and disagreements echoed around the room. Logan remained stubbornly silent, voicing no opinion, although anger still burned in his eyes. It clearly showed the disgust he felt at everything both Bryce and Lois Knight had said.

The only person in the room who seemed to sit blandly by without an opinion at all on the subject was Adrian Strange. In fact, he was still nibbling at a carrot stick, his napkin tucked jauntily into his collar, his plate balanced precariously atop his iPad.

As soon as the uproar began to wane, he set his plate aside and raised his hands.

"Now, now," he said, just loud enough to grab everyone's attention. "This is a heated subject, and we all tend to get a little carried away. Bryce is a passionate young man, and he has his opinions. Mr. Hunter has his as well. Just as I have mine."

"As do I," Lois Knight snapped, more to herself than to the crowd.

"Yes," Adrian sighed in her direction. "As do you."

"What *is* your opinion?" someone in the crowd asked Adrian. "And what do you think is going to happen next?"

Adrian Strange tucked a final carrot stick into his mouth. Noisily chewing away at it, he said evasively, "My opinion is my own. And as for what happens next, I suppose it depends on the killer, doesn't it? Since he's obviously on a mission of retribution, that could be anything." Adrian's long face erupted into a merry grimace. "As we all know, that's why literary madmen are so much fun to write and read about. You never know *what* they're going to do next."

"Or who they might actually be," Lois Knight muttered, eyeing both Adrian and Bryce with evident suspicion. "After all, in a really good book, the killer would be the last person you'd ever expect."

Chapter Thirteen

WHEN THE discussion erupted all over again, Logan tugged Milo into the kitchen away from all the other attendees of the South Park Reading Club. Out of sight of the group, he clutched Milo's shoulders, and pleaded, "We need to leave *now*."

Milo had never seen Logan so upset. "Why? What's wrong?"

Logan didn't answer, but by his stubborn stance—head erect, shoulders squared, eyes determined—Milo figured there wasn't much point in arguing.

"Let me just say my goodbyes to the hostess before we go."

"Good," Logan said. "I'll wait for you outside."

Milo laid his hand to Logan's chest, as if trying to glean what the hell was going on by touch alone, sort of like a lover's braille. Since Logan clearly wasn't going to explain it, Milo finally stepped back. Logan, shoulders slumped now, scuttled down the hallway toward the front door. From there he stepped out into the night without looking back. Milo, in turn, headed for the living room to corner the hostess and quietly plead her forgiveness for ducking out early. Two minutes later, Milo found Logan sitting on the front steps, waiting. Milo pulled him to his feet, and they headed for the car. They both breathed in the cool night air, relieved to be away from the crowd inside.

"I need a cigarette," Logan said.

"No, you don't!" Milo snapped. "Now, then. Tell me what made you mad? Was it talk of the murders?"

Logan slipped his hand into Milo's. He seemed reluctant to answer, but he finally did. "I wasn't mad."

"Could have fooled me. If you weren't mad, then what was it?"

"It was a lot of things."

"Name one."

Logan gazed at him as they passed beneath a streetlight. His normally generous mouth was a thin, tight line. Clearly, he was still angry, whether he chose to admit it or not. To Milo that was a little intimidating.

The guy was a mountain, after all. Mountains are scary when they're mad. Not that he could ever be scared of Logan, of course. That was an impossibility. Still, Logan's anger was a humbling thing to watch.

As Milo stared and Logan avoided his gaze, he was relieved to see the rage begin to dissipate, the fury fade. Logan's innate kindness seemed to help bring it under control. For the first time since their confrontation in the kitchen, a self-deprecating smile twisted Logan's mouth. He looked embarrassed. When he spoke, his voice was in its normal range again. Perhaps even softer than normal. His lips were fuller. They were starting to look kissable again, just the way Milo liked them.

Logan hooked a thumb over his shoulder to indicate the people inside the house behind him. "First off, Adrian Strange is an asshole. He seemed to find it amusing that there's a madman out there killing people, like it would make a nice plot point for a book, but insinuating that in real life it didn't really amount to much."

Milo chuckled. "I have to admit he's perfectly named, because he really is strange. But that's not all there is to it, Logan. I know there's more to what happened in there than what Adrian said. You started tensing up long before the group started talking about the killings."

At that, a bit of Logan's anger returned. He fell silent. And in Milo's opinion he fell silent for too long.

"Well?" Milo prodded. "What was it? What pissed you off?"

Logan's grip tightened around Milo's fingers. He edged closer until their shoulders touched as they strode along. He emitted a long-drawn-out sigh, as if a great weariness had suddenly settled into his bones. "I need to check something out when we get home. Bear with me until then. If I'm wrong, I'll spend the rest of the night finding new and exciting ways to apologize to you for ruining your night."

Milo waggled his eyebrows. "That's an intriguing promise. But you didn't ruin my night. And you don't need to apologize either. I would just like to know what happened. Are you sure you can't tell me now?"

Logan's silence returned, and by the stubborn tilt to his head, Milo knew he might as well stop pressing the guy. Logan would explain everything when Logan *wanted* to explain everything. Not a minute before.

THEY DROVE home without another word being spoken, although there was no animosity in their silence. Logan's hand never once left Milo's thigh, and Milo never once stopped stroking the back of Logan's hand as he drove. Upon entering the house, Logan didn't even kick off his shoes before he began sorting through his scattered bookcases, plodding methodically from one to another. While moving in a few weeks earlier, his books had been stuffed onto the shelves any old way. Logan had promised himself he would put them back in the order in which he once had them memorized, but he hadn't done it yet. Consequently, the particular book he was looking for gave him a merry chase before it finally turned up.

When it did, Logan cried, "Aha!" and yanked it off the shelf.

He found Milo sitting by the pool in the chaise lounge wearing a terry cloth robe. Every stitch of his clothing was tossed in a pile on the patio tile. Both Spanky and Emerson were squeezed onto his lap receiving much-needed belly rubs.

Milo looked up when Logan stepped through the sliding door leading out to the pool. He eyed the book in Logan's hand but didn't say anything. Reaching over, he dragged a lawn chair closer and motioned for Logan to sit. Before he did, Logan tossed the book on the chair and strode back into the house. Less than a minute later, he was back and pulling the robe around himself that matched the one Milo wore. Beneath it, he was just as naked as Milo.

Without speaking, Logan dragged his chair even closer and dropped into it. Leaning down, he placed a kiss on each of the dogs' heads. He then made a side trip to separate the folds of Milo's robe and apply a third kiss, this one a little more lingering, on Milo's appendectomy scar, always a favorite destination of his. Pleased seeing Milo's cock begin to lengthen in response, Logan flipped Milo's robe shut again and leaned back into his chair.

"Tease," Milo grumped. He lifted one of two freshly opened beers from beside his chair and offered it to Logan. Logan accepted gratefully, taking a long drink while settling back and opening the book.

MILO SAT playing with the dogs and sipping at his beer while Logan did whatever the hell Logan was doing. Milo was confused as to what the book had to do with anything. He had shot a glimpse at it while Logan was inside the house getting undressed, but he didn't recognize it or the author's name. Nor did he recognize the publisher's faded logo on the spine. The book was old and well read, or possibly just limp and tattered with age, Milo couldn't be sure. By the cover, it appeared to be a thriller. By the font and the style, it appeared to have been published back in the forties, maybe, or possibly even earlier. It was a hardback, the corners bent and frayed, the cloth binding slightly torn. A circular stain in the upper right-hand corner of the cover appeared to be from some long-forgotten coffee cup spilling its contents onto the book and being left to dry. Logan flipped through the pages, occasionally reaching over to pet one of the dogs absentmindedly. Sometimes, as he skimmed through the book, he would lazily reach out a hand and run his fingers through the hair on Milo's thigh.

When Logan bellowed, "There!" and shook the book in Milo's face, Milo was so startled he almost fell off his chair. Spanky clearly didn't like it either. He grumbled in annoyance and crawled arthritically off the chaise to disappear underneath. Only Emerson seemed unconcerned. He lay sound asleep with his head on Milo's knee and his four little feet sticking straight up into the air. By the way his feet were twitching, he must have been chasing dream rabbits dredged up from some genetic memory bank, since his experience with *real* rabbits was patchy at best.

Logan was looking so pleased with himself, Milo found it hard not to laugh. "There *what*?" he asked, more amused than curious. Logan sat back in the chair and stared at him. He glanced down at the book and cleared his throat. He began to read the words on the page before him aloud. As he read, Milo sat, confused, wondering what the hell his lover was getting at. As Logan turned a page and continued to read, Milo's attention sharpened. His eyes slowly, but inexorably, began to widen. The beer bottle rested forgotten in his hand. He stared at Logan's beautiful mouth, reciting words he had heard delivered just an hour or so before.

When Logan came to the end of a paragraph, he lifted his eyes and studied Milo's reaction. He clearly saw what he expected to see, because he briskly snapped the book shut even as a smile twisted his lips.

"He stole it!" Milo gasped, his gaze burning into Logan's. "Every word of what Bryce read, every word of what he passed off as his Work in Progress, he *stole*."

Logan nodded. "His name wasn't the only thing he lied about in that room tonight."

Milo reached out and grabbed the book from Logan's lap. "Page 56," Logan softly said, and Milo flipped the pages there. As he sat reading the words for himself, his whole body tensed. At long last, he closed the book and lifted the beer to glug half of it down in one long noisy gulp. While he drank, his eyes found Logan.

"I'm sorry," Logan said.

Milo set the bottle aside and once more stared down at the book. "*Sunset*, he called it. *Sunset*, my ass. He plagiarized it."

"Damn near verbatim," Logan said.

Again, Milo lifted the book and studied the spine, the title, the author's name, the publisher's logo, none of which he had ever heard of before. "Where did you get this?"

Logan shrugged. "I've had it for years. It was a book I loved as a kid. The author is what they would call today a one-hit wonder. Obscure at best. Totally forgotten. An unknown. He never published another book. I'm not even sure how many copies he sold of this one. Suffice it to say, it wasn't a bestseller. Still, I've always loved it. It's a hell of a thriller. Spooky, bloody, well written—at least I thought so when I was a kid. Apparently Bryce loved it too."

"Yes," Milo said. "Loved it enough to steal it and pawn it off as his own. I can't believe he would do such a thing."

Logan laid gentle fingers on Milo's arm. "You said yourself his writing wasn't that good."

"But plagiarism!" Milo cried. "Whatever made him think he could get away with it?"

Softly, Logan said, "There's another question we should be asking ourselves."

Milo's eyes were still narrowed in fury and shock. He only reluctantly tore them from the book to center them on Logan's face. "And what is that?"

In a whisper, as if afraid even the dogs would be offended, he said, "I'm sorry, Milo, but I think we need to know if his first book was plagiarized too."

Milo's jaw dropped open as the logic of what Logan said flooded through him. "My God, you're right. But could he really be that stupid?"

Logan sighed. His fingers never left Milo's arm. "If he didn't plagiarize the first, why would he risk everything by plagiarizing the second?"

Milo blinked. Once more he stared down at the tattered old book in his lap. He had an almost uncontrollable urge to throw the fucking thing in the pool.

"Yes," he said quietly. "Why would he?"

As Logan and Milo lay in bed, the moon cast a bar of pale blue light across the rumpled covers. The windows were open and a breeze stirred the curtains, causing the bar of moonlight to undulate across the bed like a snake. Since spring was in full bloom, the air was filled with the sweet scent of honeysuckle from the canyon abutting Milo's property. Flat on his back and wide-awake, Logan stared up into the shadows above his head, fully aware that Milo was doing the same beside him. Their hands were clasped. Their feet touched as they stuck out from the foot of the bed, dangling there in midair, Logan's protruding farther than Milo's since he was taller.

They had scooted low on the mattress because the dogs were sprawled out sound asleep on the pillows, hogging the headboard like the spoiled little shits they were. They had grown so close during the last few weeks that Spanky and Emerson hardly ever left each other's side. They ate together, slept together, and played together. They had even begun swimming in the pool together, whether the humans were around or not. While Emerson had grown quite a bit, Spanky still could have swallowed him whole. A few days earlier, Milo had expressed his surprise to Logan that Spanky, in dealing with Emerson, seemed to have resurrected a bit of his own puppyhood. The fact that they were now all but inseparable was even more of a shock. But, God knows, a welcome one.

This was the first night since moving in together that Logan and Milo did not make love, and Logan was feeling guilty about it. Still, his thoughts were too muddled for sex. He doubted he'd be able to concentrate even if he tried.

After last night's meeting of the South Park Reading Club, he and Milo had spent the entire day researching Bryce's first book for any sign that he had stolen parts of it like he had the so-called Work in Progress he chose to read from at the meeting. Only hours before, they had found the proof they needed. Undeniable proof. By googling and cross-referencing passages online from Thomas Giles's first release, they found verbatim paragraphs, whole chapters in fact with only the characters' names changed, that matched another forgotten book by another forgotten author published decades earlier. They had spent long hours proving and reproving their theory until there was not a shadow of a doubt that they were right.

Everything in Bryce's book, from the opening sentence to the closing paragraph, was stolen. Only the characters' names and the title were changed. Not only had he plagiarized it, but he had been lazy and cocksure enough to copy it word for word!

Neither Logan nor Milo had had a decent night's sleep since the night before, so tonight, twenty-four hours later, out of sheer exhaustion they decided to turn in early and hopefully get some rest before they decided what to do with the knowledge they had unearthed.

But sleep was still far beyond the grasp of either.

"Why did he do it?" Milo asked for the hundredth time, edging closer on the bed to press his lips to Logan's shoulder. "Why would he risk everything to do that? And look at us! Now because of what he did, we're put in the uncomfortable position of having to destroy a friend's hope of ever having a career in the field he always said he loved."

"Is he?" Logan asked, hearing the hurt in Milo's voice. "A friend, I mean?"

"He was once," Milo said with only a slight hesitation. "Hell, once he was *more* than a friend. No matter how badly love affairs end, they still leave feelings behind, whether we choose to admit it or not."

Logan rolled over onto his side and draped an arm across Milo's chest. "Baby, there's no reason in the world for you to be involved in exposing Bryce for what he's done. I'm the reviewer. The duty falls to me. I don't want to do it either, but I honestly feel the truth needs to come out. It's the only way to be fair to all the other writers who achieve their success the hard way."

Milo scooted farther down in the bed and laid his face to Logan's chest. "I know. But it still seems wrong. He was so proud of finally being published."

"And his pride was based on a lie. Every bit of it."

"I know. I just hate to be the one to pull the rug out from under him. He'll be blackballed for life, you know. Even a nom de plume won't save him from the fallout of being labeled a plagiarist."

"Nor should it." Logan slid his fingers through Milo's hair, hoping to comfort, hoping to calm. "That's why I don't want you to be involved in exposing him. You know, if you hadn't pressed me at the meeting, I might have let it go. I might not have dug into his first book to see if it was plagiarized. I might have just let his reading stand, figuring he wouldn't go any further than lying to a roomful of people. But now we know that's not the case. I didn't want to tell you about it at all, because I knew it would hurt you if I did. But you pressed, and now here we are."

Milo sighed. "It's true. I did." He tilted his head up to Logan's face in the shadows. "I don't blame you for this. I don't. It's just too bad one of the murder victims didn't run across the truth about Bryce instead of us. Since they were doomed anyway, let *them* be the ones to expose him. Hell, for once they could have honestly trashed somebody who actually deserved it."

"So you're admitting he deserves to be exposed."

"Y-yes. I'm afraid there's no way around it. But isn't there some way you can be clandestine about it. I mean, without exposing yourself in the process?"

Logan laid a hand to Milo's cheek. He lowered his voice to a whisper, hoping that would make his words less hurtful. "That would be just as underhanded as what Bryce is doing. Don't you see? I pride myself on my honesty as a reviewer, Milo. Never in my life have I intentionally set out to harm anyone by the words I write about their work. Usually if I really hate a book, I don't post a review at all. But this is different. This goes beyond reviewing. Plagiarism can't be allowed to stand. And I can't be the one to make the charge of plagiarism if I'm not going to do it out in the open, putting my own reputation on the line when I do. I've always stood behind what I write. I can't stop doing that now."

On a deep sigh, Milo muttered, "I know."

The silent darkness settled over them while Logan thought about the logistics of what he would have to do. In his head, he had already begun writing the article for his blog, the article that would expose the fictional Thomas Giles as a plagiarist—and destroy Bryce's career forever.

He wrapped Milo tightly in his arms and whispered softly, "I'm sorry."

Milo pressed a kiss to Logan's chin. "You're only doing what you have to do. I know that."

"Do you?"

Milo nodded, and a moment later, he sat up wearily in the bed and swung his bare legs over the side, reaching for his robe.

"Where are you going?" Logan asked, reaching out to stroke Milo's warm back, dipping his fingers into the hair at Milo's nape. "Why are you getting up?"

"I'm going to do what *I* have to do. I can't let Bryce be sucker-punched by this. I have to give him a heads-up."

With that, Milo eased himself off the bed. His bare feet rustled across the carpet as he walked slowly out of the room.

"Of course," Logan muttered softly, sadly, his heart aching. Not for Bryce, but for Milo. "Of course."

WITH THE living room lit only by moonlight, Milo sat bleary-eyed in the shadows. The night had barely begun, but thanks to his lack of sleep the night before, coupled with the stress of what they were about to do, Milo thought he had never been so tired in his life. He could hear Logan moving around in the bedroom. A moment later, Logan padded naked into the office and softly closed the door behind him. Milo didn't need to question what he was about to do. Logan was going to write the blog post. The blog post that would forever shatter Bryce's dream of becoming a true writer.

Bryce had to be warned, at least. Even if what was about to happen was Bryce's own fault, he had to be warned.

Sighing, Milo braced himself and punched in the numbers on his landline. Bryce answered on the fourth ring.

"Yes?" Bryce's voice was croaky from sleep. He sounded as weary as Milo felt.

Bryce mumbled something else, something Milo couldn't understand. He cleared his throat, and his words came out stronger, clearer. His voice didn't sound so sleep damaged anymore. Milo heard the squeak of springs, as if Bryce were sitting up in his bed, checking the clock, blinking himself awake, maybe, trying to figure out what the hell was going on. Then Milo thought he heard a second voice, rising muffled out of sleep, muttering a questioning curse. "Who the fuck is it?"

Milo knew that voice. It was Adrian Strange. So it was true. He and Bryce were having an affair.

Before Milo could pick at the mystery anymore, Bryce got grumpy, all but growling into the phone. "Who is this? What do you want?"

Heart aching, Milo knew immediately he couldn't be the one to do this. Carefully, with only a slight tremor in his hand, he hung up the phone, ending the call before he uttered a word. He sat holding the receiver while the sound of his own heartbeat thudded inside his head. Turning to gaze outside, he stared up through the living room window at the blanket of starlight draped across the sleeping city.

The sight was so innocently beautiful, and in such opposition to everything he felt inside, Milo closed his eyes and blocked it out.

Chapter Fourteen

BARELY AN hour later, Logan sat naked before his computer—naked because it seemed appropriate for revealing so bare a truth—held his breath for a long moment, then reluctantly tapped the Return key with his index finger. There. The blog post was live.

There was nothing unequivocal about the tale he had published for his many followers to read. It was pretty straightforward. The facts were laid out in a clear, concise, and unemotional manner. Still, he had passed no judgments. Logan had simply copied passages from the two manuscripts side by side—the original prose from the 1940s novel and Bryce's plagiarized version that had been released only the year before. Nothing was mentioned of Bryce's so-called Work in Progress, which he had read from at the meeting of the South Park Reading Club. Logan knew he had every right to mention it, but what would be the point? What he *did* put in the blog post would be more than enough to sink Bryce's career. And for that, Logan was truly sorry.

While Logan had worked at honing his words, Milo had joined him. Each man sat slumped at his own desk in their joint office while the dogs played and splashed in the pool outside, apparently having decided since their humans were up, they might as well get up too. The room was lit only by moonlight and the glow from Logan's computer screen.

Logan interrupted his work long enough to ask how Bryce had reacted to the news when Milo called him to tell him what was about to happen.

Milo sighed in the darkness. "I couldn't do it. I hung up."

Logan stared at Milo across the gloom of the dimly lit room. "Are you all right?"

Shaking his head, Milo refused to say anything more. It was as if he couldn't bear to talk about it. Logan had never seen such guilt in Milo's eyes. And worse, he couldn't believe he was the one who had caused that guilt to be there. Still, he knew—and Milo knew as well—that the truth had to come out. Sooner or later it *would* come out, either by Logan's pen or someone else's.

By the time Logan published the entry on his blog, the clock on his desk read 10:00 p.m. He powered down his computer and unplugged his phone. Milo did the same. They sat in the silent darkness inside the cluttered office while the California moon hovered outside, illuminating the dogs through the office window overlooking the pool. They had played themselves into exhaustion and were resting now, their coats wet, sprawled together on one of the chaise lounges. Emerson was lying on his back, his head propped against Spanky's tummy, both dogs sound asleep.

"How many followers do you have on your blog?" Milo quietly asked.

"Just shy of twenty thousand."

"Then the news will spread fast."

Sadly, Logan said, "Yes."

"And what about Bryce's publisher?"

This time it was Logan's turn to sigh. "I emailed Horizon Home Press a copy personally, outlining the proof of what I had posted. There is probably a shitstorm of damage control going through their offices even as we speak, or will be when they check their emails in the morning."

"Do you think either Bryce or the publishing house will be sued?"

Logan shrugged. "The original author is long dead. I looked him up. If he has family, who knows what they will do? But I have to say, I doubt this will end up in the courts. The original book wasn't particularly well received. It's not like the author's descendants are going to lose out on a lot of money because a plagiarized copy has come to light. A plagiarized copy, I might add, which was *also* pretty much a flop."

Milo didn't respond.

Still naked, Logan rose and quickly crossed the room, rolling his desk chair along behind him. He parked it directly in front of Milo's and dropped into it. Scooting forward so their knees touched, Logan leaned in to push Milo's robe aside and laid his hands on Milo's bare thighs, the feel of which, even after all their time together, still sent a tremor of hunger coursing through him. Staring at Milo's downturned face in the moonlight, he waited until those beautiful sad eyes came up to meet his own.

"Are we going to be all right?" Logan whispered. "Will you be able to forgive me for this?"

At that, Milo finally offered Logan a semblance of a smile.

"There's nothing to forgive," Milo softly said. "You're doing what you have to do. I understand that. And you're the one I love, Logan. Not Bryce. You seem to be forgetting that. Whatever you do, I'll stand beside you."

"But I've hurt you."

"No. If anything, I think Bryce is the one who hurt me. He hurt me by hurting himself. I'm surprised I care, but I do. I can't believe he would destroy himself like this. Could he really want something so badly he would risk his own reputation to achieve it? And how in God's name did he ever think he could get away with it?"

"He's not the first," Logan said sadly. "And I doubt he'll be the last. Plagiarism pops up every now and again. Sometimes even successful authors fall victim to it. You have the talent to have earned what you've made of your career, Milo. You're a successful writer. You've proven it with four wonderfully crafted, beautifully imaginative books. Unfortunately, everyone else isn't so blessed in their abilities."

They let the silence flow back into the room for just a minute. Then Milo reached over and clasped Logan's hand. "This will kill him, I think. Bryce won't survive this. To be a writer is all he's ever wanted."

"Let it go," Logan said in a barely audible hush. "Bryce is the one who decided to do what he did. The consequences of that decision have always been there waiting to bring him down. He must have known that. Now that the truth has come to light, he has to find the courage to face his mistakes."

Milo nodded, and once again the silence flowed in to replace the sound of their voices, stirring the echoes of their sorrow for what was about to happen.

"Come to bed," Logan pleaded, gently lifting his hand to caress Milo's neck. "You're exhausted. Let me hold you until you fall asleep." At those caring words, a single tear slid down Milo's cheek as Milo rose and shrugged his robe away.

Pressing a gentle hand to the velvet smoothness of Milo's back, Logan led him toward the bed.

HOURS LATER, they were wrenched from sleep by a howling uproar from the two dogs.

Milo's eyes flew open to the tinkle of glass and the thud of footsteps inside the house. Human footsteps. He reached out in the darkness and found Logan's familiar bulk next to him in the bed, right where he was supposed to be. Logan lay there as tense as Milo. The noise had woken him too.

"*Somebody's in the house!*" Milo hissed.

The dogs were going crazy now. In a panic, Milo threw himself out of bed. He tried to blink himself awake while hastily groping around in the dark to find his robe and pull it on. Across the bed, Logan did the same. The sounds were coming from the living room. The intruder was treading softly, but still the quiet, careful scuffle of his footfalls and the crunch of glass could be heard. The footsteps were drawing closer, approaching the hallway now as if the intruder knew exactly where Milo and Logan could be found inside the house. The dogs were out there too. Milo could hear them prancing around. Spanky had fallen silent. Only Emerson was now yipping and baying in his little Yorkie voice. Whoever approached muttered a string of whispered curses at the racket Emerson was making.

Milo whirled around to scan the room, seeking a weapon, *any* weapon, but Logan didn't bother. Hands balled into angry fists, he hurled himself through the bedroom door, so Milo hustled right behind him.

The house was dark. Emerson's piercing cries filled the shadows. Past the end of the hall, a figure crossed the path of moonlight seeping through the living room window. It looked like a man. A tall, thin man. He was moving toward them. Spanky was at his side. Oddly, Spanky's tail was wagging even while the Yorkie still danced and bayed around the intruder, threatening him with mayhem if he proceeded any farther.

When the figure stepped away from the noisy little dog, Milo instantly recognized him by his gait and his silhouette.

"Bryce!" he bellowed, stepping forward and pushing Logan behind him. "What the fuck are you doing here, and how did you get in?" Then he remembered the crunch and tinkle of broken glass. Incredulous, he said, "Did you break a window?"

Between Emerson's yapping and Spanky's happy hello barks aimed at the man he knew only as a friend, Milo could barely hear himself think. Angrily, he cried, "You, dogs! Come!"

Spanky and Emerson slunk toward him, momentarily cowed by their master's command. At the same time, the hall was suddenly flooded with light as Logan reached around Milo and flipped the wall switch.

Bryce stood in the archway leading from the living room. The moment the lights came up, he froze in his tracks. Milo had never seen him so wide-eyed and unkempt. His hair was a mess, his clothes disheveled. There was a cut on the back of his hand. Blood was dripping from it onto the floor at his feet.

"You've cut yourself," Milo declared.

Bryce stared at him. His expression was a mixture of stunned surprise and a little boy's guilt at finding himself caught. With the first hint of rage twisting his features, his gaze trailed away from Milo to glare at Logan standing behind him. The fury in Bryce's eyes morphed to hatred in an instant. His voice was ice. "I thought if I got inside, I could stop you. Make you delete the post. It's the middle of the night. Maybe no one has read it yet."

Word had indeed traveled fast. There was no need to wonder what he meant. This time it was Logan who stepped into the lead, easing Milo to safety behind him. His eyes never once veered away from Bryce's hateful gaze. "You know that's impossible," Logan said. "Even if I wanted to, it can't be taken back now."

Bryce continued to stare at him. Then suddenly the hatred on his face began to fade, his gaze softened into emptiness, his eyes dulled. A tiny, horrendous smile arose, twisting the corners of his mouth. "So my goose is truly cooked, then."

Logan nodded. "Your publisher knows too." His words were gently uttered and laced with pity. "It's all over, Bryce. You can stop living a lie now. You can let all the subterfuge go, take a step back, and just be who you were meant to be."

"Who I was meant to be," Bryce echoed, his shoulders slumped, his voice drained of emotion.

Logan took a step forward, arms out in a consoling gesture. "Come into the kitchen," he said. "Let Milo treat your cut while I make some coffee. Then we'll talk."

At that moment, Milo spotted the gun in Bryce's other hand. It was a small Saturday night special, so tiny that it fit snugly in Bryce's fist, rendering it almost invisible. Milo recognized it as a Raven Arms MP-25, the .25 caliber semiautomatic Bryce had owned when they were together. Tonight was the first time Milo had ever seen it out of its box.

Milo stood there, his eyes riveted on the gun. He stared at it for what seemed like hours. Then he reached forward and plucked at Logan's sleeve, pulling him to a stop. Of Bryce he quietly asked, "What are you planning to do with that gun?"

Milo's words caught Logan's attention. His gaze snapped to where Milo was staring at the gun. He stiffened.

Bryce glanced down at the pistol in his uninjured hand as if surprised to see it there himself. He handled it clumsily, as though it felt alien in his hand. Still he never once took his finger off the trigger. "I guess you'll find out soon enough what it's for," he said with a smirk. "But before all that, I thought I could scare you with it. That's what people usually do with guns, isn't it? Threaten? Frighten? Bully? I used it to break the window too, but still, a shard of glass fell and...."

He tore his gaze from the gun and stared at his bleeding hand with a funny expression, as if realizing for the first time that breaking a window probably wasn't the smartest thing he'd ever done. Nor was packing a weapon. His eyes rose again, centering on Logan's face. There was no anger in them now, just a weary acceptance, as if everything he had tried to do had come to naught and he was just beginning to realize it. "I thought I could stop it, is all," he mumbled, his voice failing. "Just somehow scare you into… stopping it."

"You can't," Logan said again. "I'm sorry. Like I told you before, it's already done."

"I know. I guess I knew before I got here." Bryce gave a sardonic chuckle, as if he were starting to see the humor in it all. "A little birdie told me."

"A little birdie?" Milo asked.

Bryce nodded.

"Was it Adrian Strange?" Milo gently asked. "Is he the one who told you? What happened? Did he stumble onto Logan's website? Is that how you found out?"

"Yes," Bryce said around a sigh. Clenching his injured hand, he caused the blood to drip faster. He didn't seem to notice. "Earlier in the evening, a phone call woke us up."

"That was me," Milo interjected.

"Oh. I should have known," Bryce said around an odd little smile. Then he picked up his train of thought. "Adrian doesn't sleep well, you know. He's up all hours of the night, roaming through the apartment, piddling with the computer. He saw Logan's post only minutes after it went live. And then… he stormed out." His eyes slid to Logan's face.

"But first, he woke me up and asked if it was true. I knew more lies couldn't save me, so I told him everything. He said he didn't want to be involved with me any longer. Not after the truth comes out. He said he wouldn't let himself be dragged down with me. And that's when he left. Without so much as saying goodbye. He practically ran out the door, never once looking back. He—he told me he loved me, you know. Not that I really believed him. People always say they love you, don't they? I think sometimes it's just the way they fill up the empty spaces in the conversation."

A sad smile turned up the corners of his mouth. "I don't suppose I can blame him, really. For leaving, I mean. He has his own pitiful career to protect. In the grand scheme of things, that's far more important than fucking a plagiarist, don't you think?"

Bryce studied Milo's face. "Want to hear something funny? It was only tonight that Adrian told me he loved me. Can you believe it?" His eyes misted over. "I guess I wasn't the *only* liar, huh?"

"I'm sorry about Adrian. I am," Milo said. "But then, why are you here? If you knew it was too late to stop it, why did you come? And why did you bring a gun?"

Incongruously, Bryce giggled. He gave his injured hand a flip as if it was finally starting to hurt. Blood spattered the wall beside him, but he didn't notice. He leveled his gaze on Milo's face once again, homing in, the anger quickly surging back.

"Oh, I'm here because of *another* little birdie who was fluttering around the internet and saw your lover's post. A birdie with ideas."

Milo glanced again at the gun. "What sort of ideas? What do you mean?"

"More death," he said, his eyes bright and teasing. "It's really very clever. Sort of a plot twist, you see. Or maybe you *don't* see. Not yet anyway."

Milo was not only confused now, he was also getting mad. He practically spat out the words. "What the hell are you talking about? And what do you mean, more death? Are you saying there's going to be more killing?"

"He means us," Logan said softly. "He means he's going to kill us."

Milo whirled around to face him. "*What?*"

Bryce stared at Logan, looking almost comically surprised. "You've got it all wrong," he said calmly, *too* calmly. "Whatever happens in this house tonight won't be done to you. Well, not really." His eyes grew cold.

"I can't take back what you've done, Logan, but I can still watch you pay for it. I can make you *both* pay for it by doing what *I* have to do."

"Revenge." Logan laughed. The word slipped through his lips as if he finally understood. "So that's why you're here. Not to apologize. Not to say you're sorry. But for revenge."

Bryce offered his most charming smile yet. It was so free of guile, it was almost sane. "Yes, BookHunter. That's exactly why I'm here."

"You're crazy," Milo said. "If you're not going to kill us, then how do you plan on making us pay? And what do you mean, do what you have to do? What the hell sort of revenge are you talking about?"

Another smile twisted Bryce's mouth. He seemed to have an endless supply, each one a little different than the others. This one seethed with a caustic irony. "You'll see," he said, while the blood dripped freely from his hand. "For now, I'll just let you in on a little secret, guys. I'm not the only one who's crazy here. That one's crazy too. But crazy like a fox."

"Who?" Logan asked. "Who are you talking about? Tell us, Bryce. We don't understand."

Milo could sense Logan trying to distract Bryce. He was getting ready to spring. *Oh, God, what if he gets himself shot?*

But at that moment, a cell phone rang. The ringtone was muted and unfamiliar. It wasn't Milo's phone, or Logan's either. It took Milo a second to realize the phone was in Bryce's pocket.

Bryce giggled, hearing it. "Oops," he whispered childishly, conspiratorially. "Speaking of the devil. I bet I know who *that* is."

"In that case," Milo said, his voice dripping with sarcasm, "maybe you'd better answer it." If nothing else, it would give him a little time to figure out what to do. Or to stop Logan from doing something crazy.

Behind Milo, the dogs must have felt the tension building in their masters. They started whimpering again, edging closer, trying to get past. Milo impatiently shushed them to silence and motioned them back.

Bryce grinned insipidly at first Milo, then Logan, as if nothing about this scenario was odd at all. The anger and hatred on his face had fled, replaced by what looked like pure, unadulterated glee. But the glee never quite reached his eyes. Instead, what Milo saw there, mixed in with fear, was a manic glimmer of determination and a renewal of purpose that scared Milo more than anything else that had happened all night. The blood was staining Bryce's pant leg now, dribbling onto his shoe. Milo could hear the slow patter of it when it fell. It was an eerie horror-movie sound that sent a chill up his spine. Without thinking about it, he edged closer to Logan. His harbor. His safe place.

The phone continued to ring.

Bryce seemed almost disinterested now, as if his mood had shifted yet again in the last five seconds. "Yes, I guess you're right. I'd better answer it. The other little birdie might be getting impatient." Suddenly his eyes danced merrily, and he gave an exaggerated shudder. "We don't want to piss *that* one off, do we?"

Bryce blithely pulled the cell phone from his pocket with his bloody hand and pressed it to his ear. A trickle of blood slid down his wrist. Milo glanced at Logan to see his reaction to everything that was happening, but Logan merely stood there staring at Bryce. Worry lines were etched into his forehead now, as if he was beginning to feel the first glimmer of fear.

Strangely enough, with Logan at his side, Milo felt no fear. The situation was simply too flat-out weird for it to harbor any danger, either to himself or to Logan. The only real concern Milo felt was for Bryce—the emptiness in his eyes coupled with the glint of determination, the slack line of his jaw, the way he could warp into hysterical laughter from one moment to the next, the way he let his wound continue to drip blood onto the floor without trying to staunch the flow. All of it put together was just… nuts. And it was a bad cut. Surely to God it hurt. Why was he not doing something to stop the bleeding or alleviate the pain?

And why is he still holding that fucking gun?

Logan stepped forward, but Milo plucked at his arm, holding him back. "Wait," he quietly pleaded.

Milo sensed Logan was reluctant to obey, but he finally did. He stopped in his tracks and pulled Milo against him, as if with closeness he would be better able to protect him. When he did, Logan's robe fell open. He casually pulled it back together, covering his nakedness, looping the cloth belt around himself to hold it in place, while with his other hand he gestured for the increasingly nervous dogs to stay back. Finished, he pulled Milo closer while his eyes never wavered from Bryce, who was still standing at the end of the hall with the phone pressed to his ear.

"We can rush him," Logan whispered. "Let me take the side with the gun."

"No!" Milo hissed. "He won't hurt us. I know him."

Logan didn't look convinced. His gaze fell again on the pistol in Bryce's hand.

Bryce spoke into the phone, his voice bright and cheery as if he were totally uninterested in what Logan and Milo were whispering about. "Yes?" The one word was lazily drawn out as if muttered by a sleepwalker. At the same time, he gave Milo an incongruous wink.

Then, clearly from the cell phone Bryce held to his ear, Milo heard the caller's sharp, agitated voice spilling out into the room.

"Don't just do what you said you'd do! Kill them first, you fool! Kill them now!"

Chapter Fifteen

"Idiot," the traveler spat.

Dressed in coveralls, latex gloves, and a watch cap in case the night got bloody, which was a distinct possibility, the figure in the shadows stuffed the cell phone back inside a rear pocket while staring up the steep canyon wall, surveying the terrain.

The undergrowth had been cleared from around the edge of the house, a common practice in drought-stricken California to limit property damage from wildfires. It made the approach far easier than it otherwise might have been. The tall figure could have simply walked up to the front door of the house and knocked, of course, but why risk being seen by the neighbors when Bryce might very well do what needed to be done without any help at all?

It was a long shot, of course. Bryce was weak. Otherwise he wouldn't be in the mess he was in. Of course, being in that mess was what made him so easily exploited.

After all, it was time to wind this up, and a better opportunity would never come along. The killings had garnered enough publicity. Trolls on the internet were holding back now, being less cruel with their reviews, showing more civility, probably out of fear of being punished for their bad manners, as they damn well should be. Consequently, the work was finished. It was time to end it now, not with a light touch, but with a grand statement, a big showstopping finale. Something they wouldn't soon forget. It was time for the traveler to tie up the loose ends and go back to a normal life. But to do that, a scapegoat had to be found. If the police weren't convinced they had unearthed the real killer, they would never give up. So it was time to cough up a sacrificial goat. And this one last explosive act, this final bloody crime scene, should very well do the trick.

If the wooden fence at the back of the property had been six inches higher, it would have proven unscalable. As it was, however, the tall figure scrambled across the top easily enough. The people inside the house would pay no heed to the sound of someone scuffling up and over the back fence. They had other things to worry about. Someone *else* sneaking onto the property would be the last thing they'd expect after good old Bryce came crashing through the living room window with all the finesse of a rampaging elephant.

The patio lights had been turned off for the night, but the underwater pool lights were still lit. Filtered through the shimmering water, they cast an eerie green rippling light across the back of the house. It was kind of creepy, actually, looking for all the world like the bilious green glow from a radar screen in a darkened com center in the bowels of some far-off ship plying a lonely sea.

The lean figure chuckled. Nice simile. Might be able to work that into a book someday. An *unplagiarized* book. And *that* thought fired up another chuckle.

Stepping carefully around the glowing pool, the shadowy figure heard voices now coming through the open patio door that led into the house. The first footfall across the threshold into the kitchen brought the dogs running. The figure hastily stepped back outside, and the dogs shot through the door in chase. As they began to bark and wail at this new intruder—jeez, it must be an exciting night for them—the figure quickly stepped back inside the house and closed the sliding door in the dogs' faces. They obviously weren't the smartest watchdogs in the world.

The traveler wagged a mocking, admonitory finger through the glass at their furious upturned faces and then quickly turned away to walk deeper into the house, letting the dogs rant and rail and scratch at the sliding door all they wanted. Once again, the occupants were too busy with their own problems to be worried about anything else, least of all a couple of moronic mutts yammering on and on...

...while a real murderer strolled in through the back door.

The figure stood frozen, listening to the sounds in the other parts of the house. Voices. Two closer, one farther away. The one farther away was Bryce. Why the hell was he still talking? He should be acting. Taking matters into his own hands. Wreaking his revenge, like he had said he would. *Owning* the situation. Not for the first time, the figure suspected the person chosen to help wrap this thing up might not be entirely up to the task. Bryce's weaknesses made him easily coerced, but those same weaknesses made him unreliable as well.

Of course, this whole plan was pretty much a fly-by-the-seat-of-your-pants operation. It had been sheer luck spotting Logan's blog post. And from there, it was the simplest thing in the world to assume that Bryce would be itching to confront his accuser. A quick phone call unearthed the fact that Bryce already knew about it, and not five minutes before, his new lover had dumped him because of it. Adrian Strange always was a selfish little prick. The figure standing in Milo's kitchen was not in the least surprised Strange had taken off running at the first whiff of trouble, leaving his poor young lover to deal with it on his own.

Deeper in the residence, the voices went on and on. Christ, what was this, a coffee klatch?

It was becoming increasingly clear that Bryce would not kill the two. Even after the traveler rushed to Bryce's apartment and consoled him over the loss of his lover, then spent long hours convincing him of other things, more *important* things, it was obvious now that Bryce simply wasn't motivated—or cold-blooded—enough to do what needed to be done. Oh, he might be desperate enough to blow his own brains out—after all, that was his idea, not the traveler's—but still, suicide was only half the task. Upping his game to murder had always been problematic at best. Truthfully, the traveler had expected it to be. But that was okay. In the end, all that was really needed from poor dumb Bryce were a few fingerprints, a little trace evidence, and above all else, a motive.

What Bryce lacked in gumption and killing skills, his newfound friend would supply. Happily. Bryce had only to provide a warm body and a convenient stooge for the cops to pin the other murders on. After all, Logan Hunter was a reviewer. All the other victims were reviewers too. It continued the pattern. As for the unfortunate Milo Cook, well, he would be simply collateral damage. Still, his bloody corpse would help make for a grand closing statement.

The newspaper story would practically write itself.

> *Author strikes back at unfair reviews, murdering three, then with the threat of being exposed as a plagiarist, goes after one more. Killing not only the reviewer but the reviewer's gay lover in the process and bringing the body count to five.*

The shadowy figure stood in the glow of the pool in the unfamiliar kitchen, eyes closed, imagining the front-page story in the *San Diego Union-Tribune*, the story that would then be picked up by newspapers across the country.

> *Stricken with guilt by the murders he had committed, the author, knowing his career and freedom would soon be over, turned the gun upon himself, closing out the last chapter of his own personal thriller. If only he could have written a story as exciting as the one he lived—and died in—he might not have needed to resort to plagiarism at all.*

The traveler grinned and took a quiet step deeper into the house, drawing ever closer to the voices in the hall.

BRYCE SLIPPED his cell phone into his pocket while gazing apologetically at Logan and Milo.

"Apparently someone is getting impatient," he said with a smirk. "So just to be on the safe side…." And with an amused little *tsk*, Bryce lifted the gun and pointed it straight at Logan's heart.

"No!" Milo cried.

Logan stretched out his arm and gently pushed Milo away. If he was about to be shot, he had no intention of letting Milo be taken down with him.

He studied Bryce's face, Bryce's eyes. There was a disconnect there, Logan thought. The guy was losing his grip on reality, if he ever had a grip on it to begin with. But it was the phone call that most disturbed Logan. And the words Logan had heard the caller say.

"Who was that on the phone, Bryce? Who called you and told you to kill us? Who is this person? Why do they want us dead? At least tell us that!"

Bryce smiled, and then he laughed outright. "What? You don't like the idea of dying? I admit it's upping the game plan a bit, but still, you don't think it's dramatic? You don't think it would fit well inside the closing chapter of a book? You don't think it makes for an exciting denouement to our little drama?"

While Bryce talked, Milo once again edged closer to Logan. He stood there now, his shoulder plastered to Logan's as if daring Logan to push him away again. So Logan snaked an arm around his waist, accepting his presence, holding him close.

Logan tried to speak calmly and patiently, like he might reason with a child. "This isn't a book, Bryce. It isn't fiction. This is your life. This is *all* of our lives. Who called you? Who put you up to this? It's not too late to back out. If someone has coerced you into doing this, you have other options. You can fight back. Or simply walk away."

Bryce gave a huff of annoyance. "That's all good for you. Saves your ass quite nicely, doesn't it? Doesn't do much for me, though. My career will still be ruined. My life will still be over."

"No," Milo said. "Your life will not be over. This isn't your closing chapter unless you want it to be. You can still write a whole new life. You can start over and do it properly this time. Find another outlet for your talents. But only if you stop this now. If you pull the trigger on that gun and hurt one of us—or yourself—you really will be lost. Think, Bryce. Please. Just think about what you're doing."

Logan laid a hand to Milo's back, taking a fistful of his robe in case he needed to pull him away in a hurry or shove him out of danger. His eyes never left Bryce's face. Or the gun in Bryce's hand.

Logan spoke up now, following the thread of what Milo had said. "If you tell us who coerced you into doing this, Bryce, we can call the police. Do what Milo says, Bryce. Think! This is your chance to do the right thing. Don't let this person exploit you because of the mistakes you've made. You're as appalled by all the killing as we are. I know you are. You're a good person, Bryce. Don't let yourself become a part of this."

"Please, Bryce," Milo pleaded. "Think."

"I am thinking," Bryce said, and with a tiny metallic click, he released the safety on the gun.

TREADING SOFTLY, the intruder ducked through the doorway to the left of the kitchen, entering a bedroom. The bed was unmade, the blankets hastily flung into a heap. At the opposite end of the room was another door. Stepping around the bed, the figure silently approached that door, easing it open to peer inside. This was an office. Two desks, two computers—currently turned off—a shitload of bookcases squeezed in here and there, each and every one of them packed tight with books.

The hallway was to the left, and the door leading out to it was open. From this vantage point, Logan and Milo were standing just outside the door in their bathrobes, facing poor old Bryce, the nitwit who had a gun but was too afraid to use it.

The traveler crossed this room too, advancing parallel to the hallway, moving stealthily through the shadows, then onward through another doorway to step out into a large living room that spanned the entire front of the house. Off to the right, shards of glass sprinkled the floor where Bryce had bulldozed his way inside by smashing a window. The figure gave a silent, exasperated cluck. What? Bryce had never heard of a doorbell? The curtains on the shattered window were billowing in the late-night breeze. The air was chilly and damp. It would be dawn in a couple of hours.

The room was unlit; the only light was what spilled out from the end of the hallway where Bryce was standing with his back to the room…

…and to the person standing unseen in the shadows behind him.

The lean figure stood stock-still, listening to how the evening's entertainment was progressing. Frankly, it didn't sound promising. Bryce was never going to shoot these people. That much was obvious. As usual, a firmer hand would be needed.

The figure in the shadows edged closer, as silent as a cat. Creeping ever nearer, the traveler pulled a gun from a jacket pocket.

This gun, unlike the gun in Bryce's hand, did not feel awkward at all.

This gun, even through latex gloves, felt like a friend.

"LISTEN TO me," Milo pleaded. "Put the gun down. Don't let this person talk you into doing what you clearly don't want to do. If you kill us, you'll be the first person the police suspect. You are the person Logan exposed tonight on his blog. They'd be crazy not to suspect you."

"Don't worry, Milo. I'm not going to kill you," Bryce monotoned around a vacant smile. "I've decided to stick to my original plan. After that, there won't be anything the police can do to me anyway. There won't be anything *anyone* can do to me."

His smile remained fixed and vacant as he lifted the Saturday night special and placed the tip of the barrel to his own temple. As if the metal felt cool and refreshing against his skin, and as if the touch had been too long coming, Bryce leaned his head into the gun and gratefully closed his eyes.

Milo and Logan both gasped.

At that moment, from around the corner of the arched doorway leading to the room beside him, a throaty voice sang out from the darkness. "Stop being so maudlin! Just do it, Bryce! Christ! *I* don't need you anymore. *Nobody* needs you anymore. Pull the trigger, and I'll finish this business myself."

Startled, and with the gun barrel still pressed to the side of his head, Bryce spun toward the voice.

The moment Bryce turned, Logan charged. But as quickly as his charge began, the second figure stepped into the light and raised a gun, aiming the barrel directly at Logan's heart as Bryce had done before.

Logan skidded to a stop, and Milo smashed into him from behind. He wrapped his arms around Logan, and they stood there together, staring in shock at the second intruder.

"You!" Milo cried in disbelief.

Lois Knight blinked coquettish eyes and gave him a perky little wink. "Hello, boys," she said coyly. "Surprised?"

NEVER ALLOWING her gun to waver from Logan's heart, she smirked at Bryce, who was standing there like a fool with the gun still aimed at his own head.

"Pull the trigger, dear," she calmly said. "If you don't, I will."

Before Bryce could make a move one way or another, Logan spoke up, once again trying to push Milo out of the line of fire.

"You don't really think you can kill all of us, do you?"

"We'll see," she said. "It shouldn't be that difficult."

"*You* killed them!" Milo exclaimed, suddenly seeing the truth for the first time, suddenly understanding *everything*. "Grace and the other two reviewers! *You're* the murderer!"

"Holy shit, you're right!" Logan mumbled under his breath. At the same moment, Bryce gaped at the woman in shock.

Lois smirked, ignoring Logan and Bryce both, aiming her reply at Milo instead. "Please, don't call them reviewers. That's far grander than they deserve. But I'm afraid I did kill them, yes. There was a lot of traveling involved, don't think there wasn't. You should see my Visa statement. But in the end it was worth it. The trolls have backed off. Have you noticed? They've learned a little humility, I think. Or maybe they're just afraid of having an ice pick stuck through their brain like poor old

BooksOnWheels. Don't look so shocked. I only did what I had to do. You know what those people were like! God knows I've seen enough of my books trashed by unfair reviews. My royalties have plummeted! Why should I stand back and let these trolls destroy my livelihood?"

"You should have been strong enough to ignore them!" Milo yelled.

"Well, I'm not!" she screamed right back. "And why should I *have* to be? They got exactly what they deserved, and I'm glad I'm the one who gave it to them."

Milo couldn't believe he was standing there arguing with a killer. He chased down memories in his head. "But at the meeting you said you were appalled by their deaths!"

Lois laughed. "No. I was appalled by the killer being called a madman, as if implying only an insane man could have been strong enough to accomplish it. It was insulting and sexist." She turned to Bryce and with a simper added, "You and Adrian Strange are both pompous asses. You're well shed of each other. Just so you know."

Then, seeing what Bryce was still doing, she impatiently slapped the gun away from his temple. "Oh, do put that down if you're not going to use it."

Turning back to Milo and Logan, she hooked a thumb in Bryce's direction. "It's because of people like this that I work alone. Totally worthless. A coward, really. And a *plagiarist*, of all things. Even I was surprised by that little plot twist. Didn't see it coming at all."

"It wasn't like that…," Bryce mumbled.

But Lois only tutted. "I'm afraid it was *exactly* like that, and you damn well know it."

"You read my post," Logan interrupted.

Turning to him, she laughed. "Not more than two minutes after it went live. Lovely work, by the way. Succinctly written. Excellent grammar. When you set out to destroy a career, you really destroy a career. Of course, I knew Bryce would have no choice but to confront you, especially if I egged him on. After all, thanks to you he has nothing more to lose. It's a shame about you two boys, though, but then Logan's exposé on little Bryce here afforded me a perfect opportunity to duck out of the murder game while I have a chance."

"The murder game…?" Bryce muttered, looking confused.

"You're crazy," Logan said, ignoring Bryce just like everyone else in the room.

Lois smiled. "Am I? Of course, ruining Bryce's career isn't all you accomplished. You've also given Bryce a reason to kill himself, and to go out with an audience to boot. He thinks if he blows his brains out in front of you, see, you and sweet Milo will spend the rest of your lives wallowing in guilt for exposing him as a plagiarist. I convinced him of that. I also tried to convince him to kill you as well, while he was at it, but no-go apparently. He'd rather have you feel guilty about his suicide. What he doesn't realize is that the rest of your lives isn't going to amount to much. A matter of minutes, if that."

"Fuck you," Milo said.

Her smile broadened ever farther. Clearly, the cursing barely jarred her composure at all. "As far as revenge goes, it's pretty pathetic, I know. But frankly, it's about all Bryce is worth. The real prize here is that you've also made him my scapegoat and given me a chance to close up shop and save myself. Not only was the fool weak enough to come up with his crazyass plan, but he even brought his own gun to the party. It's all just serendipitous as hell, don't you think?"

"N-no," Bryce stammered. "What the hell are you talking about? It's not supposed to be this way. This isn't what you told me."

She let her gaze slide from Milo to Logan, then back again, ignoring Bryce completely, as if he simply did not matter. "At least I got him here. By doing that, half the battle is won. Otherwise I'd have had to kill him somewhere else, if he didn't do the job himself, then schlepp his body into your house. No easy task for a lady. Anyway, where was I? Oh yes. The trolls. I knew my work was done, you see. I had made my point. Taught those three assholes a lesson. Like I said before, trolling on the internet has now decreased substantially. Reviews are nicer. Not that I've ever had a problem with professional reviewers such as you, Logan. You've always been a gentleman. But some of the others! How nasty they could be. Anyway, when I saw your post about poor stupid Bryce, I knew he'd come after you. For a confrontation, at least. Maybe a bit of last-minute whining and wheedling. What better chance for me to wrap up the last chapter in this melodrama and retire? With poor Bryce taking the blame for everything. It was just too good to pass up."

"So instead of trying to talk him out of killing himself, you convinced him to kill himself here in front of us," Logan said. "And once he's done that, you'll set things up to look like he killed us too. And the other three victims as well."

Lois offered a bashful smile, as if she'd been given a compliment. "Brilliant, isn't it? And as for Bryce, it's the best thing for him, really. Save himself a lifetime of humiliation after you branded him a plagiarist. Of course, I had really hoped he would kill you too, but at this point in the evening, I think that's a bit of a long shot, don't you?"

"That's impossible!" Milo seethed. "You won't get away with it! Bryce, you don't have to go along with this!"

Bryce's gaze skittered to Milo's face, then quickly returned to the woman beside him. A dawning hatred flared in Bryce's eyes, on Bryce's weary, handsome face. The muscles clenched in his jaw as he stared at her, obviously appalled by the way she talked about him, *mocked* him, treated him like nothing, as if he weren't even there. And most of all, how she had manipulated him.

Seeing Bryce's fury swell, a flurry of hope surged through Milo. Lois was too busy gloating to notice Bryce's growing anger. She still stared at Logan and Milo, her eyes veering continually from one to the other while the cocky smile remained plastered on her face.

"Oh, I'll get away with it," she said. "A little rearranging of the evidence. A few extra fingerprints, gunpowder residue transferred from the murder weapon to Bryce's hand after a final errant shot. That's all it will take. I've written mysteries," she added sagely. "I'm not a novice. I know what to do."

Milo cried out, his words pleading. "Bryce, don't let her pin this on you!"

At that, Lois truly did laugh. And with cold-blooded grace, she swung the gun around and pressed it neatly to Bryce's head. "Oh, he'll let me pin it on him, all right. He won't have a choice. He'll be dead. And as the pirates in all those swashbuckling sea stories used to say, dead men tell no tales. Like I said, our sweet little Bryce has decided to kill himself anyway. Why the hell shouldn't I profit from that?"

Bryce's eyes popped open wide. The loathing in them was almost staggering now, but still Lois didn't notice. Or care. Oddly, Bryce still let his own gun dangle uselessly from his hand, seemingly forgotten.

"Shoot her!" Milo yelled. "Shoot her before she shoots you!"

But Bryce would not. He simply stood there, his gaze suddenly filled with a terrible clarity, reeling from the realization that he had been played for a chump from the very beginning. The truth of it was written plainly across his tortured face.

Still holding her gun to his temple, Lois studied Bryce's expression as if she had never seen a creature more pathetic.

"See?" she said, watching Bryce but speaking to Milo and Logan. "See how easy it is? People see death approaching, and they simply shut down. Rarely do they fight back. Especially the cowards."

Speaking in a coldly mocking tone, as if she had not the least expectation in the world of having her request refused, she said, "You'll do what I say now, won't you, dear? Lift your gun, Bryce. Lift your gun, press it to your temple, and pull the trigger. If you don't, I'll do it for you. I can mimic a suicide victim's contact wound if I have to, but it just dawned on me that it will simplify matters greatly to have the gunpowder residue already on your hands. Then I'll use the same gun to dispose of the others. Or I can shoot you and the others with my own gun and leave it in your hand when I leave. It'll be a little more work, but I don't mind. Really I don't. The choice is up to you, dear. Just make a decision. I'm tired of waiting."

"Bryce!" Milo yelled. "For Christ's sake, fight back! Shoot her!"

Bryce's gaze never once veered from Lois's face.

To Milo's surprise, tears suddenly spilled from Bryce's eyes. As if hypnotized by her words, he began to raise the gun.

"Bryce, I loved you once," Milo pleaded. "Don't do this. Don't hurt yourself. I don't want to see you die."

Lois snorted at that. "Unfortunately, Bryce doesn't hold the same reverence for you. Or even for himself. Do you, Bryce? You really will be better off dead, you know. Your career is ruined. You'll be a laughingstock for the rest of your life. You'll never publish another word. Not that you ever really did. Not your *own* words anyway."

"She's mocking you!" Logan bellowed. "Fucking shoot her!"

But Bryce simply stood there, slowly raising the gun, turning the barrel toward himself now, preparing to nestle it against the side of his head again, exactly as she commanded him to do.

"I'm going to stop this," Logan hissed in Milo's ear, but before he could spring forward, Lois snapped toward him, leveling the gun this time directly at Milo's throat.

"If you move an inch, there will be no more deep-throating from your precious Milo because he won't have a throat left to deep-throat *with*! Of course, your deep-throating days are pretty much over anyway, don't you think? I mean, what with you both about to be dead and all."

Milo and Logan froze. In the same instant, Bryce blinked the tears from his eyes and straightened his shoulders. He glanced at the gun in his hand, then back to the woman standing beside him.

"It's time I did one thing right," he said quietly, and as soon as the words were fully uttered, he raised his pistol the rest of the way. Swiveling it quickly away from himself, he pulled the trigger.

Before the least amount of surprise could register on Lois's face, a perfectly round, cherry-red hole appeared in her forehead. At the very same moment a rosette of blood and brain matter, far less neat than the wound in the front, exploded from the back of her head. The blast of the gunshot echoed through the house. The brimstone reek of gunpowder filled the air, and a teeny wisp of smoke wafted from the barrel of Bryce's Saturday night special, just like it might in the movies.

As if the Great Puppeteer had snipped her strings, Lois Knight collapsed in a heap at Bryce's feet.

Still in shock, Logan and Milo took a step forward. Only one. For no sooner had they taken that one step than Bryce spun gracefully toward them. Once again he aimed his gun directly at Logan's heart.

"No," Milo gasped. He clutched at Logan's hand, pleading, refusing to let him go. "No, Bryce. Please. Don't take him from me."

But Bryce merely smiled as a tear slid down his cheek. It hung sparkling from his chin, catching the light like a tiny star.

When he spoke, his voice was strong and hale again. It was almost as if nothing had happened at all. He brushed the tear from his chin with the back of his bloodied hand, and his face sweetly softened.

"I loved you once too, Milo. You made me happy for a while, and not many people have done that." He paused for a moment as a hint of sadness touched his eyes, but only a hint. "What's about to happen isn't your fault. It's mine. So don't blame yourself. I'll be happier for it. I know I will." With a final, truer smile lighting his face, he said jokingly, "I'm sorry about ruining your carpet, but then I never really liked it anyway."

As his eyes narrowed in a tiny flash of self-mocking laughter, he at long last did what Lois Knight had told him to do. Never letting his sweet gaze leave Milo's face, he lifted the gun to his head, pressed the barrel snugly to his temple, and fired it once again.

The silence that followed was deafening.

Chapter Sixteen

EXEUNT OMNES... and the actors leave the stage

Logan and Milo strolled along the promenade in Seaport Village, staring out at San Diego Bay while dusk dimmed the water from blue to black. The navigation lights of sailboats blinked on here and there as darkness deepened. Up ahead where it was docked permanently at Navy Pier, the lights of the massive aircraft carrier, the *USS Midway*, now a museum, flashed into life at the foot of Broadway. The reek of low tide lay heavy on the air, smelling vaguely of sea tales and tall ships. As if mocking their imaginations, seabirds made raucous comments high above their heads.

"It's so beautiful here," Logan murmured, tightening his fingers around Milo's hand.

Emerson and Spanky led the way. Emerson, never still even in sleep, was making a game of weaving in and out between Spanky's legs and ducking under Spanky's belly, purposely tangling their leashes, which he seemed to find highly amusing. For the umpteenth time, Logan and Milo stopped to unsnarl them, and no sooner were they finished than Emerson set about tangling them again.

As they resumed their stroll, once again hand in hand, Milo's voice blended softly with the cries of seagulls and the a cappella song of a buoy bell chiming merrily in the distance.

"We walked along here on our first date. Do you remember?"

Logan's eyes softened. "Yes, I remember. I think I loved you before that first walk was over."

Milo scoffed. "No, you didn't."

Logan simply smiled to himself, a little superciliously, refusing to argue. He knew what he knew. If Milo didn't believe him, it was no skin off his nose.

They stopped and leaned against the sea wall, gazing out at the water. Milo dug two dog biscuits out of his pocket and dropped them at his feet. Emerson and Spanky snatched them out of the air before they ever hit the ground.

"I keep thinking about Bryce," Milo said.

Logan agreed softly, "I know you have."

Milo snuck a glance at Logan's face. "Has it been that obvious?"

Logan lifted Milo's hand and pressed it to his lips. "You wouldn't be human if you didn't. It was a sad thing all around. Lois Knight destroyed a lot of lives. I don't imagine she's enjoying a cup of tea in heaven tonight."

"No," Milo agreed. "I don't suppose she is." After a moment, he added. "Bryce was right about the old carpet, you know. It sucked. I never did like it either."

Logan offered a weary chuckle while laying a soothing hand to Milo's arm. "Well, it's no longer there, so you don't have to hate it anymore."

They had just spent six days trapped in a motel with the two dogs. First, the police had thrown them out of their own house for three days while the crime scene was processed. When the cops were gone, it had taken another three days for the carpet in the house, irreparably soaked in blood, to be removed, the hardwood floors refinished, and the furniture put back in place. They had talked about simply repairing the bloodstained area in the hall, but Milo had pointed out that every time he looked at it, a host of unwanted memories would come flooding back. That was the last thing Logan wanted for him. Now that the work was finished, they liked the hardwood floors better anyway.

"He wasn't a bad person, you know. I think if Bryce had one overriding fault, it was weakness. I also think if he had lived, if he had stuck to his dream of being a writer, he might even have succeeded, even *with* a charge of plagiarism sullying his past. He could have overcome it if he worked hard enough. He might have one day seen his dream become a reality. If only he hadn't… done what he did."

As they resumed their stroll, Logan edged closer and draped a comforting arm over Milo's shoulder. "He didn't want you to feel bad about what happened to him at the end. He said as much, Milo. And I think you're right. It was his weakness that killed him. He wasn't strong enough to face what was about to happen to him. The disgrace and shame brought about by the plagiarism charge was too much for him to handle. I suppose he felt he was taking the only way out he could. At least he chose not to hurt you. For that, I'll always think well of him."

Milo's eyes turned to Logan. He stopped and stepped into Logan's arms while the dogs milled about their feet.

Logan kissed Milo's hair and smelled the sweet scent of his shampoo. He cupped his fingers around the back of Milo's neck, gently holding him close while tourists strolled past, purposely averting their gaze.

"Thank you for saying that," Milo whispered, his face buried in the front of Logan's shirt. "He didn't hurt you either." He lifted his gaze to Logan's eyes. "I thank God for that every day."

Logan laid his fingers to Milo's cheek. "Then he did *two* good things in the end. That's probably more than most of us accomplish."

"Yes," Milo said sadly. "I suppose it is."

He eased himself out of Logan's arms and stared down at the dogs. The leashes were tangled again.

"You'll have to carry Emerson home, you know. It's too far for his little legs."

Logan smiled down at the Yorkie, who was gazing back as if he knew what they were saying. Nobody liked a free ride more than Emerson. "I don't mind," Logan said. "It's not like he's a burden. He weighs about the same as a Big Mac."

"Ooh," Milo said, wiping the residue of tears from his eyes. "Good idea. Let's stop for a sandwich on the way home."

"We'll have to eat it on the street. No restaurant is going to let these mutts inside."

"I don't care if you don't."

That settled, they walked on. They hugged the bay for a while, but soon veered inland, aiming for the hill that would eventually lead them home. There was a Jack in the Box along the way. They'd stop and grab a couple of sandwiches as they passed.

Milo cast a final glance back at the water. Logan thought he looked sad when he did.

"Logan?"

"Yeah?"

"Do you think the trollers will come back in full force now that they know they're safe again?"

"Yes, I suppose they will. But there are still a lot of honest, caring reviewers out there. People know the difference, I think. In spite of what Lois Knight did, I think readers always know when a review is written from the heart, and not from jealousy or hatred or whatever other emotion the trolls tap into. People don't stop loving their favorite books or abandon their favorite writers because of one or two bad reviews.

They never have. And writers really do need to be a little more tough-skinned if they want to survive. There's no other way to live the life they've chosen."

Again, Logan's hand found Milo's. He clutched it as if it were a safety line to every ounce of happiness in his life. As indeed it was.

"I love you, Milo Cook. I hope you know that," Logan whispered, just as a streetlight blinked on above their heads.

Milo leaned against Logan's shoulder as their fingers intertwined, more tightly this time.

"Yes," Milo said, his eyes gentle. "It so happens I *do* know."

Logan bent and scooped Emerson off the sidewalk. Tucking him under his chin, Logan smiled and pulled Milo just a little bit closer.

Together, the four of them grew smaller and smaller as they strolled off into the distance. In their wake, the seagulls swooped and cried, and the final gasp of dusk turned to night across the bay.

Arm in arm, and walking slowly in deference to Spanky's age, Logan and Milo spoke quietly of inconsequential things while the memory of their horrible adventure blessedly, and surprisingly, began to recede inside their heads.

While the darkness gathered around them and the towering lights of the city blinked on in their wake, laughter and the gentle murmur of soft words followed them up the hill.

JOHN INMAN is a Lambda Literary Award finalist and the author of over thirty novels, everything from outrageous comedies to tales of ghosts and monsters and heart-stopping romances. He has been writing fiction since he was old enough to hold a pencil. He and his partner live in beautiful San Diego, California, and together, they share a passion for theater, books, hiking, and biking along the trails and canyons of San Diego or, if the mood strikes, simply kicking back with a beer and a movie.

John's advice for anyone who wishes to be a writer? "Set time aside to write every day and do it. Don't be afraid to share what you've written. Feedback is important. When a rejection slip comes in, just tear it up and try again. Keep mailing stuff out. Keep writing and rewriting and then rewrite one more time. Every minute of the struggle is worth it in the end, so don't give up. Ever. Remember that publishers are a lot like lovers. Sometimes you have to look a long time to find the one that's right for you."

Email: john492@att.net
Facebook: www.facebook.com/john.inman.79
Website: www.johninmanauthor.com

It's not easy breaking into show biz. Especially when you aren't exactly loaded with talent. But Malcolm Fox won't let a little thing like that hold him back.

Actually, it isn't the show-business part of his life that bothers him as much as the romantic part—or the lack thereof. At twenty-six, Malcolm has never been in love. He lives in San Diego with his roommate, Beth, another struggling actor, and each of them is just as unsuccessful as the other. While Malcolm toddles off to this audition and that, he ponders the lack of excitement in his life. The lack of purpose. The lack of a man.

Then Beth's brother moves in.

Freshly imported from Missouri of all places, Cory Williams is a towering hunk of muscles and innocence, and Malcolm is gobsmacked by the sexiness of his new roomie from the start. When infatuation enters the picture, Malcolm knows he's *really* in trouble. After all, Cory is *straight*!

At least, that's the general consensus.

www.dreamspinnerpress.com

THE HIKE

JOHN INMAN

Ashley James and Tucker Lee have been friends for years. They are city boys but long for life on the open trail. During a three-hundred-mile hike from the Southern California desert to the mountains around Big Bear Lake, they make some pretty amazing discoveries.

One of those discoveries is love. A love that has been bubbling below the surface for a very long time.

But love isn't all they find. They also stumble upon a war—a war being waged by Mother Nature and fought tooth and claw around an epidemic of microbes and fury.

With every creature in sight turning against them, can they survive this battle and still hold on to each other? Or will the most horrifying virus known to man lay waste to more than just wildlife this time?

Will it destroy Ash and Tucker too?

www.dreamspinnerpress.com

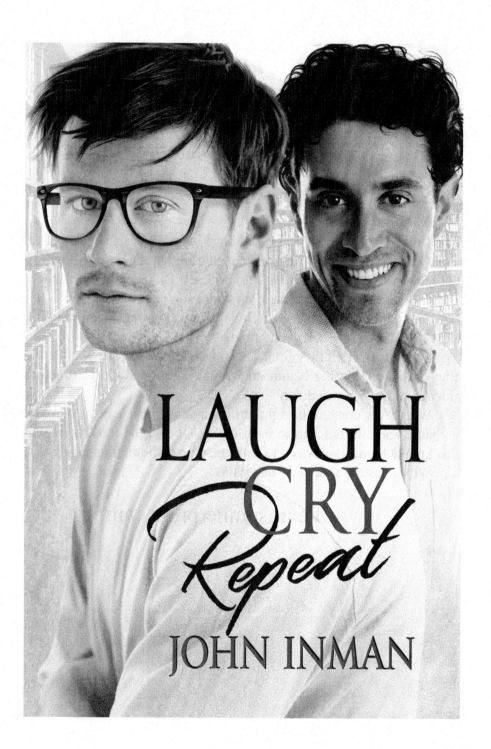

Wyeth Becker is a quiet man. Staid, serious, calm. A librarian. When he meets preschool teacher Deeze Long, he discovers joy for the first time in his life. With joy comes laughter, excitement, and a new way to look at the world through the eyes of the kindest, most loving man he has ever met.

When tragedy strikes and Deeze loses his joy, it is Wyeth who helps him find it again. It is Wyeth, the man who never truly understood happiness, who pays that gift back. Giving all he can of himself to the man who changed his life. Restoring in Deeze what he now so desperately needs.

But the road of their relationship doesn't end there. The joys and sorrows of life are never-ending. As they set out to weather the highs and lows together, Wyeth and Deeze hang on to the one thing that makes all the tears and laughter worthwhile.

Love.

For only through love can life be truly savored at all.

www.dreamspinnerpress.com

When it rains, it pours. Not only has Larry Walls been evicted from his apartment, but his hours have also been cut at the department store where he works, leaving him facing homelessness.

Meanwhile, Bo Lansing, a total stranger to Larry, toils at a dead-end job as a fry cook while attending night classes to become a certified chef. When the school closes its doors without warning, leaving Bo in the lurch for thousands of dollars in tuition, his dream of becoming a chef is shattered and his financial troubles spiral.

Desperate for a new beginning, each man answers an ad for live-in help posted by a wealthy recluse, and wonder of wonders, they are both hired! Just as their lives begin to improve, a young Kumeyaay Indian named Jimmy Blackstone joins the workforce at the Stanhope mansion.

When Mr. Stanhope's true reason for hiring the young men is discovered by one of the three, a fourth entity makes its presence known.

Greed.

With all these players vying for position in a game of intrigue orchestrated by one lonely old man and a mischievous ghost, can a simple thing like love ever hope to survive the fray?

www.dreamspinnerpress.com

Danny Sims is in over his head, torn between his abusive lover, Joshua, and Jay Holtsclaw, the bartender up the street, who offers Danny the one thing he never gets at home: understanding.

When Joshua threatens to get rid of Danny's terrier, Danny knows he has to act fast. Afraid of what Joshua will do to the dog and afraid of what Joshua will do to *him* if he tries to leave, Danny does the only thing he can do.

He runs.

But Danny isn't a complete fool. He has enough sense to run into the arms of the man who actually cares for him—the man he's beginning to trust.

Just as their lives together are starting to fall into place, Danny and Jay learn how vengeful Joshua can be.

And how dangerous.

www.dreamspinnerpress.com

FOR MORE OF THE BEST GAY ROMANCE

dreamspinnerpress.com